PICTURING DIFFERENT

A Raymere Grove Novel

Nikki Kwiatkowski

Cover designed by Karis Drake

This book is a work of fiction. Names, characters, places, and incidents either are products of the author's imagination or are used fictitiously. Any resemblance to actual persons, living or dead, events, or locales is entirely coincidental.

Nikki Kwiatkowski
Visit my website at www.NikkiKAuthor.com

Printed in the United States of America

First Printing: November 2020

ISBN-13 978-1-7332165-2-4

To my husband, Chris, and son, Lochlan

To my parents, Angie and Raymond

With loving memory, to Kevin and Kaci

CONTENTS

CHAPTER 1

Ashlyn was livid when she found out what Eric did, but ultimately she told herself that he had his reasons. Getting kicked off the baseball team before tryouts even started had been hard on him. She never expected his stupidity to get him suspended for two weeks.

She had intended to get to school earlier; however, it had been a long week, and she still had to get through today and Friday. With only ten minutes until the bell rang for students to head to first period, Ashlyn rushed into Principal Willis' office.

The receptionist was on the phone, surrounded by disheveled papers everywhere. Ashlyn attempted to wait patiently, wondering if Principal Willis was behind his closed door or not. After another minute, she figured there couldn't be much harm in knocking.

Just as she approached the door and brought her hand up, it swung open.

"I'm looking forward to it," the boy called out as he backed himself from the office, closing the door behind him, and colliding into someone he had not expected. He quickly turned and reached out to the person he had nearly knocked over, grabbing her by the forearms and steadying her. "Whoa, I'm so sorry. I didn't expect–"

"Do you always walk backwards," Ashlyn snapped.

He shook his head and laughed. "Not usually. Again, I'm sorry. Are you okay?"

Ashlyn looked down to where his hands were clasped around her forearms. Through her sweater she could feel the heat from his palms soaking into her skin. She quickly yanked her arms away and stepped around him toward the door, not saying another word.

"Miss Jennings," Principal Willis greeted, quite surprised by her presence. Upon glancing at his watch, "The bell will be ringing soon. Perhaps make an appointment with–"

"I'm here to talk about Eric's punishment," she blurted out. The idea of talking to Principal Willis was frightening.

"I'm sorry, but I don't think it's appropriate to discuss another student's behavior. If you'd like to speak with a counselor about your relationship with Mr. Weaver, we can make arrangements."

"No sir," Ashlyn replied. She waited a second more, took in a deep breath and started again. "I was hoping that since he's not allowed on school property for the next two weeks, that maybe I could fix his wrong, and maybe...and maybe he could come back early?"

"He won't be playing baseball this year, regardless if he's back in time for tryouts or not."

"But–"

"Miss Jennings, he vandalized school property. Two weeks suspension is nothing compared to if we would have gotten police involved," Willis insisted.

"I'm saying, I'll repaint the sign. I'll make it beautiful," Ashlyn stressed.

When Principal Willis said nothing in response and appeared to think about it, she took it as a miniscule victory.

"I like that idea. We'll add it to your college application," he finally announced, quite pleased with the idea.

Ashlyn groaned. It wasn't what she had in mind when she decided to bargain with Willis. For some reason, he was obsessed with students having a wide variety of garbage for their college applications.

He turned serious. "Miss Jennings, defacing the field's sign was bad, but we both know that isn't why he's not playing. Every student athlete was required to submit to a drug test within seven school days at the start of the semester. He ruined his chances on his own."

Ashlyn sighed. She and Eric hadn't talked about that. Lately they didn't talk much at all. His new group of friends weren't helping matters any. She just hoped that maybe if he was able to play this coming season that things would go back to the way they were when they met freshman year.

Just as Ashlyn turned to leave, feeling defeated, although knowing what her chances were walking in, "One moment." She turned back as Principal Willis grabbed the phone on his desk. "Dora. Yes. Is Mr.

Scott still out there? Does he have his schedule yet? Wonderful. Tell him to wait." He hung up the phone looking pleasantly pleased. "If you could do one more thing."

Ashlyn let out a sigh. It didn't matter what she did, Eric wouldn't be coming back to school any sooner, nor would he be playing baseball. She felt like telling Principal Willis to shove it, but that was just a thought. She'd never be so bold as to tell an adult no.

Just then, the bell rang and both Principal Willis and Ashlyn looked up at the small dinging box in the center of the room. Willis grabbed a couple slips from his desk and initialed them.

Great, at least he wasn't going to allow for her to be counted as tardy.

"We have a new student. Here are two late passes," he said, walking around his desk toward her. "If you could take about ten minutes or so and see to it that he knows the general area of everything."

"Yeah, sure," Ashlyn said rather somberly as she took the passes.

"Also, I admire you. It is important in life for us know where our loyalties are; however, loyalties, as well as people, have a way of changing." When he saw the hope in her face, he added, "And sometimes that change isn't for the best and isn't what we want."

"Thank you, Principal Willis," was all Ashlyn could manage as he held the door open for her and she made her way out toward the receptionist's desk.

Dora appeared a bit calmer when Ashlyn walked up to her desk and she pointed her toward the chairs across the room to a face she recognized. She didn't really recognize him, only from that brief encounter, but if she was being honest, he looked pretty unforgettable. His dirty blonde hair had a clean cut and was styled to perfection. His skin had just enough of a glow that she guessed that he came from somewhere like California or Florida. He was tall and lean. Though he had on a stylish v-neck sweater with a button-down underneath, Ashlyn easily assumed he was muscular. He looked like he'd be good at sports. That thought alone crushed her. Her boyfriend was missing out on two crucial weeks of school and here she was about to get lost in a set of light brown eyes staring back at her.

She swallowed heavily. So what if she thought he was cute. She was allowed to think that other guys were attractive.

Before Ashlyn made it half the distance toward him, he stood, a cocky grin already spread across his face.

"Principal Willis wanted me to quickly show you around," she announced, already motioning to the door.

Instead of moving, he held out his hand. "Sorry we got off to a bad start. Tripp Scott."

Ashlyn looked down at his hand. The polite thing to do would be to shake it, but something inside her head was setting off all kinds of alarms telling her how dangerous that was.

When Tripp saw that she clearly wasn't going to take his hand, he dropped it with a sigh. Anytime he found a girl attractive, she always had to have some kind of issue.

With the silence growing uncomfortable, "And you are," he pressed.

Ashlyn snapped out of whatever daze she was in. She hadn't gotten a lot of sleep the night before. "Ashlyn Jennings, but my friends just call me Ash."

"Does that mean that you anticipate us being friends," he teased.

"Everyone calls me Ash," she snapped back.

Ashlyn walked out the open door and into the hallway, already dreading the next ten minutes or so. She really needed to learn how to politely decline more often.

CHAPTER 2

Ashlyn didn't pay too much attention to Tripp's schedule. She didn't bother showing him each class, rather showing him the English and history wing and so on.

"How did you get office aide? That usually fills up a semester in advance," Ashlyn gasped when she saw his second to last class.

With a shrug, "I guess someone dropped it."

Ashlyn glared at him. She knew the people who lived in Raymere Grove and the people who moved to Raymere Grove. Almost, but not always, the people in the town had one thing in common, money. She couldn't help but wonder exactly who Tripp Scott and his parents were.

"Athletics, 8th period." It was a statement, not a question. "Are you in offseason?"

"No," he chuckled.

Ashlyn didn't know why that was funny to him. Before she could ask anything else on the matter, he told her, making her sick to her stomach.

"Baseball."

Ashlyn closed her eyes and let out a huff, which only made him laugh more.

"I take it you don't like baseball, or maybe sports at all," he speculated.

"It's not that." Not wanting to give him any details concerning her personal life, "But you should know, tryouts were this week. They end tomorrow."

"Who said anything about trying out," he scoffed.

His face held a confidence that was unnerving. Ashlyn couldn't believe that he could possibly think that he could move here, snap his fingers, and get a spot on the team.

"Good luck with that," Ashlyn snorted.

Tripp stepped in her space, his smile fading to a cocky smirk. "I don't need luck. I'm good and I know it."

Ashlyn wasn't much for confrontation, but after spending ten minutes with the guy, she had decided that he rubbed her the wrong way and he should know it. "I see you're humble as well," she said with more attitude than she expected.

He took one more step toward her and she was hit with the subtle freshness of his cologne. It was crisp and clean. And different. Everything about him was different.

"I don't flaunt much, but I know when it comes to the sport, I'm good. No point in beating around the bush about it."

"Here's your late pass for class," Ashlyn hurriedly spoke. She also took the opportunity to take a step back as she stretched her arm out to hand him the slip of paper.

"That's it?"

Ashlyn desperately wanted to get to class. Her first class of the day was newspaper. It was the one class she never wanted to miss. "Yeah. Just give it to your first period teacher."

There was that stupid chuckle again. "I meant, we're done with this?"

"Yes. Believe it or not, classes started almost fifteen minutes ago," Ashlyn stressed.

He watched as she grew more uncomfortable by the second. She wasn't the typical girl he generally went for. He tended to like flair, which usually included girls that spent too much time in the mirror on their hair and makeup, ones that went shopping every weekend, but always looked incredibly sexy in overpriced attire.

The girl before him...She looked different. She had a simple beauty about her. Her oversized sweater and slim jeans concealed most of her body. Though she was taller than a good portion of girls, she appeared tiny standing in front of him in a pair of flat shoes. Her makeup was simple and subtle, no smokey eyes or blazing red lipstick. He wasn't sure how long her hair was; she had it in a cute side braid that hung over her left shoulder. Though during most of their conversation she refused to meet his eyes, he was certain they were one of the most beautiful shades of blue he had ever seen.

"Can I get your number," Tripp asked bluntly.

"What?! Why?!"

"In case I get lost," he laughed.

Ashlyn recovered from her shock at how bold he was and turned serious. "Just find the front office. They'll help you." She adjusted her bags and turned to leave.

"Can I still have your number?"

A surge of giddiness raced through Ashlyn, but she was quick to squash it. She knew guys like Tripp Scott without needing to know him. He was overconfident, cocky, and far too proud. He was used to getting his way and probably one of the biggest jerks on the planet.

When Ashlyn didn't turn to respond, Tripp calmly followed her and walked in front of her. "Well," he pressed.

"I have a boyfriend," Ashlyn blurted out.

For a moment she thought she saw the confidence fade in his face, but if it did, he found it back rather quickly. "That's great and all, but still not answering my question."

Ashlyn huffed in annoyance, and stepped away. "If you can't do the math on that one, then I feel sorry for you."

* * *

"Wow. You look like crap," Emory pointed out as soon as Ashlyn sat down at the lunch table.

June and Kayla immediately looked up and put on their sweetest smiles.

"Thanks," Ashlyn said, sticking out her tongue in the process.

"I guess you didn't convince the principal to let your loser boyfriend back to school early."

Ashlyn glared at Emory. Of all their friends, Emory was the only one who ever spoke out about her very obvious dislike for Eric.

"Worse," Ashlyn began, already stuffing her ham sandwich in her face. "Somehow, I still managed to volunteer my time to repaint the sign, and he had me show around a pretentious jerk. Now I'm behind on my assignment for newspaper."

All three girls surrounding her now perked their ears up at that last bit.

"Wait," June began, quickly trying to swallow the bite of food in her mouth before continuing. "The new guy?"

"Ugh," Ashlyn scoffed. "Yeah. Tripp Scott." She shook her head as those wasted minutes flashed through her mind.

"Lucky," Kayla hissed.

Ashlyn gasped. "Lucky? He's a jerk."

Emory raised a brow and leaned forward with a mischievous look on her face. "Well, when it comes to jerks, you would know."

Ashlyn smiled and shook her head. "I'm serious. He thinks he's the greatest baseball player on the planet. He thinks that he doesn't even need to try out for–"

"He doesn't," Emory quickly interrupted.

Silence ensued and three sets of eyes waited for her to continue.

"Deacon came over for supper last night and told Ellis all about him." Emory said with a shrug, as if that explained everything.

Ellis was Emory's twin, and so as not to hurt himself for his senior year of football, he had opted out of playing baseball in the spring. Deacon, his best friend, didn't share the same sentiment, and was trying out for the team again, although he was one of the few people that practically had a spot if he bothered to show up.

"Deacon said that Tripp stopped by their practice yesterday and met with the team. He's played all over the place," Emory added.

"What do you mean," Kayla quickly asked.

"His dad is in the tech industry or something, some bigshot, and they've lived all over. I guess baseball was the one thing he tried to keep consistent."

"All over," June now inquired.

"Gosh, if you want to know so much about him just ask," Emory teased. "I think he's lived in the Dominican Republic, Canada, Australia, and some country in Asia," she added with a wave of her hand. "He's lived solely in the states for the last couple years." Before either girl could ask anything else, "That's all I know! Oh, except that," she began directing her words to Ashlyn. "Yes, he's on the team, without a tryout."

Emory watched as Ashlyn tried to hide her reaction. Knowing that had to cut her a little, especially after she would have done anything to get Eric on the team for this season.

Ashlyn couldn't help but allow her attention to drift to a table nearby. Several of the guys there would be playing for the team. Though Deacon and Byron did football in the fall, they also chose baseball in the spring. Both, as well as a few others, seemed to have already taken Tripp under their wing. Despite not playing, Ellis usually hung out with the guys, or occasionally he and Deacon would join Emory for lunch.

After a quick scan of the cafeteria, Ashlyn saw that he was seated with Abby and her friends. That was another relationship that Emory wasn't fond of. She disliked the idea of her brother dating a girl on the same cheerleading squad as her; however, with Abby being a senior, none of them expected it to last for more than a few more months.

Ashlyn froze when she scanned back to the boys she had been carefully watching moments earlier. Their attention was all directed to one thing. Her.

CHAPTER 3

Ashlyn took her time getting to class after lunch. She sent a text to Eric to see if he was at least working on his assignments that had been sent home with him; however, she didn't expect a response before her next class started. At least she was thankful that the day was more than halfway over, and tomorrow was Friday.

"Barely made it," Mrs. Cohen greeted Ashlyn just as she slipped in the room with two other students upon the ringing of the tardy bell. "Looks like today is your lucky day," she said, causing Ashlyn to stop immediately.

All science rooms had tables of two instead of desks. Upon returning for the spring semester a few weeks ago, Mrs. Cohen made all the students draw numbers for a new seating arrangement. With twenty-one students in the class, one person had to be the odd man out. Ashlyn didn't mind that she didn't have a seatmate, and when it came to partner work, Mrs. Cohen always let her join and make a group of three.

She wouldn't have used the word lucky to describe her situation when she looked at her table near the back window.

"But, Mrs. Cohen," Ashlyn began, her voice full of panic.

"Please take your seat," she insisted. "We have a full lesson today and can't waste a minute." Mrs. Cohen then grabbed a handful of dry erase markers from a container on her desk and went to the white board, already rambling about geology.

Ashlyn could feel his eyes upon her, but she refused to acknowledge him. Instead, she placed her overly large tote bag on the edge of the table and dropped her backpack to the floor. She quickly rummaged through it and withdrew her earth science notebook and a pen. Mrs. Cohen meant business and unless she went off on a tangent, her notes could be hard to keep up with.

"I think the universe is trying to tell us something," a joking voice whispered.

Ashlyn tightened her lips and dug her pen into the paper a little harder than usual. "We're on geology. Astronomy isn't until later. Check your syllabus."

"Cute," was all Tripp said in response.

Thankfully halfway through class Laura asked a rather simple question, but it led to a huge explanation from Mrs. Cohen. This was generally why every class period was a full lesson, as they never really got through the planned lesson; however, everyone gave Laura praising smiles at getting the chance to rest their hands.

Unfortunately for Ashlyn, this meant that Tripp took Mrs. Cohen's long and drawn out explanation to engage in unwanted conversation on Ashlyn's part.

Tripp brought his hands up like in prayer so that they mostly covered his face and turned toward Ashlyn. "I asked about you."

That got Ashlyn's attention and she snapped her head toward him. "Oh, yeah," she whispered back. "What did you find out?"

A sinister smirk came to his face. "That you have a boyfriend."

Ashlyn couldn't stop a smile from spreading across her lips. "I told you," she shrugged.

"I was hoping you were lying," he said with a seriousness that Ashlyn didn't expect.

"Well, I wasn't. Are you always so forward? You know nothing about me–"

"Hence why I asked you for your number."

"You know what I think," Ashlyn paused, still thinking.

Tripp rolled his eyes. "I guess you're going to tell me."

"I think that you think you can come in here all charming and attractive and get any girl you want because you're the new guy. You're something different, but I can see through that. You're just a flirt, and I have no intention of playing whatever little game you're trying here." She let out an exasperated breath.

Tripp raised his eyebrows to silently ask if she was done. When she didn't respond, he replied with a soft chuckle that only she could hear. Her angry scrunched up face only made him laugh more.

"What," she hissed. She intended to put him in his place. He wasn't supposed to be laughing at her.

He leaned in more closely, so close that Ashlyn could see the little flecks of gold that made his brown eyes appear lighter. "You just called me charming *and* attractive."

Ashlyn's jaw dropped and she thought over what she just said. While technically she used those words, she was not saying that *she* found him to be those things.

Before she could find a way to respond, "It's all good. The guys told me all about your boyfriend. They said if I knew any better, that I should back off before ever starting. They also noted that you were extremely loyal, and I didn't stand a chance anyway," he concluded, just as the bell rang.

Tripp made it seem as though it was no big deal and he had already gotten bored. As Ashlyn gathered her things, she couldn't help but watch as he casually left the classroom, two girls already scurrying after him.

He'd have no problem having his choice of girls. With his confidence and looks, Ashlyn knew that it would only be a matter of time before girls were fighting over him.

"Nice work on the sign," Ellis scoffed, plopping down at the lunch table.

"Ugh," Emory huffed, although she still made room for him. "Why aren't you eating with Abby today?"

"She has an attitude and I don't feel like dealing with her. Where are the other two?"

"They have names you know. June is at lunch tutorials for band and Kayla got sick over the weekend," Emory said, filling Ellis in.

Just then, Deacon and Tripp strolled up. Deacon rarely ever joined the girls anymore unless Ellis was gracing them with his presence. Usually that only occurred when he and Abby were having a fight, which seemed to happen on a weekly basis now.

"As I was saying," Ellis began. "Your sign sucks."

"Shut up, Ellis," Emory shouted.

"It's fine," Ashlyn told her friend. "I worked on it all Saturday. It's a big sign and I had to get all the base work done. Not like you'd know anything about art," she snapped back at Ellis.

"It's just a sign. Don't go all Picasso on it," he huffed.

"I'm confused," Tripp chimed in.

Ashlyn went back to her food and said nothing. So far, she had done a pretty good job of ignoring his unwanted and uninvited presence. Unfortunately for her, Emory wasn't shy in filling him in.

"Oh, you know the sign for the ball field? Ash's *wonderful* boyfriend defaced it with derogatory writing. Then, because she's an idiot and thought she could get Principal Willis to ease up on Eric's suspension, she volunteered to repaint it." She playfully nudged Ashlyn.

Ashlyn didn't mind it. What Emory said was basically true. She looked up to find Tripp with little to no expression on his face, staring at her.

Even though his eyes never left hers, he directed his question to Emory. "When does he get back?"

"Next Monday." Then Emory quietly teased Ashlyn, although her level of quiet wasn't all that so. "Aww, he won't be here for Valentine's."

Ashlyn rolled her eyes. Their school didn't do anything special for Valentine's anyway.

"Back to Ellis," Ashlyn started. "I'll finish the sign this Saturday. Well in time for the first game." She couldn't imagine why he'd care. It was Ellis just being Ellis.

"Excuse me," a dainty voice called from behind Ashlyn and Emory. It was a bit foreign to Ashlyn, but all too familiar to her friend, who proceeded to roll her eyes and go back to her chicken tenders. "Could I talk to you girls. Privately," Rachel added.

Rachel was on the cheerleading squad the past fall with Emory. She was also Emory's biggest competition for head cheerleader for their senior year, despite Emory expressing that she absolutely didn't want that title.

Ashlyn gave Emory a look and rose from her spot, Emory grumbling and throwing down her tender and following.

Once they were near some glass doors leading to the courtyard. "Okay," Rachel began with a giggle.

"The new guy. Laura told me that you sit next to him in earth science," she said, pointing out the obvious to Ashlyn. Then she turned to Emory. "And he seems to be good friends with Deacon and your brother."

"And," Emory huffed, pretending not to follow.

"I mean, come on. Help a girl out. Every girl wants to get her claws into him, and you two are having lunch with him," she squealed. "Put in a good word for me?"

"What was that about," Ellis asked when they got back.

With a full mouth, "Oh, she wants us to make her sound like an angel in hopes that your buddy here will fall for her psychotic self. Seriously, crazy nut-job," Emory said, enunciating each word carefully in Tripp's direction.

Emory then looked across the room to an eagerly smiling Rachel and gave her the thumbs up, eliciting laughter from Ashlyn.

Tripp looked in the direction and the girl immediately turned away, her face red as could be. He could say that she was attractive, but so were lots of girls. Not wanting to be rude, and not saying it outside of his own head, he could also admit that she was easily forgettable. For some reason she didn't capture his attention like the girl before him that he was thankful for bumping into days earlier.

"What do you think," he asked Ashlyn, putting her on the spot.

Her eyes widened. "About what?"

Tripp nodded his head in the direction of Rachel. "Worth pursuing?"

A strange feeling ran through Ashlyn. She knew the mayo on her burger smelled funky. She just didn't expect the queasy feeling taking over her stomach. She shrugged. "Yeah. Emory just doesn't like her because she's going to be in charge of the cheer squad next year and she's already letting it get to her head."

Ashlyn wished she wouldn't have looked up and met his eyes. The way he was looking at her, combined with that devilish smirk, told her that he found humor in her response.

CHAPTER 4

That Monday was the only day of the week the guys ate lunch with the girls. Once Ellis and Abby made up, just in time for Valentine's, he went back to sitting with her during most of lunch and some of the baseball team toward the end of lunch. Ashlyn was thankful for that; sitting beside Tripp in earth science was already all she could stand of him.

As she finished her lunch that Friday afternoon and made her way to class, she realized that after Monday's lunch, and the mentioning of Rachel, Tripp had barely spoken more than a handful of words to her.

While walking down the hall, she felt her phone go off.

Eric: Sorry I missed your text during lunch. I just got up.

Ashlyn: You do realize you have to be here by 8 starting Monday.

Eric: Ha. Anyway, going to go play some Call of Duty. Happy V-Day!

Ashlyn sighed. She wondered if he would have said anything had she not said something first. Lately he had been messing up a lot, and though Emory liked to tease her about how Eric wasn't the same guy she met during freshman year, she was slowly wondering about the truth to that.

Tripp didn't say anything to her when she sat down. He was engrossed in something on his phone, but Ashlyn greeted him anyway.

"Hey," he responded, not bothering to look away from his phone. "Crap," he quietly hissed to himself pulling his hoodie up over his head and answering his phone.

Ashlyn's eyes widened. The tardy bell would be ringing in less than a minute. Phones were allowed during lunch and passing period, but if Mrs. Cohen were to see him with his phone out after class started...Scratch that. He didn't just have his phone out, he was having a conversation on the phone!

"Yes. That's correct. Thank you," he concluded, rushing through the conversation.

Tripp then removed his hood and tossed his phone into his bag, letting out a sigh of relief.

Ashlyn couldn't help but note his change in demeanor. When she first came in, Tripp looked almost irritated. Now he appeared his usual self, albeit, a little hyper. He kept bouncing his left leg, which Ashlyn found just a tad annoying.

Mrs. Cohen, while always in a good mood, was in an especially good mood. It probably had a little something to do with the vase of a dozen red roses on

31

her desk. Notetaking was surprisingly easy with no one complaining of carpal tunnel.

"Alright, we have fifteen minutes of class left," Mrs. Cohen announced as she handed stacks of papers to the tables in the front. "Take one and pass it back," she instructed. "This is a short worksheet. You'll be able to finish it before the bell, and because I'm feeling generous, today you may work with your seatmate."

Tripp immediately gave Ashlyn an out. "I can work on my own, if you want."

"Oh…" She was quite surprised. While she didn't know much about Tripp, there seemed to have been a shift in him ever since Monday. It's not like she cared, but Ashlyn did find herself wondering if it had anything to do with Rachel. "Or, I can do the first half and you can do the second, then we'll share? Half the time?"

Tripp narrowed his eyes on her. "What if I'm really stupid?"

Ashlyn motioned to his notes. "You take great notes. You actually pay attention. Plus, if you're playing a sport, you and I both know you have to keep up the grades."

"Wow. Was that a compliment," he teased. It was the most they had spoken all week.

Ashlyn found herself smiling ever so slightly. "Don't get used to it."

When their papers finally reached them, "Do you want to work together then?"

Ashlyn didn't see the harm, and it would save time. "Sure."

Tripp slightly scooted his chair a little in her direction, but the look on his face and the way he began talking about the assignment, made Ashlyn shake any thoughts of it being a flirtatious gesture.

It wasn't until they were nearly done with their work that Ashlyn heard her name being called by Mrs. Cohen from the front of the classroom. She looked up with many of the other students, only for the room to fall mostly silent. The once vigorous talks of trying to complete the assignment turned to whispers when the office aide handed Mrs. Cohen the exquisite vase.

Mrs. Cohen held it up, meeting Ashlyn's stunned expression and repeated herself. "Ash, these are for you."

Ashlyn nervously rose from her seat. She didn't have to look around the room to feel all eyes on her as she walked up to the front. Lots of girls might like that sort of attention, but she most definitely did not.

Mrs. Cohen smiled sweetly when she handed Ashlyn the bouquet. "I'd say that you're a very lucky girl," she whispered.

Ashlyn couldn't make eye contact with anyone on her way back to her seat. Several girls along the way complimented her on the flowers, but it wasn't until she placed them on the table and sat back down, that she really got a good look at them.

They were...different. Students throughout the day had received deliveries, some from friends and significant others, some from family and parents. They were all the same thing that you see for Valentine's, red roses. This was something else entirely. The vase was overflowing with unimaginable flowers that Ashlyn had never seen. Every color under the rainbow poured throughout the beautiful leaves and petals. Most of the stems were tropical and exotic, as their names escaped Ashlyn. The only ones she could clearly identify were the lilies and bird of paradise, but even the lilies weren't the standard ones that she was used to seeing in the market.

She was shaken out of her bubble when the girl in front of her leaned back in her chair and turned to her. "I guess Eric feels pretty bad for not being here."

Ashlyn smiled. "I guess so."

At that, she grabbed the card, only to be disappointed. All it contained was her name and the address to the school. The inside was completely blank.

Ashlyn couldn't wait the few minutes until the bell rang and quickly retrieved her phone.

Ashlyn: Thank you so much! The flowers are gorgeous.

Eric responded rather quickly with back to back texts, only for Ashlyn's heart to stop for a beat.

Eric: Dude! I told you I was playing Call of Duty!

Eric: What flowers?

Ashlyn: You didn't send me flowers today?

Eric: No. Was I supposed to?

Tripp pretended to still be finishing his worksheet. The truth was he had already done the last two problems on Ashlyn's as well.

From the corner of his eye, he could see the texts coming and going from her phone beneath the table. Just as he read the last one, Ashlyn tossed the device into one of her bags.

"Uh, here," Tripp said, pushing her paper towards her. "I finished writing your last two."

Ashlyn's brows were furrowed, and her face scrunched in a combination of thought and disappointment. "Thanks," she mumbled.

Tripp cleared his throat. "Your boyfriend did well," he said, gesturing to the large vase with his pen. When she didn't respond, only continue to stare at the flowers, "For someone who just got spoiled, you don't seem to be in a very good mood."

"They're not from him," Ashlyn replied quietly.

"Oh?"

The rise of pitch in Tripp's one word made her instantly regret filling him in on that piece of information.

She tried not to show her disappointment. "They're probably from my parents."

Thankfully the bell rang. "Do you want me to hand in your paper," Tripp asked, already sliding it on top of his.

"Yeah. Thanks."

Just then another girl walked by. "Wow, Ash. Seriously, best boyfriend ever. That's totally like sweet and sensitive bad boy."

Tripp watched Ashlyn's jaw tighten, no doubt finding the girl's comment annoying.

Ashlyn looked up only to meet Tripp's serious, and oddly unemotional, face staring back at her. If she expected him to give her a hard time or tease her, she was pleasantly surprised.

"Despite them not being from the sender you wanted, they really are gorgeous. I'm sure they'll make for some great pictures."

Tripp turned to leave, but his last comment rattled Ashlyn. "Wait!"

He stopped and only turned halfway. The classroom was dwindling down and at this rate, they'd both probably be late to their next class.

"Who told you I take pictures?"

Tripp raised a brow and shook his head. "First of all, that comment alone tells me," he chuckled. "Secondly..." He pointed to her oversized shoulder bag with her camera inside. When she eyed him suspiciously, "Relax. I was just making an observation. You've made yourself perfectly clear. I'm not secretly digging up information on you."

Ashlyn reddened with embarrassment and looked away. "Sorry. I'm just...Today is just," she started.

"I get it," Tripp said softly. "Anyway, have a great weekend."

Just like that, he left her. He didn't give her any grief or tease her that her own stupid boyfriend couldn't send her anything for Valentine's Day. He just calmly strolled out of the classroom.

Ashlyn looked down at the flowers as she grabbed them and hurried to her next class. They really were exquisite. Who cares that they weren't from Eric? They were still hers, and Tripp was right about one thing; they really would make for some great pictures.

* * *

Ashlyn nearly bolted off the sofa when she heard the front door open.

"Mom," she gasped with complete shock. It was only 5:30. "What are you doing home so early?"

Poppy Jennings worked as a therapist, specializing in marital and family counseling. She split her time between Raymere Grove and the big city. Mondays, Wednesdays, and Fridays were her days where she had to drive the hour long or better drive into the city. Sometimes both of her parents shared the ride those days, as Ashlyn's father, Daniel, worked for a law firm there.

"Oh, my last client of the day emailed the office early this morning that they wouldn't be able to make it. Your dad still won't be home until 7 or so. I was hoping that I could make a lovely dinner."

Ashlyn just now noticed the grocery bags in her mother's arms. "Do you need some help," she quickly asked.

Her mother eyed her suspiciously as she made her way to the kitchen. It wasn't even 6 on a Friday night, and Ashlyn was already in a pair of sweats watching television.

"You don't have a date tonight," Poppy asked with great skepticism.

"No. Eric already had plans with some friends, and I didn't feel like joining them." She left out the fact that Eric never even bothered to invite her along in the first place.

Her mother didn't even respond with a word, just a grumble of irritation. Needless to say, her parents weren't overly fond of Eric, at least not anymore. Up until the summer before, he was great. Then he went with his cousins for summer break in California, and he seemed to change.

"Oh my," her mother gasped when she saw the bouquet of flowers on the table.

"Ugh. Yes. Thanks, mom," Ashlyn grumbled.

"I'm sorry," Poppy laughed. "What?"

"You and dad did not need to send something, especially something so over the top. I mean," she began to ramble. "Don't get me wrong, they're absolutely gorgeous, but everyone thought they were from Eric, and–"

"Oh, sweetie," her mother interrupted, shaking her head. She continued to unpack items from the bags. Ashlyn was thankful that she wasn't going out when she saw the steaks and shrimp. "You got so mad at your father and I when we did that your eighth-grade year."

"Wait. You didn't?"

"No," Poppy continued to chuckle. "You were so embarrassed then."

Knots formed in Ashlyn's stomach and her eyes drifted back to the curious bouquet on the table. If it wasn't Eric, or her parents...Maybe Emory, June, and Kayla? Maybe they expected that Eric wouldn't do anything. Emory did mention that he wouldn't be there on Valentine's.

A group text and ten minutes later confirmed that it wasn't them.

Emory: We love you and all, but that looks like $200 or better. No way.

Kayla: Personally, I would have gotten you chocolate if anything.

June: Sorry. I'm with Emory!

Ashlyn knew just how to solve the mystery. She wasn't in newspaper for nothing. The one thing she found oddly intriguing about the class: research and investigative journalism.

Once she got to her room, she flipped the card over and dialed the florist's number. It rang several times before a soft and exhausted voice answered the phone.

"Hi. Um...I received one of your arrangements to-day–"

"Did you order red roses instead of pink? I'm so sorry," the woman began apologizing. "We ran out at the last minute. I can offer you a discount for any future–"

Ashlyn quickly interrupted the woman's rant. "No, no. It's nothing like that. I got an arrangement at school today, and the card was blank. I know it's probably not in your policy, but I'd really like to know who sent it."

There was a moment of silence. "What's your name?"

"Ashlyn Jennings."

"Oh," the lady gasped. "That one I remember. Quite an odd request for Valentine's."

"Could you tell me who ordered it," Ashlyn asked with hope.

The sigh on the other end already told her before any words. "I'm sorry." Ashlyn figured. Her mom worked all the time with people in extramarital affairs. Imagine if a spouse could find out how his wife got a mysterious bouquet of flowers. "I mean, I would," the woman continued. "You're just a kid after all, but that was a specific request on the sender's part."

The called ended with Ashlyn left even more intrigued, and strangely, more frustrated. Why would someone send something so beautiful and not take credit for it?

CHAPTER 5

When Ashlyn returned to the field after lunch, she was thankful for the dry breeze and rather warm sunlight. She'd definitely be able to get the final touches on before the first game in a few days.

It wasn't the ideal way to spend an entire Saturday, but she did enjoy painting. Though the air was still a little chilly, the sunlight made up for it, and she found that she felt more at peace than she had in a long time.

She was always rather artistic, but after her freshman year, she switched from so many art classes to newspaper. Newspaper was the closest thing that the school had to photography. In the end she was torn about the future. She loved to paint, and she knew she was good at it, but something about a camera, and capturing things in a different way, felt like a calling as well.

Tripp was mildly out of breath when he approached the field. He thought she would have heard him, but the closer he got, he realized that she had earbuds in, and he couldn't help but wonder what kind of music she listened to, if their tastes were similar, and if not, would it be something he'd like.

Rather than make his presence known, he hung back, getting some air, so he didn't look out of shape, despite that he was far from it. He remembered her telling her friends at lunch how she'd be spending her Saturday. It wasn't a coincidence that he jogged in the direction of the school. He just didn't think of what he'd do or say if he saw her.

His heart continued to race, long after he thought he had cooled down from his run. He hesitantly stepped closer in her direction until he was just close enough to tap her on the shoulder.

Ashlyn jumped in shock from the contact and spun around with flailing arms.

Tripp flew back, his black t-shirt now covered with a light blue splatter.

Ashlyn yanked out her earbuds. "What the hell are you doing," she screamed. She grabbed her chest. "You almost gave me a heart attack!"

Tripp glanced down at his shirt and pulled it from his body in Ashlyn's direction.

"That's your own fault," she continued to scream.

"Sorry. I called out, but I guess you didn't hear me," he lied.

"Of course I didn't hear you!"

"Anyway, hi," he began again, more awkwardly.

"Hi?! Seriously?!"

He took a deep breath and stepped to the side, pretending to admire her work. "I went for a jog and happened to see you working."

Ashlyn rolled her eyes. "Well, I'm a little busy. If you don't mind–"

"Want some help," Tripp quickly offered. He could tell his question surprised Ashlyn, as her eyes grew twice their size.

Ashlyn stumbled for words. "Why would...I...No," she finally managed. "No, thank you."

He picked up one of the brushes and twirled it around. "It'll go much faster. I'll do the easy stuff."

"I'm sure you have better things to do on a Saturday afternoon."

He shrugged and turned back to the sign.

Ashlyn didn't know how to get rid of him. She needed to get rid of him. She still had a couple hours' worth of work and he would only serve as a distraction, a distraction in the sense that she'd have to waste her time explaining and telling him what to do, not that she found him distracting in the way half the girls at school did.

Tripp noticed that she had the lettering stenciled out. "What color do you want the letters?"

He had to be kidding. "First of all, no. You have to have a very steady hand for that," she began, reaching for his brush, only for him to hold it up in the air above his head, teasing her like a child.

"How do you know that I don't have a steady hand?" Ashlyn ignored him and stepped forward, reaching for the brush above his head one more time. It was no use. He was easily half a foot taller than her, and with much longer arms. When she finally gave up, "And secondly?"

"Secondly," she began with a great amount of irritation in her voice. "What's it going to take to get you to go away?"

"Come on," Tripp laughed. "After we got along so well with that assignment? I thought we were making progress."

"Progress?"

When Tripp realized where Ashlyn's mind was probably going, he quickly corrected her. "Yeah, to friendship? To you not hating me?"

"I don't hate you," Ashlyn blurted out. She could have slapped herself on the forehead. It would have been better if he continued thinking she did.

"You don't," he asked teasingly.

"Maybe a little," she said, unable to help smiling as she did. She sighed. She could not believe what was happening. "If you really want, it's the sky blue." She pointed to the small bucket of paint that was for the letters.

Tripp smiled. Without saying another word, he went to the bucket, knowing that Ashlyn was carefully watching him, just waiting for him to make a mistake. After several minutes he had the large letter R completed. When she said nothing of the skill or quality, he continued on.

They worked in silence. Ashlyn hadn't put her earbuds back in, just in case Tripp did decide to say something to her. She was quite surprised that he was being rather normal, doing just as he acted like he intended, simply helping her complete the sign.

Ashlyn was so focused on her details of the bear that she didn't notice Tripp coming closer and closer as the lettering went on across the sign.

Tripp didn't want her to mess up, so he waited until she was dipping her brush into the paint before he seized on an opportunity that had crossed his mind since they first started.

"You did not," Ashlyn screamed as soon as Tripp's brush grazed her cheek.

He erupted into a fit of laughter to the point that he was doubled over and clutching his stomach. When he finally began to compose himself and look up to no doubt a livid expression on Ashlyn's face, she shocked him further by swatting his forehead with her brush.

"Hey!" Tripp wasn't mad in the least; he just didn't expect Ashlyn to play along. The only difference was, she didn't stop her assault on him.

Ashlyn dipped her brush back in the black paint and swung at Tripp again, this time hitting him across his forearm. He took a step back, still laughing, but now with his hands up in surrender. Ashlyn sliced her brush through the air once more, now nicking him ever so slightly at the neck, and then below his right eye.

Tripp lunged at her from behind when she bent for more paint and wrapped her into a bearhug, making it impossible for her to move her arms. Surprisingly, she was laughing.

"Let go," Ashlyn squealed, jumping up and down.

"Truce?"

"You started it," she laughed. Trying to break free from his arms was not going to happen. He was way too strong for her, no matter how much fight she had in her.

Tripp spun Ashlyn around and their chests collided, all the while keeping his grip on her arms firm so that they remained at her side. He could feel her fit of laughter radiating through his body, and it felt unlike anything he could ever recall with her in his arms. Then suddenly it stopped.

Ashlyn brought her eyes to meet Tripp's, and that's when their predicament clicked. Their faces were only inches from one another. She could feel his heavy breaths coming through the cool air, and she was certain that he could feel the same from her. She glanced down at their bodies pressed together, his arms around her, now loosening, as if he knew they were in dangerous territory as well.

Alarms blared in Ashlyn's head, more loudly than they had ever done before. She quickly stepped back, and when she did, Tripp's arms easily fell from her.

"Sorry about that," Tripp apologized.

He wasn't sure what to say. The look on Ashlyn's face showed sheer horror, and her beautiful blue eyes that stared up at his so sweetly moments ago, wouldn't even look in his direction.

"You just looked so serious," he went on. "I thought you could use a little fun."

"I need to finish this," Ashlyn grumbled. She wiped her cheek but did a poor job of removing the blue paint.

Tripp knew it would be pushing his luck, but why not. "Ash?" Thankfully she turned to him. He took a step forward and lifted the bottom of his t-shirt. "Hold still," he softly instructed as he brought his shirt up to her cheek.

Ashlyn told herself to step back a thousand times in that moment. She just couldn't. For starters, the small and shallow girly part in her could see most of his abdomen with that gesture, and he looked absolutely incredible, like a model for some expensive jeans that didn't need a shirt. Secondly, the gesture was sweet and innocent. For a moment she thought he might be bold enough to kiss her. If that were the case, more than likely his face would have met her closed fist. The look on his face, however, was serious. He was really concentrating on removing the paint from her cheek, not even caring that he was covered in ten times as much.

"There," he said, pulling his shirt back in place. "All good."

What Ashlyn found to be incredibly unnerving, Tripp stepped to the side and went back to the letters, like nothing had happened. Maybe it was her, she told herself. Maybe he was simply being playful, and she and her own messed up mind had taken it to mean more, to be a moment between them, and she had to go and make it awkward.

More time passed and Ashlyn made the final touches to the Raymere Grove Bears Baseball signage for the field.

"Hopefully no other idiots mess it up," Tripp spoke without thinking.

"He was just upset," Ashlyn huffed.

Tripp shrugged. "Well, it was pretty immature, regardless."

Ashlyn let out a deep breath and spun to face him, her eyes flaring with annoyance. "He's paying for it, okay?"

Tripp hated the direction their conversation was going. He especially hated that he had inadvertently brought up her boyfriend, but now that he had, "Do you always make excuses for him?"

Ashlyn sucked in a breath at that. Tripp didn't know anything about her and Eric to go around making assumptions like that. "Just mind your own business," was all she could come up with.

He was frustrated, but now that he had already ruined it and pissed her off, why not go all the way? "Come on, Ash! He makes a mess, you clean it up, and I bet he doesn't even care. I mean, he didn't even care enough to send you something for Valentine's! Did he even take you out?"

"Shut up! Just shut up!" She slammed the lids onto the buckets of paint and placed them into a box. "I was actually quite surprised that you didn't throw that in my face yesterday. Guess you couldn't hold it in much longer," she spat. Deep inside along with the anger boiling out, his words really hurt her.

Tripp couldn't help but take in a deep breath and calm down. Though Ashlyn tried not to show it, he picked up on the sadness in her voice. "Look, I'm sorry. I never meant–"

"Was it you," Ashlyn found herself interrupting. The idea had come across her mind, but she couldn't possibly see it being true.

Tripp's eyes narrowed, appearing to be deep in thought. "Was what me," he slowly enunciated.

Ashlyn stood after she placed the last container of paint in the box, and met his eyes, his legitimately confused honey colored eyes. "The flowers," she hesitated, already feeling like she knew the answer, and feeling like an idiot for thinking that it could have ever been him.

"No." Tripp watched Ashlyn's expressions and body language carefully. He couldn't figure out what was going on in her head, but his answer appeared to fill her with relief, much to his disappointment. "Even though you seem to know very little about me, I believe that first day you had me pegged as cocky and overconfident. If I'm going to give a girl something, you should know, I'd at least take credit for it."

"That's what I thought," Ashlyn sighed, her eyes falling to the ground. That was her last idea of who could have sent them. She'd just resign herself to the fact that maybe she wasn't meant to know. It was an incredibly sweet gesture and that's all it was supposed to be.

"I know I pissed you off just now, but let me help you get this stuff–"

"No." Ashlyn's voice was firm. "Please, just go."

Tripp wanted to protest, but this time, he got the impression that he wouldn't be able to sway her. Instead he allowed their time together to end on her terms.

CHAPTER 6

Tripp was forced to watch as the wavy dark-haired guy took his place next to Ashlyn. She seemed happy, full of smiles, as he put his arms around her shoulders and gave her a peck on the cheek. He hated how painful it was for him to see. He hated it even more that Deacon, Ellis, and now Byron, decided to sit with the girls on Monday. Maybe it had to do with Eric being back and wanting to see how that was going to go after all the trouble he had gotten into.

Tripp tried his best to ignore his surroundings, and instead fell deep into his own thoughts. It was always easy when it came to girls. He was stupid to think that Ashlyn would have fallen head over heels that first day when he asked for her number. Just looking at her, just her showing him around the school for those few minutes, he knew she was different. The worst of it was, she had completely captured his attention, and he couldn't even get a small percentage of that on her part for him.

When he managed to look up, he was surprised to see that she was watching him. After Saturday, he fully expected her to gloat, to flaunt Eric around; however, the look on her face, her eyes on his, showed nothing but concern, and maybe a little something else. She bit her lip uncomfortably and quickly glanced away. What he wouldn't give to know every thought racing through her mind right now.

"Saw the sign," Deacon said with a nod in Ashlyn's direction. "Looks way better than before."

Eric nudged Ashlyn. "Maybe I'll spray paint what a loser Willis is over it and the next one will be even better yet," he joked.

Ashlyn didn't find it funny. "Don't," she insisted seriously. "We worked really hard on it."

Eric was quick to catch one particular word. "*We*?"

Tripp held his breath and looked down at his food. There was no way that Ashlyn would tell her boyfriend that she spent her Saturday with another guy, even if it was strictly of a friendly nature, at least for the most part. He still had a hard time convincing himself that when she was in his arms, they didn't have a moment.

Before Ashlyn could answer, "Yes, we," Emory spat. "So, leave it alone or I'll kick your–"

"I cannot deal with her right now," Eric groaned. "I told some of my friends I'd see them today. I'll catch you later, babe."

Tripp smiled ever so slightly at the disgust that spread across Ashlyn's face at the word babe. He had never called a girl that, but he couldn't imagine Ashlyn being one of those that would like to be referred to as such.

Tripp tried to be inconspicuous about it, but he was curious as to where Eric was going, and glanced up every now and then until he exited the glass doors to the courtyard. He found himself intrigued as to why he'd leave Ashlyn to go anywhere else.

He tried not to judge books by covers, but the table of friends that Eric joined did not at all seem like the people Ashlyn and her friends would fit in with. They honestly didn't look like they cared to be in school at all. Even though he knew he was looking for even more excuses to dislike the guy, he couldn't help but be rubbed the wrong way at how excited one of the girls got upon seeing Eric, and how close he sat to her.

He shook his head and went back to the conversation before him, knowing that he was imagining something that wasn't there.

"Thank you, Emory," Byron exclaimed, holding up his hand from farther down the table for a high five.

Ashlyn rolled her eyes and smiled. Comments like that didn't bother her, but when she thought about it...Shouldn't they?

"Assuming no one is going to say anything, Emory was with me this weekend," June began, adding a fake cough at the end.

Ashlyn could feel her cheeks reddening at the attention. They were all her friends. It wouldn't hurt if they knew. Right?

"By you taking that long to respond, you have us all curious as to that *we* comment..." Kayla added teasingly.

Ashlyn attempted to discreetly shoot Tripp a look, wondering if it was okay for her to say anything.

Though there was a playful look in his eyes, he must have sensed her uncertainty.

"I happened to be out for a run," Tripp offered. At that point everyone's attention shot toward him. Perhaps he should have added more, but he wasn't sure where he was going with it or how much he wanted to say. For some reason, he wanted to keep a lot of that day private, something just between Ashlyn and him.

"Well that says nothing," Emory scoffed.

"Yeah, and what kind of running do you do on the weekends? I thought you live like five miles from the school," Byron pointed out.

Tripp only got a glimpse of Ashlyn's face when Byron made that comment, but he couldn't ignore the combination of speculation and intrigue behind her brilliant eyes.

"Anyway," Ashlyn began rather slowly, her eyes narrowed onto Tripp who suddenly couldn't look at her. "He happened to run by the school and saw that I was a little behind. He helped with some of the lettering," she concluded with a shrug. She tried her best to make it look like it wasn't a big deal, and it wasn't. Really it wasn't.

However, when she looked up, she saw how carefully her best friend was watching her every movement. There wasn't a doubt in her mind that Emory was going to grill her about every little aspect of that day.

* * *

Tripp tried not to be too cocky when his teammates congratulated him on the 4 to 2 win, but he would have been surprised if he hadn't have gotten at least one home run. He was ecstatic that he was able to get two; however, the team they played didn't seem all that good. He thought the score should have been much higher.

Had the game been on a weekend, no doubt there would have been further celebration; however, a Thursday night meant there was still one day of classes. He did go out for a quick bite to eat at a local grill with a few of the guys. Though Ellis didn't play baseball, Tripp realized that he was an essential part of the group he had fallen into. He was a little surprised that Emory tagged along, and a little disappointed that a particular friend wasn't with her. Unfortunately for him, Ellis' girlfriend, Abby was also present. While she was a senior, he knew that she and Emory were both on the cheerleading team, and not necessarily the best of friends. It seemed that Emory wasn't friends with many of the cheerleaders at all.

Tripp had to come to the painful conclusion that since Emory didn't do a good enough job with Rachel's request, Rachel had found another way in. This now led to a very awkward meal with a girl beside him that he didn't know or care to know.

"I heard you were supposed to be good, but wow," Rachel gasped. "That was some game!"

"Thanks," Tripp grumbled.

Ellis gave him a thumbs up, but Tripp shook his head in return. If he had to be honest, Rachel was just like most of the girls he had dated, but lately he wanted something different.

Rachel sipped on her diet soda to cover the lull in conversation. Tripp was thankful for that and created conversation with the girl across from him.

"So, Emory. Do you come to a lot of the games?"

Emory looked up surprised. Usually when she went out with her twin and his friends, she wasn't included into much of the conversation. Knowing that their father wouldn't be home, she only tagged along this time because she needed food and didn't feel like cooking.

Tripp saw Emory's eyes narrow, and she took a minute to respond. "Yes. *We* do."

His stomach turned to knots with the way she was looking at him and the way she cooed her words. She knew why he was asking. The smart thing would have been to drop the conversation. It was already uncomfortable with Rachel right next to him. Though the guys didn't seem interested in whatever he had to say to Emory, eventually someone would overhear the wrong thing and take it in a way he didn't want.

Emory seemed to sense as much. She gave Tripp a knowing smirk and went back to her burger.

It was at that moment that another presence took Tripp away from conversation with Rachel. He hadn't noticed the person talking with Byron and Deacon until now. Now...Now Eric's words were directed to him.

"Heard you're quite the hotshot," Eric called out from across several people. He was standing between

Deacon and Byron, obviously he wouldn't be staying long.

For the first time, Tripp decided to nix his over-confidence. "I'm okay," he shrugged.

"I'd say more than that if my girlfriend is staying in to write a stupid article about the game," Eric laughed, although he didn't seem to be amused.

Tripp perked up at the mentioning of Ashlyn. He didn't expect to have a noticeable reaction to Eric's comment, but he must have, because the next thing he knew, someone's foot collided with his shin. When he looked away, Emory was glaring at him.

"Ash was at the game tonight for the school's online newspaper. When she joined sophomore year, she went to a lot of the football games because I had to be there, and in the spring, she went to pretty much every baseball game because..." She stopped and nodded in Eric's direction.

Right. Of course. Tripp clenched one hand beneath the table in frustration. Ash was only at his game because Emory was there and, apparently, she was doing an article for the school's paper. They definitely weren't on a friendly enough basis for him to think that she'd come to see him. At least she wasn't at the game to see Eric, and even better, she was at home right now tapping away on a computer, not picking up food with Eric.

Eric proceeded to ask Tripp questions. Normally, Tripp would be flattered, but something about Eric's questioning rubbed him the wrong way.

It was a little after nine when everyone started breaking off and heading out. Tripp was relieved that Rachel had received a text from her mother earlier, saying that she was needed home. He was even more relieved that Abby and Rachel left together. She had hinted about possibly needing a ride home, and there wasn't a single part of him that wanted to be left alone with her.

He was within feet of his G-Class when a pitter-patter of footsteps rushed up to him.

"Hey," a voice called out.

Tripp was stunned when he turned around and found Emory approaching him. She halted feet before him and took in his vehicle.

"Whoa, no wonder you came to Raymere Grove," she scoffed.

Okay, his dad was rich. It was a surprise that came with the move. If it had been up to him, he would have been fine with a newer model Mustang or Corvette. He never expected something upwards of a hundred and thirty thousand.

He didn't care to talk about his father's wealth. He was exhausted and still had one assignment that needed completing before second period.

"Did you need something," he asked, trying not to show any irritation.

"Oh, yeah. Duh. Here you go," she laughed, handing him a napkin with the Flip's Grill logo on it.

He narrowed his eyes not understanding, and that's when she turned it over. Ten numbers were written neatly and clear as day. Tripp felt sick to his stomach when he looked up and saw the bright smile across Emory's face.

"Uh," he began, swallowing heavily. "Thanks, but...I should let you know, I think you're cool, but I'm not really–"

He was interrupted by a fit of shrieking laughter. Was this some kind of prank? He didn't understand what could be so insanely funny about the situation. A second more and she was dabbing at her eyes, crying from laughing so hard.

Tripp stood there, still holding the napkin, with a nervous and uncertain expression across his face.

"Oh gosh. Wow." Emory coughed trying to catch her breath. "You should have seen the look on your face."

Tripp held the napkin up.

Emory turned into a mix of playful and serious. "No, that's not my number, you idiot," she scoffed. "Don't get me wrong, I think you're cool," she said, mimicking his own words.

Tripp rolled his eyes and shook his head. "Ugh. Rachel."

"No. Eww. I thought we cleared that up at lunch. The girl is crazy. She put on a cute show tonight, but that's just until she's got you in her web."

Tripp looked at the number on the napkin. Thank goodness it wasn't Rachel's. "Then I'm confused."

"Oh, come on," Emory screamed, gesturing with her hands. "If you could have anyone's number, who would it be?" She watched as Tripp's eyes lit up like a kid on Christmas morning.

"She told you to give me–"

"Whoa," Emory interrupted. "Definitely not." Tripp's eyebrows furrowed in confusion.

"She tells me everything, you know. Well, almost everything," Emory went on. Everyone had their secrets after all. "I know that you asked her for her number on your first day. She ranted about it for several days, about how you could be so bold, and then not caring that she had a boyfriend." Emory raised a brow and shook her head. "Anyway, there you go."

"Why are you doing this," Tripp was quick to ask.

Emory simply shrugged in response, acting as if she didn't care. In the distance Tripp heard Ellis and Deacon screaming from a car. "Do what you will," Emory said in one rushed breath, then turned and bounded off toward the car.

Tripp got into his vehicle, still staring at the napkin. Maybe he should have played it cool, waited a few days, but something inside him was bouncing like the Energizer bunny at the idea of talking to Ashlyn outside of the occasional lunch or that one class. Without thinking it over too much, he put the number into his phone and fired off a text he should have run through his head a time or two.

* * *

Ashlyn just closed her computer when a vibration from nearby startled her. She reached for her phone, anticipating one of her friends, or possibly, but not holding her breath, Eric.

The text was none of what was expected.

Unknown: It was great seeing you today.

Ashlyn sighed and quickly fired a text back. Poor guy or girl.

Ashlyn: Wrong number. Sorry.

Tripp had never thought about the anonymity of starting a conversation with Ashlyn, and only then realized that he could potentially have a little fun. He knew that she'd throw a bit of a fit when she found out it was him regardless.

Unknown: No, Ash. I've definitely got the right number.

Ashlyn's heart raced as she climbed into bed, about to put her phone on silent and on her nightstand.

Ashlyn: Who is this?

Unknown: Who would you like for it to be?

Ashlyn: This isn't funny. Either tell me who you are or lose my number.

Unknown: Goodnight, Ash.

CHAPTER 7

Unknown: You look incredible today.

Ashlyn nearly choked on her water when the text came in. Her friends, as well as Eric, who was joining her for a few brief minutes at the start of lunch, all looked at her in the same confused way.

"What was that about," Eric immediately asked, nodding to the phone Ashlyn had below the table.

"Nothing. Just...my mom," Ashlyn lied.

The statement was good enough for June and Kayla, and possibly Eric, who seemed consumed by his own device.

"Oh, tell Poppy I said hi," Emory spoke up.

Ashlyn eyed her friend suspiciously, but Emory held a look of pure innocence.

Ashlyn had a difficult time sleeping the night before. For some odd reason, the number that had text still made her body buzz in excitement. As strange as the texts were, she looked forward to the mystery. Despite feeling a sense of guilt, she waited until Eric joined his friends outside before replying.

Ashlyn: So, we go to school together?

Unknown: Yes.

Ashlyn: And are you in the cafeteria now?

Unknown: Yes.

Tripp had to look away once he saw Ashlyn's head pop up. She wasn't stupid, if she saw him staring at her, she'd know right then and there who the number belonged to. He was a little surprised that she hadn't guessed already; however, since last Saturday, he had tried to be more standoffish and distant, even feigning loss of interest.

She reminded him of a wounded animal, which probably wasn't the best way to describe her. He'd never tell her that, but the little bit he had known about her in that short time, she seemed hesitant and vulnerable. He wanted to come on strong; that was his usual way. He didn't see the point in beating around the bush. He found her interesting. The first time he saw her, something clicked in his head. He wanted to get to know her better. Was he head over heels in love? Definitely not. Did he find her attractive and wonder what it would be like to touch her again? To kiss her? Absolutely.

Tripp waited until lunch was over before checking his phone.

Ashlyn: How long are you going to keep your identity a secret?

Unknown: It hasn't even been twenty-four hours. I'll add impatient to what I'm learning about you.

Tripp silenced his phone and threw it into his bag as soon as Ashlyn walked into their class. He was pleased to see that she was on the phone, no doubt reading the message he had just sent. He found it cute how she bit on her bottom lip slightly upon looking at the device.

"Hey," he acknowledged when she sat down. Without another word he retrieved his notebook and pen from his bag.

Ashlyn eyed Tripp with a great deal of skepticism and a bad feeling came over her. She waited until the bell rang and the class fell silent while Mrs. Cohen called attendance. She then shot off a text to the number and waited.

She heard nothing. She recalled that Tripp had his phone on vibrate the time she had seen him texting in class. Either that wasn't the case, or it wasn't him. A bizarre mixture of relief and disappointment came over her.

Mrs. Cohen started to talk about an upcoming project, but Ashlyn was tuned out. She found herself to be a very curious person, and she was more curious than ever about the person texting her and how they got her number.

Tripp smirked when he finally dared to look at his phone after class.

Ashlyn: I know you're in a class right now. This is just a test.

Did she really think that he'd be so careless to have his phone on ring or vibrate? However, this also meant that a part of her suspected him.

Unknown: A test?

Ashlyn: Sorry. Stupid. Ignore that.

"Ashlyn," an authoritative voiced called out. It belonged to Mr. Reynolds, the newspaper and journalism teacher. "I'm so glad I caught you before the end of the day."

Ashlyn closed her locker and refrained from pointing out that the school day was over.

"I was just about to email you, but if you could come to my classroom really quick. I have tutorials going on, but I needed to give you something," he went on.

Ashlyn agreed and followed Mr. Reynolds back to his room. At least a dozen students were in there for after-school tutorials. Several of them Ashlyn recognized as ones that didn't need tutoring, they were just overachievers.

"I anticipate you'll probably be at the baseball game this Saturday," Mr. Reynolds asked as he dug in a file cabinet for a folder.

"I haven't decided. I can be."

There were probably twenty games that their school would end up playing, both at home and away. Ashlyn had no intention of going to the away games. In fact, since Eric wasn't playing, she probably would only go to a couple more with Emory. Eric had already been upset that she went to the first game.

"Well, if you are, I was hoping you could do an interview with next week's student athlete of the week," he said, handing her a paper of questions. They were the standard questions that were repetitively asked of most of the athletes of the week. "However, if you don't get around to it, that's fine. It can wait until next week, but athlete of the week is always in Thursday's edition."

Ashlyn smiled and took the paper. "I'll see what I can do. Who is it?"

"Oh, the new guy, Tripp Scott. I've heard great things about him, mostly on the field, but off the field as well," Mr. Reynolds gushed.

Ashlyn's brain scrambled for something, anything, to get out of the assignment. She felt strange when she was around Tripp. She didn't want to have to sit down with him and ask all those questions.

"Actually, sir. I'm pretty swamped. If there's someone else–"

Before Ashlyn could finish her sentence, one of the overachievers staying after school on a Friday for no good reason, rushed up to Mr. Reynold's desk.

"Mr. Reynolds! If Ash doesn't want to, I'm able," Grace said in one excited breath.

Mr. Reynolds gave Ashlyn a sharp look, clearly not happy, and directed his words to Grace. "That won't be necessary."

"It's fine with me," Ashlyn chimed in.

"See! It's fine with her. I can interview Tripp," she squealed. She wasn't doing a very good job at containing herself with the idea of getting a chance to talk to a guy that most of the female body at the school was falling all over.

"Thank you for...your enthusiasm," Mr. Reynolds began. He looked back over to Ashlyn. "I handed this assignment to you. Is there a problem?"

Ashlyn's first thought was no. There wasn't a problem. It was all in her head. She had interviewed lots of athletes in the last two years. This one shouldn't be any different, but it was. She just couldn't explain that to Mr. Reynolds when she had a hard time explaining it to herself.

"No. Sorry. I've got it," Ashlyn finally concluded.

Grace shot her the nastiest of glares when she folded the paper up and put it in her bag. Ashlyn couldn't see how she had managed to offend someone who had never been part of the conversation to begin with.

* * *

Unknown: How was your day?

It was stupid, so stupid. Ashlyn couldn't contain the excitement that rushed through her when she looked at the text. Earlier in the day, Eric had told her he wanted to take her to a movie, but shortly after school, his plans changed. She should have asked her friends to do something, but she had already told them she had plans with Eric. She could only imagine the grief that Emory would give her if she told her that he canceled again.

Desperately wanting to engage in conversation with the mystery person, she knew she'd have to come up with more than a one-word answer.

Ashlyn: It was long, but thankfully it's the weekend.

Unknown: Big plans?

Ashlyn: A friend and I are going to the baseball game tomorrow.

Unknown: You like baseball?

Ashlyn: I'm honestly not sure. I think. I usually just go because she goes.

Ashlyn hated putting it like that, but it was the truth. Oddly, she decided to leave out the part that she first started going to the games for Eric. If this person went to the same school, chances were, they knew she was in a relationship, or could easily have found that out.

Unknown: Doesn't seem like the best reason.

Ashlyn: Well, now my newspaper teacher gave me an assignment for student athlete of the week. I'm supposed to try to do the interview after the game tomorrow, but it isn't due until Wednesday evening, so it can go out Thursday.

She groaned and fell back into the couch. She did not need to babble all that in a text. Saying that also made her think of Tripp, and she did not want to spend her Friday night thinking of him; however, the next text made her think of him even more when she told her mysterious friend who she was interviewing.

Ashlyn: Tripp Scott. Ugh.

Unknown: Haha. Do you not get along with him?

Ashlyn didn't want to rant away about Tripp to some stranger. It wasn't that she didn't get along with him. In class, they did pretty well when they worked on assignments together. It was something about that first day. The way he looked at her was unnerving, and he completely ignored the fact that she had a boyfriend. Then there was that playful moment with the sign, which Tripp had to ultimately ruin.

Ashlyn: He can just be a bit much.

Tripp didn't entirely understand what that meant, but it probably had something to do with his forwardness and confidence, which Ashlyn thought to be cockiness. Okay, maybe he was a little cocky.

"Sweetie, it's Friday night," Tripp's mother, Eliza pointed out.

"Thanks for informing me," he said, continuing to swipe away on his phone.

"I just thought you'd want to be out with friends."

"Tripp doesn't have any friends," Cason yelled as he plopped on the couch beside Tripp and reached for the remote.

"I do too," Tripp grumbled. It was his only response to his little brother. There was no way he was going to argue with an eight-year-old. With respect to his mother, "I went out to eat last night after the game. I'd just rather stay in tonight."

"Stay in and text," his mother questioned with a teasing hint in her voice. "You do realize if you get off that thing you could just go and talk in person."

"She's busy," he sighed before he could catch himself.

"Ooooh," Cason cooed.

"Ah, the reason there's a $250 florist charge on the credit card..."

Tripp playfully kicked at his brother, who was now making gross kissy noises. "I asked dad first."

"I know. He told me. I didn't know you had a girl-friend," Eliza shrugged. She went back to organizing a bookshelf.

"She's just a friend."

Eliza spun around to face her son, her eyes narrowed and her lips tight. "Do you want to talk," she hesitated.

"Oh my gosh," Tripp laughed. "I'm going to my room."

Tripp couldn't believe that Ashlyn continued to text him throughout the night. A part of him felt like it was probably because she wasn't out with her boyfriend or friends, and he was just a cure to boredom. He'd take it for now.

It wasn't until after one in the morning that he finally had to tell her goodnight. They had text for more than six hours. There were a few breaks, but for the most part, the conversation was steady. He was careful with what he told her to some of her questions. When it came to school, all he told her was that they were in the same year. He made sure to not mention anything about playing baseball. Aside from that, he was very honest and open with her, and he felt like she was as well. Although he did wonder why she not once mentioned anything about her boyfriend.

CHAPTER 8

"You look strangely happy," Emory pointed out as Ashlyn made her way up the bleachers to their usual spot.

"I take it the movie went well," Kayla asked with a wink.

There was no point in lying to her friends. "Eric canceled on me, so I stayed home."

"What," June gasped. "We all could have done something."

"It was late and at the last minute," Ashlyn said, attempting to brush off the conversation.

"Wait," Emory began, dragging out the one word for much longer than the one syllable required. "Why are you blushing?"

Ashlyn tried to hide her face and took that moment to dig her camera out of her bag. "I'm not blushing," she insisted.

"Oh my gosh, yes you are," June squealed.

"Totally! What are you hiding," Kayla pressed.

Ashlyn wanted to tell them. Maybe she could tell them just a little. She could trust all three of them. It would never get back to Eric. That thought alone made her feel like she was doing something wrong, but she wasn't. Was she?

"There's been this person texting me," she vaguely began.

June and Kayla leaned in, and in unison, "And?"

"Well, that's what I was doing last night. Just texting," Ashlyn admitted leaving out all the details, especially the last message she received, which only kept her up feeling giddy.

"That sounds ominous," June said in a whisper.

Ashlyn looked to Emory. She hadn't said anything so far, but she was doing that thing where she was listening and evaluating. Ashlyn hated when she did that.

Just as Ashlyn put a new memory card in her camera, Emory swiped her phone.

"Goodnight, beautiful?!"

"Hey," Ashlyn yelled, lunging toward Emory and yanking the phone away. "Don't go through my phone."

"You let Eric go through your phone," Emory pointed out with great seriousness. When Ashlyn's eyes widened in panic, "Yeah, remember last semester when he saw that I text you that he was a loser jerk. He flipped out and wanted you to break off our friendship."

"It's just some texts. I'll delete them before–"

"You shouldn't have to." Emory shook her head. "Just because someone calls you beautiful doesn't imply anything, but we both know he won't see it like that. Honestly, put a lock on your phone. It's annoying that even we have to be careful about what we say to you, just in case he sees it. It's one thing for him to have access to your phone, it's another for him to go through what we talk about." Needless to say, Emory was still mad about the ordeal from the semester prior.

"Well maybe if you'd stop calling him names," Ashlyn pointed out.

Emory shrugged. "I call them like I see them."

* * *

"Hey, Tripp," Ashlyn called out to him as he crossed the parking lot.

He was a little surprised, most everyone had cleared out after the game. She came jogging up to him with a giant purse. He didn't know what it was called, but he knew she kept her camera tucked safely inside.

"Hey," she repeated, once she was within normal talking distance.

The way she positioned herself in front of him and turned, blocking the sun from both their eyes, allowed him to face the original direction he was headed. This also meant that he could see his parents and little brother waiting for him at their car. Cason was already making duck faces that were supposed to resemble kisses.

"Hey," Tripp softly addressed her.

"Yeah, so," Ashlyn nervously began. "First of all, good game." It was almost painful to say. She knew Tripp had a big head when it came to baseball. Sadly, after seeing him play for a second time, he had every right to think he was as good as he claimed. "Secondly, I'm supposed to interview you for student athlete of the week."

"Oh, cool," he said, pretending to be surprised.

"Yeah, do you have a few minutes?"

If he did the interview now, it would be rushed, and he really wanted some alone time with Ashlyn, regardless what the context was.

He nodded behind her. "My parents are waiting."

Ashlyn turned and gave a sweet smile, mostly because once she turned, she didn't know what else to do.

"We're going out for an early dinner," he continued.

Ashlyn tried not to be disappointed. "Oh, I see." When given an assignment, she liked to get it out of the way sooner rather than later.

"You're welcomed to come with us," Tripp offered. He couldn't help but burst into laughter when Ashlyn's jaw dropped, and her giant blue eyes grew twice their size. "I'm kidding," he began trying to compose himself. "Well, I'm not. You could come, but I knew you wouldn't."

Ashlyn wanted nothing more than to go, only to prove him wrong. This, however, was one challenge she could not allow herself to accept.

"I just don't know your parents." She glanced back to them, now having a conversation between themselves. "Or your brother."

Tripp shrugged. "That's how you get to know someone. You talk to them, spend time with them."

Suddenly, Ashlyn didn't like the direction the conversation was going. There seemed to be an underlying meaning to his words, and she didn't want to overthink what he was saying.

"Anyway, just give me your number and we can set something up. Assuming you agree to be interviewed," she added, taking out her phone.

Tripp raised a brow, and a smirk came across his face.

"What," Ashlyn questioned, quite surprised.

"I don't know. I wouldn't feel right about that."

"What are you talking about?"

Tripp pretended to think. Ashlyn knew right away he was playing some kind of game that she didn't have the time for. "I mean, you have a boyfriend. You probably shouldn't be asking other guys for their number."

"Ugh! You are impossible! I'm asking so we can set up a time and place," she continued to scream in frustration.

"You could just wait until I see you in class on Monday," Tripp said quietly, taking a step closer.

His proximity caused the spring air to feel much warmer than Ashlyn knew it to be. "Or, this could be done by then."

"Sorry. I have plans the rest of the weekend," he said. He took a step around Ashlyn. From over his shoulder, "See you Monday."

CHAPTER 9

"You seem to be in a good mood," Tripp pointed out when Ashlyn sat down.

"I'm always in a good mood." She made note that several people in the last four days had already said something to the same effect.

Tripp hadn't gotten a good look at Ashlyn from across the cafeteria at lunch, but now that she was seated next to him, he saw how adorable she was. She wore a plaid button up in bright shades of blue, pink and purple. Over that she had on a slender pair of overalls with decorative patchwork at one of the knees. What he found to be strangely cute was that today she had her hair in haphazard pigtails. In a sea of contoured faces and beach waves from a metal rod, she stood out.

"What," Ashlyn asked, now looking at him after preparing her area for the lesson.

Tripp didn't realize that he had been staring. "Nothing."

"Oh, before class starts, I wanted to talk to you about meeting up for just a few minutes."

"Just a few minutes?"

"I'm a fast writer. The questions shouldn't take long," Ashlyn pointed out, reminding Tripp of the interview for the school's online paper.

He tried to hide his disappointment. "Oh, yeah, that. I can meet after school today."

Just before the bell rang, Ashlyn glanced back at her phone. She had hoped for a message, but had to figure that her mystery friend was already in class.

"Something wrong," Tripp asked.

"No. I was just expecting–" Ashlyn quickly stopped when she realized what she was about to say.

"Ah, the boyfriend. Gotcha," Tripp teased.

"No. Not *the boyfriend*. He has a name by the way," Ashlyn spat.

Tripp leaned in, closer than Ashlyn ever expected. "So, not *Eric*. That's odd."

Quickly finding her words, which seemed difficult with his proximity, "What's odd?"

"You just looked hopeful, and then disappointed, like a girl expecting a message from her boyfriend." Tripp held a smirk that Ashlyn suddenly found to be rather attractive. At the realization, she wanted to smash her notebook in his face to make it go away. "And now you're blushing."

Ashlyn huffed and turned away with the ringing of the bell. "Just shut up."

Then he laughed. He laughed a lot. Hearing that laugh did something to Ashlyn that she didn't like, not one little bit.

As Mrs. Cohen called roll, Tripp whispered into Ashlyn's ear at an impossibly close distance. "After school? Library?"

She could feel his breath. She was positive that when he said those few words, she felt them beat across her neck.

"Ash Jennings," Mrs. Cohen repeated.

Ashlyn jumped and raised her hand. "Here!"

Tripp shook his head. "Wow."

"What?"

"Something about you seems off," he pointed out.

"First of all, library, yes," Ashlyn said, remembering that she was in such of a daze that she had forgotten to answer his question. "Secondly, you don't know me, so I don't know what that comment is about. Lastly, personal space." With that, she pushed at his arm to make him go back to his half of the table.

She wished that she wouldn't have touched him. Through his button down she could feel his arm tense and it felt harder and more muscular than she had imagined.

Tripp was sad that their banter had to end once class started. It didn't have to. There had been times that they made stupid comments to each other during the lesson, but today was different. Tripp could tell that Ashlyn had a battle going on inside. She had the strangest combination of looks running across her face. Anxious. Hopeful. Disappointed. Confused. Her thoughts seemed to be a million miles away from earth science.

Unknown: I loved your outfit today. You looked amazing.

Ashlyn sat at a secluded table near the back windows of the library and read over and over the text. Her heart raced as she pondered her response. She had to do it. It drove her crazy all weekend thinking about it.

She didn't care who it was, all she had to offer was friendship anyway. She hated that the thought crossed her mind. She had a boyfriend. She felt like every time in the past few days that this person text her, she had to remind herself of that fact. The person behind the screen, whoever they were, was so easy to talk to. He was fun, caring, and very complimentary. Did she wish that Eric was more like him? Or did she wish for something entirely different?

Ashlyn: Please tell me who you are.

Unknown: Sorry. I'm enjoying us getting to know each other.

Ashlyn: That's not fair. You have a name and a face to put to everything I say.

Unknown: What if I'm really ugly?

Ashlyn: If you know anything about me, then you'll know I'm not that shallow.

Unknown: If I tell you who I am, will you spend one day with me outside of school.

Ashlyn swallowed heavily and looked around the library. She knew Tripp had athletics at the end of the day, but could he possibly take any longer?

She went back to her phone and reread the message. Her skin felt like it was on fire. Butterflies rode rollercoasters in her stomach. As much as she didn't want to send the next message, she knew she had to. She had already felt pangs of guilt over the last few days.

Ashlyn: I have a boyfriend.

Unknown: Which is why I didn't use the word date or anything to imply that it would be more than two friends hanging out.

Ashlyn: But you'd want it to be.

Unknown: Wouldn't any guy? I'll take what I can get though.

Before Ashlyn could think of how to respond, Tripp fell into the chair next to her, startling her so much that she jumped.

"Whoa," he laughed. "Calm down."

"Don't sneak up on people," Ashlyn huffed.

Tripp watched her carefully as she took out a folded piece of paper and her pen. Her breathing was heavy and rushed. Redness made its way from her cheeks down to her neck.

He had an effect on her. He knew it. Well, maybe not him so much as his words, masking him behind the screen as a stranger.

"Okay, I'll try to make this quick," Ashlyn began.

"It's all good. Take your time."

Ashlyn rolled her eyes and went to ask the first question, but before she could get one word out, "How was your day?"

A question so simple practically fried her brain. "Excuse me?"

Tripp chuckled and leaned back in his chair. "I asked how your day was? Terrible? Great? Just okay?"

"Umm. Good. Yeah, good."

Tripp watched how flustered she became. He wanted to know why. He wanted to know a lot of things. Instead, "Anything interesting?"

"Not out of the usual," Ashlyn answered. She felt strange with him being so normal. He was being normal, right? Or was this a tactic of some sort?

"I saw your write-up about Saturday's game. You take really good pictures."

Now Ashlyn was intrigued. "How so?"

"It's hard to explain," he began.

Ashlyn knew it. He didn't care. He was just looking for something to compliment her on. It was clearly one of his flirting devices, just like when girls pretend to like sports for a guy but don't know the difference between a touchdown or home run.

"I guess," he continued, much to her surprise. "I know you didn't just go out there with a camera, click it a few times, and pick whichever one turned out the least blurry. Some of the photos you have symmetrically balanced, but with others you clearly wanted them the opposite, like the one after Byron scored the last run. You had everyone on the left of your photo, but on the right, you had the opposing team's pitcher on the mound. It was strangely balanced even though it wasn't. It was a good picture." When Ashlyn didn't say anything, and looked at him with her mouth slightly agape, Tripp awkwardly ran his hand over the back of his neck and fiddled with the bill of his ballcap. "I know I'm not saying it right, but–"

"Thank you," Ashlyn interrupted. Strangely he was saying everything right, since the moment he sat down. "Anyway, on to–"

"You like photography more than the journalism aspect, am I right?"

Ashlyn couldn't help but smile and shake her head. "There isn't a photography class here, but yes. I like taking the pictures; however, oftentimes, like with the games, that means I'm stuck writing the articles too."

"And the painting?"

Ashlyn put her pen down and eyed Tripp skeptically. "We're wasting a lot of time talking about me and you not answering these questions."

Tripp chuckled. "I wouldn't call it a waste."

Ashlyn swallowed heavily and took in a deep breath. "All I did was paint a stupid sign."

"Oh, whatever! You did the bear freehanded and it came out amazing."

Ashlyn blushed at the compliment. "Okay, I am in art. I like art and photography. Sometimes it's hard to remember what something looks like, so most of my drawings or whatever, are just copies of what I've photographed."

She continued to amaze him. "That's really cool." Seeing a slight way in, but not wanting to come off as too strong, "I'd really like to see some of your stuff one day." Ashlyn's eyes shot up and her face went flat. Before she could say something that would no doubt ruin the last ten minutes, "Anyway, what questions do I need to answer?"

Ashlyn rapidly blinked a couple times and went to the sheet of questions before her. "First question, age?"

"Seventeen. You?"

Ashlyn couldn't stop the smile from coming to her face. "This is about you, not me. But, sixteen."

Tripp saw her continuing to write something. "What's that," he asked, taking the chance to scoot his chair closer in her direction. "You didn't ask–"

"Sport and position. Baseball and first base. I didn't need to ask," Ashlyn confidently pointed out. "Favorite class?"

"Earth science," Tripp answered a little too quickly.

Ashlyn paused, her pen on the paper but not moving. Tripp waited for her to say something, to give him a deathly glare which he'd only find humor in. He was surprised and disappointed when she simply wrote the two words down and moved on to the next question.

After what seemed like an hour later, largely in part because Tripp kept interrupting to ask Ashlyn questions about herself, they were nearly done.

"Okay, last question. Where do you see yourself in ten years?"

Tripp thought for a minute. He looked out the window and saw that the afternoon would soon be fading. The school library closed at five, so they'd be needing to leave momentarily. He hated that his time with Ashlyn would soon be over; however, he had gotten almost an hour of her time. It didn't matter that it was only for a stupid assignment.

"Tripp?"

Tripp looked from the window back to Ashlyn. He wanted so badly to tell her how beautiful she was. Instead, "Happy."

"I'm sorry?"

"You asked where I see myself in ten years. That's my answer."

"Wow. Okay," was all Ashlyn could say as she wrote the one-word answer down.

Jokingly, "Is that a bad answer?"

Ashlyn looked up at him with a serious face. "No. It's actually really good."

Tripp didn't say it to try please her into thinking he was deep and sophisticated, but he was happy that it seemed to surprise her. She probably thought he'd say something overly cocky, like winning the World Series.

Ashlyn put the paper back in her bag and brought out her camera. "I just need a picture now."

Tripp's face scrunched up. "Seriously?"

"Yeah." Noticing his expression, "Why? Is something wrong with that?"

He shrugged and stood. "I'm not really good with pictures. Plus, I just got done with practice."

"You've showered. I can smell your bodywash, or whatever," she mumbled. "You'll be fine." She quickly added and began fumbling with her camera settings. She did not want to think about Tripp's bodywash.

"I'll make you a deal."

"This isn't something negotiable," Ashlyn laughed.

"Take a picture with me first."

"Nope," Ashlyn responded immediately. She was certain with the playfulness of his words that if she looked up, he'd have that stupid grin on his face.

"Come on, what's the big deal?"

Ashlyn looked up and glared at him.

"Just a quick and simple selfie," he added, like what he was asking for was so effortless.

"On your phone, I presume?"

Tripp nodded.

"Why? What will you do with it?"

Tripp shook his head and held up his hands. "Whoa, it's just a picture with you. Nothing sinister about it, but I get it."

Ashlyn clutched her camera and crossed her arms. "What do you get?"

It was low. He knew it was, but he went there anyway. "I'm sure your boyfriend would be pissed if he ever found out," Tripp said with a cool shrug. Immediately he saw flames dance across her eyes that often mirrored the ocean.

Ashlyn set her camera on the table. "Get your phone," she growled.

Tripp tried to hide his excitement over his win, but inside he was doing the most ridiculous happy dance.

Ashlyn stood in front of him and he stretched out his arm with his phone so that it was in front of the both of them. That's when Ashlyn grabbed the wrist of his hand attached to the phone and his whole body tensed from her innocent touch.

"It's too dark. Turn," she instructed. "Face the window. Ugh. Now there's a shadow from the phone. Just a little more. Move slightly to your left. There! What's so funny," she sighed.

"Nothing. I didn't mean for it to be a big deal."

Though Ashlyn had her back to him, he saw her eyes fall from the screen in embarrassment. "It isn't."

"On the count of three," he asked.

"Sure."

"You'll smile?"

Ashlyn took a deep breath in annoyance. "I don't have all day, Tripp."

"One...Two..."

Just as Tripp got halfway through the count, he snaked his free arm around Ashlyn's stomach and drew her in until her back collided with his chest.

She held her smile for a second more, until he hit the screen and she knew the moment was captured.

Her head screamed for her to move, to step away, but his warmth around her kept her feet frozen in place. A second or two more and a chill rushed over her when he dropped his arm and stepped away.

"Not bad, right," he asked showing her the picture.

Ashlyn couldn't think straight and just nodded. Tripp acted so calm about it. Was she the only one who read into the gesture more than she should have? He made it seem so innocent, but it didn't feel that way. In those few seconds, Ashlyn felt as though something else had passed between them. The way he held her, something about it felt...nice.

When she didn't immediately step away after the picture, Tripp knew that she had to feel something close to what he did. While he tried to pretend that it was nothing, Ashlyn had gone silent and nervously chewed on the bottom corner of her lip.

"Here," he said, holding her camera out to her.

She yanked it from him and pointed where she wanted him to stand. He followed her directions, but when she looked into the lens, she didn't look happy.

"Take off your cap," she told him.

"Nope. My hair is a mess," he tried to say in a playful tone. He hated how tense she looked now.

Ashlyn took in a deep breath pretending to be irritated, but Tripp could see that a smile tugged on her lips. She stepped forward and reached for his cap and yanked it off.

"Hey!"

"There, better."

Tripp ran his fingers through his hair and tousled it back and forth.

"Stop it and stand still," Ashlyn huffed.

"Give me my cap or fix it!"

Ashlyn made a noise that could only indicate frustration, but she stepped forward a few feet and reached up to straighten his hair. As soon as her fingers touched the smooth strands of deep gold, she realized how intimate the moment felt. Her heart pounded erratically.

Tripp couldn't take it anymore. He knew she'd pull away soon, take her picture, and that would be the end. He didn't want that to be the end.

Ashlyn froze when Tripp lightly grabbed her wrist and gently pulled it from his hair. It was only then that their eyes met, and the look on his face was one she had never seen from him. In the next passing moment, his golden eyes darkened to the deepest brown.

When he stepped forward and closed the space between them, Ashlyn found that the tiny voice in her head, the one that was supposed to tell her to step away, was silent. Completely silent. Though she didn't want to admit it, she was glad.

After Tripp lowered her arm, he slid his around her waist while the other reached up and slowly traced from her shoulder to her neck, his eyes never leaving hers.

It was then that the fine and patient thread that restrained him every time he was around her, finally snapped.

CHAPTER 10

It was unlike any kiss that either of them had ever experienced. At first Tripp barely pressed his lips to Ashlyn's and drew back after the smallest of pecks. When she didn't pull away, or slap him, as he had thought she'd more than likely do, he kissed her again.

Ashlyn felt like she was on a rollercoaster spiraling out of control throughout the starry sky. His kiss was filled with so much passion and hunger. His arm at the small of her back drew her impossibly close, so close that she could practically draw a map of the muscles that trailed down his chest, just from her hands sliding over the tightly fitted t-shirt.

When Tripp lightly bit at her bottom lip, she parted her mouth just enough and the taste of spearmint burst inside as their tongues met.

Tripp couldn't contain the animalistic growl he let out when Ashlyn not only let the kiss continue, but allowed it to go so much further than he could ever imagine. His whole body could go up in flames at any moment with the heat radiating between the two of them. Needing to steady himself, he took a step backward and hit the window, immediately welcoming the cool glass pressed against his back.

That slight movement must have shaken something loose on Ashlyn's end, and she quickly pulled away, not just out of Tripp's arms, but several feet backwards.

When she looked up, despite her haggard breaths matching those of Tripp's, he could see the truth written clear as day across her face. *Mistake.*

Tripp was further surprised when, after touching her lips and shaking her head, she was actually the first of them to speak.

"Crap!"

It wasn't exactly what Tripp was expecting after what just happened between them.

Ashlyn placed her camera in one of her bags and began rushing to get her things together to leave. "That did not just happen."

Tripp didn't know if she was talking to him or to herself. "That was amazing." He clenched his eyes and took in a sharp breath when he got a glare full of lightning bolts at that comment.

"No. No. No. That was a mistake, a huge mistake."

There it was. That's exactly what he expected her to say and it tore at his insides to hear that.

"Ash," he sighed. He couldn't think of what to say in the few seconds before he knew she was about to run away from him. Though it was futile, "Can you just wait a second? Can we talk?"

A part of her wanted to scream, another wanted to slap Tripp, and another wanted to cry. There was also a part of her that hated that the kiss ended, but she squashed that little piece so fast.

"That's the first and last time something like that will ever happen between us," she hissed at him.

Tripp took a step toward her, but before he could get another word out, she rushed out of the library.

He raked his hands through his hair in frustration before slapping his cap back on. Maybe the kiss had clouded his judgement, but he reached for his phone knowing the devastating blow he was about to deal.

* * *

Ashlyn thought her heart might fall out of her chest from beating so hard and so fast as she made quick steps through the parking lot toward her car.

In the pocket of her overalls, she both felt and heard her phone going off like crazy, but ignored it. Thinking of who it could be, her mind flew to Eric.

She had cheated on him. That's what that was. One of the best kisses of her life was completely tainted. She shook her head. No. The kiss was horrible. It was too...It just didn't...She didn't feel...

Ashlyn stopped midway through the parking lot and screamed. That was followed by jumping up and down and stomping her feet like a child. Her body was shaking with frustration and she wanted it out.

Thankfully, the school was nearly deserted by now and no one had witnessed her little fit. When she was done, she took in a deep breath. Another alert from her phone piqued her curiosity. She reached for it, and when she saw the screen, froze.

Missed call – Unknown

Missed call – Unknown

Unknown: I'm sorry, okay?

Unknown: Where are you?

Unknown: Ash, please don't leave. I need to talk to you.

Ashlyn could feel the thumping in her head from the blood flow. When she was able to swallow, it felt like a brick sinking from her throat to the pit of her stomach.

She scrolled and looked over the messages again, hoping that the person she had been messaging like crazy the last couple days had not just been the one to send those messages.

She couldn't explain why, but tears stung at her eyes. "No," she whispered.

Stuck in a strange universe, oblivious to everything around her, Ashlyn didn't hear Tripp's fast approaching footsteps; however, the faint sound of her name from a voice she was beginning to recognize all too well, snapped her back to reality. She spun around, only to come face to face with a breathless and panicked wreck of a guy.

"You," she managed to say.

Ashlyn stayed firmly in her place as Tripp took steps toward her; however, she had no intention of letting him get close enough to touch her.

"Yeah."

She held up her phone. "You're the only who's been texting me?!"

Seeing how skittish Ashlyn looked, Tripp stopped about three feet in front of her before answering. "Yeah."

"So, none of this was real," she said softly, looking down at the phone in her hand.

Her words annoyed Tripp. "Are you saying that because it's me?"

Ashlyn searched his face. For once it was firm and serious, something she rarely saw when it came to him. Usually he was lighthearted and full of laughter. Not thinking her words through carefully, only speaking as they came to her, "Yes. The person that I've been messaging is nothing like you."

"How would you know," Tripp growled, his voice deep and gruff. "You never even gave me a chance to be your friend."

Ashlyn laughed. He was mad. Good. He deserved to be mad. It wasn't fair that all these emotions were hitting her, and he acted unaffected. "I know guys like you. You don't want to be my *friend*. Girls are just another thing for you to collect."

Tripp shook his head in disbelief. "After everything I've told you, that's what you think of me?"

A part of Ashlyn hated the hurt that flashed in his eyes, his beautiful eyes that became lighter with the slowly descending sun. "This mystery person is a joke. If it's you, it's just a lie, just a game for you to play to mess with my head."

Tripp couldn't take the venom she was injecting directly into his veins. "I think you're scared."

Ashlyn appeared shocked. "Of what?"

"Realizing that I am that person."

"That doesn't scare me," she huffed.

"No. What scares you is that you liked that person, but you don't want to like me because you have this idea of me stuck in your head from the first ten minutes of meeting me. It scares you that you're wrong, and that maybe I am a great guy."

She couldn't take the way his eyes were latched to hers. It was more than simple eye contact. "I can't do this." Her words were barely more than a whisper as she turned from him. "Please, just leave me alone."

Tripp forced himself to let her walk to her car, get in, and drive away. As much as it frustrated him, he knew what he had to do next. Wait.

After that kiss, and now knowing that he's the person she's been messaging, he had to believe that despite what she was thinking and feeling right now, in the days to come she'd realize that there was something between them.

He laughed at how ridiculous he was being over a girl, but from the moment he met her, all he wanted was to get to know her. An instant attraction was quickly leading to something more for him, and the softness of her lips, now just a memory on his, was proof of that.

Ashlyn didn't text Eric that night. She couldn't. What would she have said? She had to say something, didn't she? The idea that she had cheated on him made her feel sick to her stomach. It was kind of an accident, but he wouldn't see it that way. All he'd see is red. Despite how she felt about Tripp, he didn't deserve whatever Eric would dish out if he found out about what happened.

"In your pajamas already," Ashlyn's mom pointed out.

Ashlyn reached for a bottle of water, the refrigerator light now overpowering the glow from her mother's laptop as she sat at the dining table.

"It's nine, and it's a school night," she pointed out.

Poppy rubbed her eyes beneath her glasses and squinted at the corner of her computer to check the time. "Wow. So it is."

"Anyway, goodnight mom."

"Come sit for a second. I'd like to talk."

Thankfully in the darkness Poppy couldn't see Ashlyn rolling her eyes. Her mother was great, but as a therapist, oftentimes when she said something similar, Ashlyn felt like she should be lying on a couch in an office.

Ashlyn pulled out the chair across from her mother and took a sip of water. The blinding light from the computer did nothing for her mother's looks. It made her appear far more tired and aged than she actually was.

"Is everything alright at school?"

It was an odd question for her mom to ask. "I guess so. Why?"

"Just checking in. I feel like something is a little off lately, especially today."

Though she didn't want to talk about it with her mom, Ashlyn knew that if she didn't say what was bothering her, her mother would only continue to pester. For a split second, she thought about lying, making up some project for one of her classes that was giving her the fits, but her mother could tell when she was lying. If she ever decided to change from a marriage counselor and family therapist, she could have a great career as an interrogator.

"There's this boy at school, and I think he likes me," Ashlyn finally admitted, feeling her cheeks warming as she said it aloud.

Poppy smiled. "This is a bad thing because..."

"He's just...He's so cocky. He thinks–"

Poppy quickly interrupted. "I don't like to speculate what other people think and don't think."

This is why she didn't like talking with her mother. There always had to be a lesson or something insightful that she was supposed to pick up on. "Ugh. Can you just be my mom for a second and not a therapist?"

Poppy rubbed her tired eyes and laughed. "That's me being a human. We shouldn't make assumptions like that. Although fine, go on," she sighed, pretending to be annoyed.

"He's just a bit much," Ashlyn said with a shrug.

"If he likes you, and you like him, there's nothing wrong with being friends."

"I have a boyfriend," Ashlyn grumbled. Needless to say, her parents were the same as Emory when it came to that particular person.

"Ah, yes. The boyfriend. Sweetie, you're in high school, you're allowed to speak to the opposite sex. You shouldn't feel bad about that because of Aaron."

"Eric," Ashlyn corrected.

"Right."

"I talk to other guys. For example, Emory's brother. I just think it's unfair if I'm friends with someone who has kind of made it clear that he might like to be more than friends," Ashlyn began to ramble. If she were to admit it, up until today, things were going along fine with Tripp. She could see themselves maybe being friends one day. Then he had to go and ruin that.

"Kind of, might...When you use words like that, you're trying to play down the truth. *Well, I kind of might have eaten the last piece of cake from the refrigerator.* You either did or you didn't," Poppy teased.

With sleep pulling at her eyelids, Ashlyn rose from her chair. "On that, I'm going to bed."

"One second." Ashlyn paused to hear what else her mother had to say on the matter. "I know you're almost seventeen and you don't like to talk about all this stuff. I just want to point out that I notice things. Today you came home more distraught and conflicted than I've ever seen; however, over the last few days, you've been happier and bubblier than I've seen in a long time."

"I'd rather not talk about it," Ashlyn mumbled, unable to meet her mother's eyes. She really didn't want to mention the kiss.

"I know that. Just know, the people we surround ourselves with, affect us, whether we want them to or not.

Ashlyn knew that, and it frustrated her. "I don't want people to have an effect on me."

"But they do," Poppy stressed. "That's why we try to have positive people in our lives, ones that lift us up and care about our wellbeing and success, and ones that make us laugh, make us happy."

"Thanks, mom. Goodnight. I love you."

"I love you, too," Poppy concluded, letting her daughter get the much-needed sleep she looked like she could use.

* * *

Ashlyn put her phone on the charger and saw text notifications. She was hesitant to click on any of them, rather, one chat in particular.

Emory: Yeah, I can meet before school. I'll come to your car when Ellis and I get there.

Eric: Hey, babe. I need help on some lame history thing. Can you help me tomorrow?

Ashlyn rolled her eyes. She'd respond to that in the morning. Lately, Eric's version of her helping him ended up with her doing it for him.

Like pulling off a bandage, she forced herself to click on the chat that was no longer an unknown person.

Tripp: I really am sorry, about a lot of things. I should have asked you before doing that.

Ashlyn's eyebrows furrowed as she stared at the odd text. What was he talking about? While it would have been in her best interest to block his number and go to bed, she was far too curious.

Ashlyn: Doing what?

Tripp: The kiss.

Was he serious? What kind of guy asks a girl before kissing her? That sounded like something people would have done in the Victorian era.

Ashlyn: Seriously?

Tripp: Despite what you think of me, I was raised to be a gentleman. I guess I just thought the signals were there, for that I'm sorry.

She couldn't believe that he was apologizing like that; however, something else in that message stood out, and an icy chill ran down her whole body.

She realized that he wasn't entirely wrong. Even when they took that stupid picture together, and he held her, she didn't say anything. She wasn't the one to pull away. If she kept thinking about everything that followed, she felt sick to her stomach. Tripp didn't misread anything. A part of her in that moment wanted him to kiss her, and if she was completely honest with herself, it wasn't the first time that she had thought about his lips on hers.

CHAPTER 11

"Geez, what was so urgent," Emory yawned as she closed the passenger door to Ashlyn's car. "Ellis was so annoyed that I asked him to leave ten whole minutes earlier."

Emory glanced over to Ashlyn sitting in the driver's seat, staring at the doors far ahead to the front of the school.

"Uh, earth to Ash," she said, nudging her. "You're the one who said you needed someone to talk to."

Ashlyn broke from the trance that had come over her. "I messed up," she finally said.

"No, please be more ominous and vaguer," Emory scoffed.

Ashlyn turned in her seat to face Emory and shuffled so that she was sitting with her right leg underneath her.

"I don't know where to start," she began, running a hand through her hair. She kept it simple and down today. After having gotten very little sleep, fixing her hair was the last thing she wanted to deal with. "Tripp kissed me," Ashlyn blurted out.

Emory's jaw dropped and then she waved her hands back and forth. "Whoa, wait. I think we missed a bunch of parts to this story."

"And I kissed him back. Oh god, it wasn't just a kiss," she groaned, slamming her head to the side into the steering wheel. "There was tongue!"

"Holy crap!"

Ashlyn closed her eyes and shook her head. "That's not even the worst part."

Before Emory could allow her to continue, "Worst part? Unless he's like a really sloppy kisser with bad breath, I'm failing to see where any of what you said is bad."

"No, he's a great kisser, wonderful breath and...No! Stop! That's not the point." Ashlyn had to quickly stop herself from any further description. "What do I tell Eric?"

Emory groaned and sank back in her seat. "Unless you want Tripp's mutilated body found in a field somewhere, you don't tell Mr. Temperamental anything."

"But if I don't then–"

"One kiss, or whatever you want to call it, singular, right? It only happened once? The two of you got caught up in the moment, yeah," Emory interrupted.

Ashlyn nodded.

"Then just let it be that and don't worry about Eric." The look on Ashlyn's face made Emory skeptical. "Unless...There's a chance that it might happen again..."

"No," Ashlyn quickly shouted.

Emory saw how distraught Ashlyn truly looked, and though she wanted to point out the redness painted across Ashlyn's cheeks and tease her, she sadly had to let that wait until this was something they could look back on and laugh about.

"You said there was a worse part," Emory back-tracked.

"You know that person that's been texting me?"

Emory froze. "Mhmm."

"It's Tripp!" Ashlyn shook her head. "Like, I don't even know how he got my number. Then, ugh. He was so nice and normal in his messages and for a split second...I guess I just wondered what it would be like to always have someone who asked about my day and told me goodnight, and...I'm such a mess."

Emory took in a deep breath, knowing that Ashlyn would be mad at her for at least the remainder of the day. "I figured."

"You figured? What part?"

"I gave him your number last week."

Ashlyn stared at her calm and collected friend, trying to process what she had just said. "You what?!"

"Ugh. Be mad at me. The guy has the cutest crush on you, and rather than speaking to him, you act like he's some deadly disease. Truth be told, I think it's brilliant that he didn't tell you who he was. For a few days, maybe you got to see the him that you wouldn't give a chance to."

"Why can't any of you understand that I have a boyfriend?! I have for the last two years," Ashlyn screamed at the top of her lungs.

"Maybe because he's never around, and when he is, he doesn't act like it," Emory coldly pointed out.

Ashlyn was about to speak but quickly closed her mouth. They both knew that there was nothing she could say in retaliation to that comment.

* * *

And so, the days went on.

Ashlyn never told Eric.

After a few awkward moments in class the first days since the incident, it became a little easier to breathe around Tripp. Thankfully, he nor any of the other guys sat with Ashlyn, Emory, June, and Kayla at lunch that week.

Ashlyn attended the two games that week with Emory. She took her pictures and made a quick exit before the end of the games, despite one of the nights Emory asking her to come along to a dinner outing with several of Ellis' friends.

As hard as it was, Tripp refrained from sending another text to Ashlyn after that day. She had his number too. If she wanted to continue a conversation outside of the classroom, she could text him; however, after several days, he knew that wouldn't be the case.

In avoiding each other with every part of their lives except for that forty-five minutes a day, they had inadvertently neglected a very important project.

"Alright class, some of my overachievers from other periods have already handed in their projects." Students in the classroom looked around as Mrs. Cohen said that. "Now you don't think I'd be so careless to leave them out and let some of you last minute people get ideas? Just keep in mind, they're due on Tuesday. If you want to enjoy your spring break, I'd consider getting them in."

Just then the bell rang.

"I guess we need to talk about that," Tripp said, bringing up the project that they only had a handful of days to both start on and complete.

"I have an entire closet full of crafting supplies. I can do the structure and you can write the paper," Ashlyn pointed out. This way they wouldn't have to work together outside of class.

Tripp zipped his backpack and tossed it on. "You want me to write a ten-page paper myself?"

"First of all, it's double spaced. That's technically only five pages," she pointed out. "And the last page is sources and citations, so now it's only four and a half."

"You sure? The paper is sixty percent of the project grade."

That got Ashlyn's attention.

"You know what, I'll do the paper."

"And I'll do the sculpture of our landform?"

Ashlyn didn't like how the dividing of the project was going. While she knew Tripp cared about his grades and would do a good job, she preferred to do all artistic aspects.

"I'll just do all of it."

They had been walking out of the classroom, but now Tripp stopped and turned, blocking Ashlyn's path.

"No, you're not," he chuckled. "Look, I know working with me is the last thing you want to do, but if you think I'm going to let you do this entire project by yourself, you're crazy."

Ashlyn stepped around Tripp and, having no desire to be late to her next class, made her way to the door. Tripp followed her out into the hall.

"I'm busy with my family this weekend, and Monday we have a game. So..."

"So, today would be the only day that you could work on it?"

"Oh, sorry. It's Friday," Tripp pointed out.

Ashlyn stopped in the busy hall and turned to face him, students continuing to flow around them. "What, you have a date?"

"No. I assumed you might."

Ashlyn lowered her eyes and shook her head. She was not about to mention anything more, ever, about her relationship when Tripp was around.

He didn't want to appear too eager. "Cool."

Ashlyn turned and they continued to walk down the hall together. She didn't know what class Tripp had next, but she couldn't ever recall leaving their class together and him going in the same direction as herself.

When Ashlyn didn't say anything more on the matter and appeared to be deep in thought, "Do you want to get together after school then?"

Ashlyn bit her lip. She hated how such an innocent question about a stupid assignment made her heart thump just a little more erratically.

"That'll be fine. Library?"

"The library closes at five. I guess we could go to the public library. I think it closes at seven on Fridays. What about the structure itself? We can't exactly pack up a bunch of supplies and work on that there," he pointed out, hoping that Ashlyn didn't see what he was trying to do.

"Ugh. Yeah, you're right." She paused and stood at a classroom, the hall growing emptier by the second. "Umm, this is me."

Tripp was a little surprised she hadn't told him to get lost prior.

"Which class is yours," she proceeded to ask.

"Oh, none. I have History, so–"

Shocked, Ashlyn abruptly interrupted him. "That's halfway across the school!"

Tripp chuckled and nervously raked his hand through his hair. Ashlyn's attention was immediately drawn in that direction and a knot formed in her stomach, thinking back to the library when her hands had been there.

"Anyway, today, after school, at?"

Ashlyn rolled her eyes. "Luckily my dad is working from home today, so you can come over."

Tripp couldn't help himself. "Are you not allowed to have friends if your parents aren't home?"

"Boys," Ashlyn quickly corrected. "I'm not allowed to have boys over if they're not home. Emory's brother is the only exception, because occasionally he's bored and tags along."

Just then the warning bell signaling a minute left until the tardy bell rang out.

Tripp began walking backwards to the direction of his class, which most definitely was nowhere near Ashlyn's. "Just text me the address, okay?"

Ashlyn nodded and turned to go into her room.

It wasn't until she sat down and began grabbing supplies from her bag that she realized what had happened. Did Tripp just walk her to her class?

CHAPTER 12

Tripp parked his G-Class on the street and looked at the painted numbers on the sidewalk. He was at the right house.

While his parents had moved into a newer and more modern looking house, Ashlyn's looked like something you'd see on a Christmas card, large and classic, giant oak trees, grand front porch, flowerbeds lining the front. It looked sweet and innocent, if a house could be described as such.

Tripp glanced at his phone. The last message Ashlyn sent him was that she was running by the library to pick up a few books. They needed at least five sources and no more than two could be websites. Ever the diligent one, at some point throughout the day, she had managed to research and reserve books that she thought they'd be able to use statistics, quotes, and references from.

Tripp also knew she wasn't home yet because her car wasn't there; however, several others were. Ashlyn had told him to simply wait for her, but she didn't exactly say where.

Adults didn't make him nervous. With as much traveling as his father did, and occasionally attending conventions along with him, Tripp was accustomed to speaking with those much older than himself. Speaking to parents of a girl he was definitely interested in, that was a little new to him.

He was taken aback when the front door swung open and a short and stout woman with black hair streaked with grey answered.

"How can I help you," she asked. Her accent was very South American; however, he couldn't place exactly where from.

"Hi, I'm a friend of Ash's. I'm here to work on a project with her."

The woman scrunched up her nose and looked Tripp over like he had crawled out of a sewer. Once she was satisfied, and he had passed whatever test she was conducting in her head, "You're not the boyfriend."

Tripp wasn't sure if it was a statement or a question, but he awkwardly laughed. "No. We're in science together."

The woman looked down at Tripp's jeans and sneakers. "You're cleaner than the boyfriend. I don't let him in."

A male voice from inside called out. "Carmen? Do I need to sign for something? I'm expecting a document this evening."

"No," she yelled back. She turned to Tripp and eyed him suspiciously. "Still wipe your feet. I just mopped. You'll wait in the living room until Ishy gets home."

Miraculously, Carmen stepped aside and held the door open for Tripp. For a minute there he thought she might ask him riddles, or spray him down with Lysol. He couldn't be too sure. He also made note to tease Ashlyn about whatever it was that the woman called her.

"Mr. Daniel," Carmen began, blasting by Tripp and going farther into the house. "Miss Ishy has a visitor."

When Tripp turned the corner along with Carmen, he was even more surprised at what he saw in the large open living room and dining room. Folders and papers flooded the place, and three men in business-like attire poured over the documents.

As they entered the room, the most casual of the three straightened and made his way over.

"Thank you, Carmen," he said, although he was looking at Tripp the entire time. Carmen quickly excused herself and disappeared in the direction they had come. The man then extended his hand, which Tripp respectfully took. "Daniel Jennings."

"Tripp Scott."

Daniel's eyes narrowed as soon as Tripp told him his name. For a brief second, he got a little nervous, wondering if Ashlyn had said something unfavorable about him.

"I thought you looked familiar," Daniel said with a small smile forming.

Tripp was more confused than ever. He was certain he had never met the man before him in his life.

Daniel began laughing at the nervous expression plastered on Tripp's face. "Sorry. I read your school's little online paper, especially the pictures and articles that my daughter does."

"Oh, I see," Tripp said, now feeling much more comfortable.

"You've done quite well in the games this year. You should be proud of yourself," Daniel went on.

Tripp didn't expect to receive such compliments from Ashlyn's father. Sure, he didn't know the guy, so maybe he liked to give compliments. He just had a preconception that all fathers would hate any guys showing up to their homes for their daughters, schoolwork or not.

Ashlyn's father went on to apologize for the mayhem. It was then that Tripp found out that Daniel was a lawyer in the city. Apparently, their entire building was being repainted, but he still had a high-profile case that needed a great deal of attention, so much so that he couldn't spare a single day off for easily the next week. It was a crucial matter that he couldn't go into, or so he said. Tripp had a feeling that as friendly as he was, if Tripp asked the right questions, the man would happily oblige to give little details. He didn't though. In just meeting Daniel for five minutes, he already had too much respect to pry.

* * *

Ashlyn nervously rushed through the door, only for Carmen to scream at her to wipe her feet. She pretended not to hear and went straight to the main living space. She had seen Tripp parked on the side of the street, but he wasn't inside his vehicle. He would have had to have been insane to go into her house without her being there. Besides, Carmen would never allow him inside anyway.

She thought that perhaps he may have gone for a walk around the block, but all the blood drained from her face when she entered the living room to tell her father that she was home, and there was Tripp, sitting off to the side from the sea of paperwork, in an armchair, with his laptop. He looked like he belonged there. Ashlyn stood speechless and confused.

Daniel was the first to notice her. "Hey, sweetie! You're home."

It was then that Tripp's eyes shot up to meet hers. He could tell that she was rattled by the situation.

"Oh, your friend got here a little while ago," her father went on, noticing how Ashlyn was staring at the boy across the room.

Ashlyn was slow to speak. "Yeah. We have a project to work on." Looking around the dining room and living room, "When you said you were working from home, I thought you meant in your home office."

"I know. With the law firm closed for painting, it was easier if Josh and Seth came over here rather than trying to video conference," her father tried to explain.

Ashlyn sighed in defeat. "Today is the only day we have to work on this project."

She wished that she would have found a vaguer way to say that. Her father's narrowed eyes let her know that he knew she had waited until the last minute.

Without scolding his daughter, "Just work in your room."

Ashlyn's jaw dropped. "What about the rule about no boys in my room," she huffed.

Daniel laughed. "Oh, that's only for one boy in particular." When he saw how Ashlyn's faced scrunched in anger he coughed and pretended he had not just said that. "I mean, this will be a one-time thing. Just...Uh...keep the door open?" When it came to rules and raising a teenage daughter, he still was uncertain what he was supposed to do and not do.

"Thanks, dad," she grumbled. She was annoyed by the entire situation.

By now, Tripp had stood and grabbed his backpack and folded his laptop under his arm. As he made his way to Ashlyn on the other side of the room, "It was nice meeting you Mr. Jennings, same goes for you two as well." He gave a slight nod to Josh and Seth.

"Keep up the good work on the field," Daniel called back with a thumbs up.

Ashlyn didn't say a word to Tripp as she stomped up the stairs leading him to her room. Just as they reached her open doorway, she spun around to face him and nearly collided with him. So as not to make things more uncomfortable for her, Tripp instantly took a step away and distanced himself from her.

"Whatever you do, don't touch anything," she hissed. She didn't mean to sound so mad, but she was annoyed and had a hard time hiding it. Her father had only met Tripp once, for a few minutes, and already he trusted him more than Eric. It wasn't fair.

Tripp watched as Ashlyn entered her room and placed her bags in the corner and six books from the library on her bed. He stood in the doorway, admiring her in her own world.

He didn't know why he was pleasantly surprised to see that there wasn't an ounce of pink anywhere. Ashlyn never struck him as being into a single color, much less that one. Her room was indeed colorful. To tone down all the artwork and the large area rug, her bedspread was a simple grey with no pattern whatsoever. Had it been full of various colors, it would have been too much for the room. He couldn't help but notice the blue frog and orange seal stuffed animals that sat between the black throw pillows at the top of her bed. It was the perfect amount of innocence and cuteness.

He slowly entered the room and placed his bag at the door.

Ashlyn didn't say anything as she left her room, and Tripp continued to make his way farther into a place that was just for her. On her desk there were an ungodly amount of pictures, some of flowers and landscapes, others of school activities, a lot of their baseball games. Despite her rule of no touching, he pushed them around, trying to get a glimpse of every one that she had taken.

Soon he gave up and wandered through the rest of the room, it was then that a large easel near the blue and green curtains covering the windows caught his attention. There was a canvas on it, but it was hidden, covered with a cloth. His curiosity was piqued. He glanced back to an empty doorway and turned once more to the easel.

Just as his fingers touched the course material of the fabric which he knew was concealing something beautiful, there was a piercing shriek.

"What do you think you're doing?!"

Tripp turned only to come face to face with a fury he had never seen in Ashlyn.

She dropped the massive amount of crafting supplies in the middle of the room and stormed over to where Tripp was standing. She slapped his hand away from the cover and yanked at his other arm, attempting to drag him away.

"I told you not to touch anything," Ashlyn continued to scream.

"I'm sorry. I just wanted–"

"I don't care what you wanted. That's mine! It's private."

Tripp help his hands up in surrender. "I'm sorry. Truly."

Ashlyn shook her head. Tripp could see the hurt in her eyes. "You can't just leave things alone can you."

Tripp's right brow rose in a questioning way, and before he could change the subject, reading into a deeper meaning behind her words, Ashlyn forced herself to say something first.

"It's my artwork and I'm not ready to show anyone yet."

"Yet?"

Ashlyn let out an exasperated breath. "Yes, yet." She didn't know what made her continue to ramble. "I'm trying to come up with something for the spring art show."

Tripp's face held a look of interest that Ashlyn hadn't seen in some time. Trying to be dismissive about what she had just told Tripp, she went back to the center of the room and began unfolding the painter's cloth so that she wouldn't make a mess on Carmen's impeccably clean floors.

Tripp knelt opposite Ashlyn and started to help unfold the cloth's other end. Not wanting her to shut down about her project, "When is it?"

"Second week in April," she answered vaguely.

"I'll need a specific date closer to it, because I'm definitely coming."

The enthusiasm in his voice pulled at something deep inside Ashlyn and she tried to swallow down the lump in her throat.

Ashlyn quickly changed the subject. "Anyway, the library didn't have many books on the Fairy Chimneys, but I did find books on Turkey and the Cappadocia region where they're mentioned. If we can find two really good websites, we should be okay."

"Already done," Tripp said, standing to go retrieve his laptop. "In fact, I started working on some of the paper." He opened his laptop and sat beside Ashlyn on the floor, watching as she placed her materials methodically.

"I'll start on the model and help with the paper as needed."

"You can make sure I have all the citations right. I'm horrible with that." It wasn't true, but he wasn't going to be an egotistical jerk and tell Ashlyn that he really didn't need any help at all.

Thankfully, she hadn't asked to see what he had written. He already had two full pages, single-spaced. He left blanks where he needed a quote or statistic to back up what he was saying, but after reading several articles on the Fairy Chimneys, he had already accomplished quite a lot.

An hour passed by. Most of the time was spent in silence, but after Ashlyn got over Tripp invading her privacy, occasionally they would ask each other random questions, nothing too invasive.

Ashlyn sat back on the floor against the foot of her bed with Tripp. Tripp glanced from his laptop to her project on the floor in front of him. "I don't know how you're so creative."

"I was homeschooled by my grandmother the first few years. She lived like she was stuck in the seventies. She was extremely artistic and down to earth. Needless to say, when I started school, I was horrible at math. She didn't teach me much when it came to math and science," Ashlyn laughed.

Tripp wanted to ask more about her grandmother, if she got to see her a lot, if she lived nearby, but the starry and despondent look in her eyes told him better. If he asked anything more about her grandmother, he'd only hear the sad truth that she was no longer around.

"I'm sure you need a citation here for that kind of statement," Ashlyn said, changing the subject and pointing to the computer.

It was a paragraph about mesothelioma and the mineral erionite.

Tripp had the book opened nearby, but wanting to make Ashlyn laugh, he ignored it.

"You're right." He talked as he hit the next few strokes on the keyboard. "Open parentheses, Scott comma Tripp." He glanced at the time at the corner of his computer. "Five colon four seven. Period. On March–"

Ashlyn couldn't take it. She playfully nudged Tripp's shoulder. "Stop it. Be serious."

She wasn't at all irritated with him. He could hear the faint laughter in her voice, and he loved it.

"Should I put location," he asked, glancing around the bedroom.

"You're impossible," she said with a smile he hadn't seen in what felt like a long time.

He reached for the book between them at the same time she did. When their hands touched, and neither instinctively pulled away in that moment, it felt like lightning bolts descended from the heavens and rained down on them at the very spot where the little bit of skin from their fingers touched.

A cough from the doorway made Ashlyn the first to not only pull away, but jump to her feet as though one of those imaginary lightning bolts electrocuted her.

"Mom. Hi."

CHAPTER 13

"Hello," Poppy began with a smug look.

She stepped over the threshold into Ashlyn's room, her eyes never leaving her daughter. Tripp quickly hit save on his document and closed his computer. He stood up and at that moment a pair of blue eyes that mimicked ones he had grown to know well shot toward him.

"We were just working on a science project," Ashlyn began, praying that her mother wouldn't say something embarrassing.

Poppy looked down at the floor and the model of some sort of rock sculpture thing. Books were scattered all about. She had no doubt in her mind that her daughter was telling the truth, but that didn't stop her from being a mother and teasing Ashlyn.

"On a Friday night?"

Ashlyn was just about to speak and was rather surprised when Tripp spoke out instead.

"That's my fault. I kept putting it off, and with other school activities I guess time got away from me. I think we're all good though, yeah," he asked, directing the last part to Ashlyn.

"Yeah."

Poppy tried to hide her smile at how uncomfortable the two appeared to be. She extended her hand to Tripp. "If you haven't guessed, I'm her mother, Poppy Jennings."

Tripp took her hand. It was rather cold. "Tripp Scott."

"I know. My husband already told me when I got home. He's a bit of a baseball fan," she said, shaking her head. "Anyway, I didn't mean to bother the two of you. I'll let you finish. I was just coming to ask about dinner."

Ashlyn's face scrunched up and she crossed her arms. "What about," she asked rather slowly. Something about her mother appeared off.

"Well, your father, Josh, and Seth have been working so hard, so I'm making a big meal tonight. Stuffed chicken breast," she exclaimed.

Ashlyn narrowed her eyes. Something was definitely off.

Poppy turned to Tripp. "You are staying for dinner, aren't you?"

And there it was.

Tripp looked to Ashlyn for help, but she was scowling at her mother who seemed to be ignoring her.

"Uh..." Did he want to stay? Absolutely. Did Ashlyn want him to? From the looks of it, a thousand percent no. "Actually, I already have plans, I should probably–"

"You do," Ashlyn interrupted, looking a little stunned. She quickly dropped her eyes and refused to look back up at him.

Tripp felt a little victorious. He turned back to Ashlyn's mother. "You know what, I'd love to stay for dinner. Thank you so much for the invitation."

"Wonderful! Everything should be ready by 7:30," Poppy said with an eager smile. She quickly made her exit from the room, but just when Ashlyn allowed the tension to fall from her shoulders, her mother's head popped back around the doorframe. "Oh, Tripp, dear. I have to tell you, those flowers you sent were absolutely gorgeous! If you can't tell, Ash loves color. Way better than the regular red roses," she said with a wink.

Very softly, "Thank you, Mrs. Jennings."

Then she was gone.

Ashlyn stared at the empty doorway for quite some time, unable to move, attempting to process the last five minutes. Finally, she spun to face Tripp.

When she didn't say anything, only stare at him with narrowed eyes and pursed lips, "Hi."

"Hi?! Why didn't you say *what flowers*?!"

Tripp shrugged and ran his hand through his hair. Ashlyn hated when he did that. It only reminded her how gorgeous and perfect his hair was.

"No point in lying to your mom."

Ashlyn took a couple steps backward and sat on the foot of her bed and stared at the mess on the floor before her. Tripp sighed and sat beside her, making sure to keep a bit of distance.

"You're upset," he asked.

Ashlyn closed her eyes and took in a deep breath. "I specifically asked if you sent them."

"Keep in mind, this was also after you just got done screaming at me." Not wanting to relive that part of that day, "Besides, in the end it didn't matter who sent them. All that matters is that you felt special."

Ashlyn couldn't believe what he was saying. She felt dizzy, like the whole room was spinning and the only thing still was the two of them, frozen in place, a good foot apart.

"But why?"

Tripp laughed at the question. "Come on, Ash. You knew I kind of liked you."

Ouch.

Kind of.

Liked.

Ashlyn quickly hid the look of disappointment that she could feel coming to her face. Past tense was good. That meant that they could move on from whatever crush Tripp had at some point. She just had to shake the idea that while he was now going backwards in his feelings for her, she had started to take a step or two forward. A very minimal step, that only consisted of her admitting it in the silence inside her head that Tripp was indeed attractive, and she was attracted to him, and that there might be a slight crush beginning on her part.

Then she remembered the conversation they just had with her mother.

Turning to face him, "Did you really have plans tonight?"

He chuckled nervously and shook his head. "Nah, but you had this look of horror and extreme annoyance all over your face when your mom asked me to stay."

"I was just surprised."

Tripp waited until Ashlyn looked up at him and held eye contact. "I can make up an excuse if you don't want me to stay. I don't want things to be awkward."

"No, it's fine."

Unable to restrain himself from lightening the mood and teasing Ashlyn, he pushed at her shoulder and she swayed just a little. "Are you saying you *want* me to stay?"

Ashlyn laughed. "I'm saying, it's *fine*," she repeated. Although there was a giddy nervousness running through her at the idea.

Tripp liked how things were going between them. He much rather would have preferred if Ashlyn could have just given him her number that day that he asked, but that's what any girl would have done. Ashlyn wasn't just like any girl.

Whatever progress he thought they might be making in their path to friendship was quickly interrupted with a text alert from her phone that sat between the two of them. She grabbed it immediately, but he had already seen who the text was from. He rose from the bed and began cleaning up their workspace below.

Eric: Hey, babe. What's up?

Ashlyn: Working on a school project.

Eric: It's Friday?

Tripp heard Ashlyn sigh. It was one of annoyance, but it wasn't his place to ask her what was wrong, especially not when she was texting *him*.

Ashlyn: It's the only time I'll have to work on it.

It wasn't lying. She didn't have to tell Eric that it was a partner project and that her partner happened to be a guy, a guy that seconds ago was sitting beside her on her bed.

Okay, so by all standards a lie of omission is still a lie.

Eric: Want to go out? Flip's Grill in half an hour?

Ashlyn: Can't. My dad has colleagues over, and my mom is cooking.

When Eric didn't respond back, she put her phone on the charger and finished helping Tripp clean up.

Tripp didn't say anything, but his whole demeanor had changed. He didn't joke around anymore and, when Ashlyn did say or ask him anything, his responses were short and to the point.

"Thank you, Tripp. That's so sweet of you," Poppy said, handing Tripp the dinner plates to set the table.

While Ashlyn's father and the two others had managed to clear out from the dining room, the living room still left something to be desired.

"Here are the forks and knives," Poppy said, placing a pile of utensils on the corner of the island and quickly rushing back to open the oven.

Without saying anything, Ashlyn and Tripp made their way to each placemat, placing all the necessary items. Poppy didn't trust either of them bringing out the food. She took that upon herself.

Poppy sat at one end, far opposite of Daniel. Josh and Seth sat across from each other on the end near Daniel, and Ashlyn and Tripp across from each other near her mother.

Ashlyn kept her eyes on her plate for the most part. The few times she had looked up, Tripp was watching her. It did things to her that she wasn't comfortable with. So instead, she focused intently on the spinach and feta stuffed chicken breast covered in a mushroom sauce with a side of roasted potatoes and another of green beans.

Tripp went on to compliment Poppy on the meal. At first Ashlyn thought he might be trying to suck up to her parents, but realized he had no reason to. For reasons unknown, they already liked him. Also, he wasn't lying about the food, if he were, there was no need for him to go back for seconds.

"Does your mother not cook," Poppy asked.

"Oh, she does. She stays home. With all the traveling we've done over the years, it was hard for her to keep a normal job," he managed between bites.

"What is it your father does?"

"He works in the tech industry. He got offered a job by McCallister Industries that was too good to pass up. For once I think we'll be in the same place for a long time."

Ashlyn couldn't help but glance up and notice the sweet smile on his face as he said that.

"Anyway," he continued. "After living in so many different places, my mom picked up a little bit here and there, and often we get strange things for our meals. Argentina, Canada, Australia–"

From down the table, Seth called out, "Hey, vegemite!"

Tripp burst into adorable laughter. "Yeah, she learned the hard way to use that sparingly."

Ashlyn didn't want to ask. She'd look it up later, but it sounded like a combination between a vegetable and termite.

Dinner went rather well. For a minute, Ashlyn thought her mother might embarrass her when it came to Tripp. She knew she didn't have a problem with her dad. He was generally oblivious to things that were right in front of his face. Poppy on the other hand, she saw everything, for instance, the flowers. Ashlyn couldn't wait to ask her how in the world she knew that Tripp sent them.

Just as Daniel, Seth, and Josh went back into the living room to wrap up a few odds and ends, and

Tripp and Ashlyn began to help clear the table with Poppy, the doorbell rang.

"I'll get it," Poppy said. She quickly dried her hands and left the kitchen.

Ashlyn continued to hand Tripp dishes to put in the dishwasher. It was so odd having him help her clean up the kitchen, yet strangely comfortable.

"Umm, Ash," Poppy began hesitantly when she returned. "You have a visitor."

The glass of tea Ashlyn was emptying into the sink fell from her hands and clanked in the soapy water. Upon instinct she grabbed for it, relieved when she lifted it from the suds and saw no cracks.

Tripp looked in Poppy's direction to see what, or rather who, had taken Ashlyn by surprise, and he had never felt more uncomfortable in his life.

Eric.

* * *

Ashlyn got Eric out of the house and into the backyard as quickly as possible. She was almost certain that if she didn't, he'd cause a scene with Tripp there. Also, something in his eyes told her that he wasn't completely himself.

Ashlyn walked across the large deck to the steps leading out into the yard and sat down with Eric doing the same seconds later.

"I thought you said you were working on a project. I didn't know that you had another guy over, having

131

dinner with your stupid parents," Eric unnecessarily screamed inches from her face.

Ashlyn couldn't help her voice rising now. She tried never to yell back when Eric went off, knowing that's what he wanted. "I told you. We were working on a project. Since it got late, my mom insisted that he stay for dinner."

"Yeah, well your mom is stupid. I wish she'd fall off the face of the earth," he spat.

"Seriously?! Then you wonder why they don't like you." Ashlyn took in a deep breath. She needed to remain calm. "Are you on something right now?" She shouldn't have asked. That question would always be a trigger.

Eric shot up and towered over her. "I come to see my girlfriend, only to find her messing around with another guy, and then you have the nerve to ask me if I'm sober."

It was a mechanism. Ashlyn had to tell herself that. He was just trying to make it out to be her fault...But...It was. She could have been less vague.

Her head turned into a battling mess of guilt, anger, sadness, every unpleasant feeling she could imagine that threatened to cause the food in her stomach to make a quick exit.

"Ash," a sweet and welcoming voice called from the glass patio doors. "Your friend is leaving. I didn't know if you wanted to tell him goodbye."

Ashlyn jumped up, apparently a little too eagerly, because when she turned to tell Eric to give her a minute, all she got was an icy stare that could kill.

* * *

Walking Tripp out, and down the driveway to the street felt a little heartbreaking. Ashlyn tried to hide all the emotions swirling around inside, but with each step, she felt like her world was crumbling.

Tripp leaned against his door and took a good look at the girl in front of him. In just a matter of minutes she had changed. Long gone was the playful, bubbly, and sarcastic girl that drove him crazy. In her place was someone unhappy and broken.

In the dark and silent night, they both heard the rather loud closing of a door. Ashlyn turned back to the house to see Eric, arms crossed, on the front porch waiting. She turned back to Tripp, nervous to see the expression on his face, surprised when it held nothing.

The end of the driveway was a good distance from the house, far enough that even in the quiet night, Eric wouldn't hear their words.

"Thanks for letting me stay for dinner. Please tell your mom again how great it was," Tripp began, as if nothing was wrong, like he was only leaving because it was time, and not because of the interruption to their night.

"Thanks for helping me with the assignment," Ashlyn responded, more robotically than she meant.

Tripp held her gaze, wanting so badly to say something, but not having the words. A part of him wanted to yell at her for being such an idiot, for being so stupid to stay with such a loser, to stay with someone

133

who didn't treat her the way she deserved, but he knew doing so would only push her further away, and he felt like they were beginning to make a great deal of progress in their friendship.

"I'd hug you goodbye, but I'm guessing that's not a good idea," Tripp said with a smile as he nodded in the direction of Ashlyn's porch.

Ashlyn's eyes shot up to meet his, and through the pain and uncertainty, Tripp saw something beautiful. Hope.

Ashlyn told herself to take a step forward and do it. She was her own person. She didn't belong to anyone. Eric would get glad just as quickly as he got mad. Despite all that, she couldn't. She didn't want to push any more buttons, so instead, she extended her hand.

Tripp took it, knowing that all she intended for it to be was a goodbye handshake. Instead of shaking her hand like he would with any other person on the planet, he softly moved his fingers along her wrist, his thumb rubbing featherlight circles on the back of her hand.

She shook a little and beneath the streetlights, he could see little goosebumps prickle across her arm. Then she pulled her hand away.

"Goodnight, Ash," Tripp said as he opened his door and threw his bag in.

Just as he was about to close the door, "Wait." Tripp turned, his door half open. "Text me that you made it home alright?"

Tripp smiled and nodded, and as he pulled away, a warmth unlike anything he had felt before came over him. He couldn't believe how much he was falling for her in such a short amount of time.

* * *

"You're disgusting," Eric growled, as soon as Ashlyn was within speaking distance, making her way up the porch steps.

"Eric, I'm really tired. Can we do this another time?"

Ashlyn wouldn't mention it again, but she knew Eric had taken or done something before coming over.

"Oh, I guess he's the reason you're so tired?!"

"Stop it," Ashlyn hissed. At this rate she'd be surprised if the neighbors didn't call the cops eventually. "My parents have been home all afternoon. All we did was work on a project. Just let it go."

"I see the way you look at him."

Ashlyn was tired and suddenly didn't bother watching what she said. "You mean with my eyes. Yes, Eric. I looked at him with my eyes."

"Don't get smart with me. I can't believe you're like that."

Eric now stood nearly chest to chest with Ashlyn. She looked up at him with cold and unemotional eyes.

"Like what," she growled.

"You're nothing more than a stupid cleat chaser. I guess since I'm not on the team you throw yourself at the new guy. I mean, I guess he was your only option. All the other guys find you repulsive. Hell, your best friend's brother could have dated you before I came in the picture, but even he didn't want you."

Ashlyn felt that. Those words went straight through her.

Eric went on, taking full control of the conversation and situation. "You know what, I can't even deal with you right now. I need some time to think." He waved his hands in front of her and bounded off the porch.

Ashlyn wanted to call him out, yell at him, tell him that she's the one who needed time to think after his behavior, but the words didn't come.

She was grateful that she managed to slip upstairs and into her room without her parents confronting her. If her mother said anything about Tripp and Eric, she was certain that she'd burst into tears.

However, tears managed to come anyway when she took her phone off the charger and saw a text message from Tripp.

Tripp: Made it home. Goodnight, Ash!

Maybe she overthought the message. It shouldn't have made her sad. He did what she asked.

When she put her head down on the pillow, she couldn't stop the silly tears that surfaced. She would

have given anything to see his text say *goodnight,*
beautiful again.

CHAPTER 14

"What was that about," Kayla asked.

Ashlyn didn't even look in the direction of the entrance to the cafeteria. She could only imagine the glaring look of hatred from Eric.

They hadn't spoke all weekend, not even so much as a text. She didn't know where they stood. Strangely, as much as it bothered her, it also didn't.

"Ash," Emory called out. "Seriously, what's his problem?"

Ashlyn simply shrugged and shook her head. The guys were eating lunch with them today, and she didn't want to discuss her relationship in front of them, especially Tripp.

"Will you cut it out," Emory yelled at Ellis as she swatted his hand from her fries. "Why are you even here today?"

"Abby's mom let her miss school so they could go shopping for spring break," Ellis told her, stealing another fry.

"Then go eat with the guys."

"They're not big on sharing," Ellis said, again taking yet another fry from Emory's plate.

"Who's all going to the game with us tomorrow," Emory asked. Kayla and June snorted a little. They occasionally went, but it wasn't a priority. "Wow, okay. Just you then," her question directed at Ashlyn.

"I guess so." Ashlyn tried not to sound too excited, but maybe the baseball game was just what she needed.

"And this time you'll come out to eat after?"

Ashlyn could feel Tripp carefully watching her, waiting for a response. She knew that he'd more than likely go out with Ellis and some of the players from the team. It's not like it would be a date.

"Definitely."

* * *

To save Ashlyn a drive, Ellis and Emory picked her up Tuesday evening before the game. Ashlyn figured it was Emory's way of ensuring that she went out to eat with them afterwards. It turned out to be a bad decision on her part, because as soon as everyone got to Flip's Grill and pushed together tables, she realized more than just a couple of the baseball guys had come.

She should have known that Ellis' girlfriend, Abby, would come, but she didn't expect that she'd bring a friend. Rachel.

Tripp tried arranging it so that he could sit on the side of Ashlyn not claimed by Emory. At the very least maybe across from her so they could talk, but that hadn't been in the cards. Instead, he had Byron on one side and Rachel on the other. Ashlyn couldn't have been farther away.

Ashlyn did a great job of pretending not to care, completely ignoring Tripp and a giggly Rachel. That's all she could hear were the giggles. The place was so loud there was no way she could pick up on the conversation they were having.

Her pretending must have worked out in her favor. For once, not even Emory got the hint that anything was wrong, and nothing was wrong, not really. Ashlyn knew she had no claim to Tripp. She was so messed up she didn't even know if she still had a boyfriend or not. Tripp deserved to move on and be happy, and they were kind of friends, so she needed to be happy for him.

There was a lot of talk about the upcoming spring break. Abby was going to Mexico, Deacon was going to spend time with Ellis, working out and playing video games. Ashlyn wasn't sure what Byron, Rachel, or Tripp had for plans.

"I'm so glad," Emory told Ashlyn once Ashlyn admitted that she was going to work on some painting. "How many pieces can you put in the art show?"

"Up to three paintings and five photographs, but I don't have even one painting," Ashlyn admitted.

Tripp watched as Ashlyn's face lit up with whatever she and Emory were talking about. He would have given anything to hear what she was saying. Instead he was caught in two conversations, one with Byron talking about his cousins in Canada, and one with Rachel talking about swimsuits. Normally, any hot girl talking about skimpy pieces of fabric would have his attention, but that hadn't been the case in a while. Not since he had moved to Raymere Grove.

Eventually Ashlyn excused herself to use the restroom, thankful to get away from everyone, and wishing she would have driven herself.

Tuesday nights weren't that crowded, so she wasn't surprised when she was the only one in the women's restroom. At least she felt like she could finally breathe.

After turning off the faucet, Ashlyn looked into the mirror, really looked. She wasn't ugly. She had nice hair that she fixed in various styles. She wore just enough, but not too much, makeup. While she didn't spend thousands on designer clothes, she dressed nicely. Her body was normal. She was just as thin as Emory, and Emory was a cheerleader. So, what was wrong with her?

She hated how much Eric's words continued to bother her. Not wanting to ruin her mascara, she quickly dabbed at her eyes before any tears could fall.

The bathroom door swung open just as Ashlyn tried to compose herself.

"Oh, wow," Rachel gasped.

Great. Of all the people that could have walked in, it had to be Rachel.

Ashlyn sniffled back any more tears from coming. "Hey."

"Oh my gosh, are you okay?"

Ashlyn had heard a great deal about Rachel from Emory. While Rachel could be a total witch when it came to the cheer squad, overall, as a person, she wasn't as bad as her predecessor.

"Yeah, I'm fine," Ashlyn assured her, hoping that she'd go into one of the stalls and cut the conversation short.

"It's Eric isn't it," Rachel proceeded to ask, shaking her head and unnecessarily flipping her hair.

If Ashlyn was to be a hundred percent honest with herself, it wasn't all just about Eric. Eric was a good portion of her aggravation and hurt, but there was something else eating away at her that had nothing to do with Eric, and everything to do with Tripp.

"I should have known something was wrong," Rachel went on. "I was out walking Diamond the other evening. She's my little maltipoo."

Ashlyn tried so hard to hide the look of discomfort that must be coming to her face at having to listen to whatever Rachel was spewing.

"Anyway, Crystal lives on my street a few houses down, and I saw Eric dropping her off. I guess that isn't so odd, like, I know they run with the same friends now, but I don't know, you know?"

Ashlyn swallowed the lump in her throat. No. She didn't know.

"Well, anyway," Ashlyn began, trying to find a way out before Rachel felt the need to tell her any more information.

"Hey, wait. Stupid question." Rachel hesitantly leaned against one of the sinks and twirled her hair. "I know sometimes a few of the guys sit at your table, and I know you and Tripp are partners in science..."

"Yeah..."

"Well, I would ask Emory, but I know she's not too fond of me."

Ashlyn wanted to tell Rachel that her statement was putting it mildly but decided against being a jerk to her.

"I guess I was just wondering if he talks about me. This is like our second date, and..."

Rachel's words suddenly blurred after that word. *Date.*

Ashlyn wanted to scream. She didn't know how she felt except that she was full of hurt, anger, jealousy. She knew it! She had known it from the beginning and she still went and allowed herself to begin to have feelings for Tripp.

The flowers, the kiss, having dinner with her parents when he didn't have to...What was all of that? Did he really have that much free time to invest in playing girls?

"So, what do you think?"

Ashlyn snapped out of it. "Uh, about what?"

Rachel sighed in annoyance. "About Tripp. He agreed to eat lunch with me tomorrow, but he seems so distant. Do you think I should be the one making the first move?"

Ashlyn couldn't give her that advice. All she knew was that she needed to get out, out of the restroom, and out of the stupid restaurant. "I honestly don't know much about him. Sorry."

Before Rachel could say another word, Ashlyn tore out of the bathroom.

"Whoa, watch it," a voice screeched, as Ashlyn inadvertently collided into someone coming out of the men's room.

Ellis.

"I'm sorry," Ashlyn quickly apologized.

Ellis looked her over carefully. She had seemed fine all during the game, even the little he saw of her throughout dinner; however, now was a completely different story.

"You don't look so good," Ellis pointed out.

Not wanting to have a serious conversation with Ellis of all people, "Thanks for letting me know. I'll try harder next time."

"Not what I meant," Ellis huffed. "I mean, you look like you're about to throw up."

She felt like she was about to throw up.

"I tell you what, go outside to the benches in the front."

Before Ashlyn could say a word back to him, he quickly went down the hallway and back to their table.

* * *

"What are you doing here," Ashlyn asked as soon as Ellis sat beside her on the bench.

"Seeing if you're ready to go home."

Ashlyn looked up at him curiously. Although he never missed a moment to annoy and tease her, for the most part Ellis always was nice to her. "You don't have to take me home. We both know that Emory isn't done eating. I can just call my mom."

"That is true," Ellis laughed. "I told her you weren't feeling good and I was going to take you home. Besides, Deacon can take her."

"What about Abby?"

"She's got her own ride with Rachel, well, unless they find a way to convince Tripp to take Rachel home." Ellis rubbed his temples. "They can both be a little relentless." He looked up at her. He had hoped to make her smile or laugh, but she looked sadder and more miserable than ever. "Come on, let me get you out of here."

For some reason, Ashlyn felt like that car ride home with Ellis was one of the lowest points in her life. She felt weak, and it was then that she realized just how weak she was, but it wasn't something where she could magically snap her fingers and wake up the next day a new person. Something had to change though, starting with Eric. She allowed him to get in her head from the start, and he managed to change a lot about her, especially her confidence and self-worth.

"Is the entire ride going to be in silence, or do you want to vent?"

"Nothing to vent about," Ashlyn lied.

"I know whatever is bothering you has to do with Eric, even if it's only a little," Ellis admitted. He glanced over at Ashlyn after he made another turn and in the faint bit of light saw that she was chewing on her lip, thinking of what to say.

Ashlyn took a deep breath, knowing that it was going to be an uncomfortable conversation. "Why didn't you ever ask me out?"

Ellis tapped his brakes a little too suddenly as he came to the stop sign. "What," he gasped in shock. "I didn't know...I thought...You liked–"

"Wait. Stop. That came out wrong," Ashlyn quickly interrupted. She could tell that she had taken Ellis by surprise. "Eric and I got into a fight and he said some things."

"Like?"

"Along the lines of, if you spent all that time with me over the years and weren't interested, why would any other guy be," Ashlyn managed, hating how awkward it was to say that to Ellis.

His outburst of laughter surprised her.

"Wow! That guy is nuts. A total tool. Come on, Ash. You and I both know that you never wanted me to date you."

"I know, but–"

"It's just his way of getting into your head, beating you down, and all so you stay with him. He's constantly chipping away at all the good parts of you and making you feel worthless." They were at Ashlyn's house now, but Ellis' rant was far from over. "I never would have asked you out because I love you like a sister, and I also love to tease and aggravate you just like a sister. You're my sister's best friend. That's a line I wouldn't touch with a ten-foot pole. I also know you're beautiful, and you're crazy if you think that Eric is the only guy in that stupid school that would want you. You know why guys aren't beating your door down asking for a date?" He paused and waited for Ashlyn to shake her head. "Because you've been stuck with that jerk for two years! I mean, before then girls had cooties, and by the time we figured out that they weren't so bad and making out was fun, you were already trapped in some sick relationship with him."

Ashlyn was stunned that all of that came from Ellis Parker. It wasn't a massive revelation, but it was enough to make her really think about where she was and who she was.

"Come on, Ash," he sighed. "You're stronger than this. You have to be if you put up with my sister." That got a smile out of the nearly broken girl sitting next to him. "Just grow a pair already. Rub some dirt on it."

And anything remotely insightful from Ellis was ruined.

Seeing the wrinkled nose and confusion, "Sorry. That's what my uncle tells me."

Ellis' uncle also just so happened to be Raymere Grove's football coach.

"Thanks, Ellis."

"So, we're cool? You don't have some age-old crush on me," he jokingly asked as he batted his eyelashes.

"Absolutely not!"

It felt really good to laugh. It's what she needed.

* * *

Tripp: Hey, how are you?

Ashlyn climbed into bed and stared at the message, debating if she should reply. A tiny voice inside her head told her she had enough boy problems. The best would be to slowly stop communicating with Tripp and let him go, because at this point, she was at an impasse. She couldn't be with him, and apparently, he no longer wanted her in his life like that, but she also didn't want to see him with someone else.

The thought made her feel gross, and like a horrible person.

Ashlyn: I'm fine.

Tripp: Ellis told us you didn't feel well. I was worried. I could have taken you home.

Ashlyn felt the butterflies fluttering in her stomach upon reading the text. She remembered what Ellis told her on the bench, about Rachel trying to get Tripp to drive her home. She couldn't ask him directly if he had. That would be too weird.

Ashlyn: Thanks, but you deserved to get to enjoy your win. Besides, I'm sure you had your car full.

It would have been more enjoyable with you.
Tripp quickly deleted the text. He couldn't talk to her like that, at least not right now. They were

making progress, or so he thought. The last thing he wanted to do was scare her away.

Tripp: Nah, I left shortly after you.

Ashlyn didn't ask if he took Rachel home. From the sound of the text, she liked to imagine that he didn't, but the fact that she cared so much only meant one thing.

Ashlyn brought up her chat with Eric and, with shaky fingers, tapped out the message.

Ashlyn: I need to talk to you. Tomorrow.

CHAPTER 15

Ashlyn wasn't surprised when she saw Ellis, Deacon, and Tripp having lunch with Abby and a few of her friends, namely Rachel.

She realized that she had to begin taking baby steps. The last thing she wanted to do was go from one relationship to the next. Though she didn't want to speculate, Tripp didn't seem over the moon to be sitting next to Rachel. He looked deep in thought and even a little disinterested. She couldn't imagine a long-term relationship coming from whatever they had going.

"Hey," a voice called out, causing Ashlyn's friends to go deadly silent. "You wanted to say something."

Ashlyn capped off her water bottle and got up from her seat. After looking around, seeing the watchful eyes of Emory, Kayla, and June, "Can we step outside real quick."

Eric's hands were shoved in his jean pockets and he shrugged like he didn't care if they did or didn't. Ashlyn used that opportunity to take the lead and head out to the courtyard. She saw the table where Eric sat with some of his unsavory friends, and she veered in a direction farther away.

"So, what's up," Eric asked casually.

Ashlyn tried her best not to show irritation in her voice, but she was livid. After the things he said to her on Friday, after not speaking to her or reaching out for days, now he was going to pretend like it never happened.

"I need a break," Ashlyn blurted out, getting to the point.

Eric cocked his head like he didn't understand what she was saying. "You're still mad?"

Ashlyn felt like the air was knocked from her lungs. "Still mad? Are you serious?"

"Oh, come on. We had a fight. Couples fight. Get over it. You're being dramatic," he groaned.

"You are unbelievable. You're the one who yelled at me and then told me that you needed time to think."

"Yeah? And? I needed to cool off," he told her calmly, which only aggravated her more.

Ashlyn didn't like yelling or arguing, but Eric was making it difficult not to scream at the top of her lungs. "Well, now I'm telling you. I need a break from you."

He narrowed his eyes and Ashlyn saw a spark of anger. "All of a sudden, you need a break. Is this about your little ball player?"

"This is about me," Ashlyn growled.

"Because you do realize he's cuddled up with some cheerleader right now. Man, you must feel like garbage for throwing yourself at him," Eric laughed.

Ashlyn had to ignore those words. All he wanted was to get her worked up and say that everything was her fault. She wouldn't play this time. "Eric," she sighed. "We need to take a break. I can't do this."

"So, we're not even going to hang out over spring break?"

Ashlyn wanted to jump up and down and ask him if he was really that dense. "No. I'm going to work on my painting for the art–"

"You can't be serious," he scoffed. "You still waste time with that?"

Eric said a lot of mean things to her, especially when he was mad. Out of all the things he said, that comment bothered her a lot. It was nowhere near as rude as he could be, but it really showed her his lack of care in anything that made her happy.

Despite Eric insisting that she'd get bored and change her mind by the start of spring break, she left that conversation feeling lighter and just a little relieved.

* * *

"Oh, I hope they made up," Rachel sympathetically mentioned to some girl next to her.

Tripp's ears instantly perked up, and he found himself inserting into the conversation. Pretending not to care, "What do you mean?" He was aware that Eric and Ashlyn probably had a fight last Friday night, but what could Rachel possibly know about it.

She turned to Tripp, eager to talk to him. "Last night, at dinner, when I went to the bathroom," she began speaking in slow and shortened bursts like she was telling a horror story. "She was crying."

That hit Tripp in the gut. Ashlyn seemed fine, from the little he could tell, when she was at the table. Then she went to the bathroom and Ellis said she was sick. Looking up at her walking back to her table of friends, she didn't look sick.

"We talked a little," Rachel went on. "I told her that I saw Eric taking another girl home, but that was after I already saw her crying. I mean, they've been together since, like, freshman year. I'm sure they made up. She looks happy, I think," she continued to ramble.

Tripp stood and excused himself to throw his food away. Suddenly he had lost his appetite.

* * *

Tripp looked at the selfie that Deacon had sent some time ago once again. It included Ellis, Emory, and Ashlyn all crammed on a couch with video game controllers in their hands.

He was excited to be visiting his grandparents in Georgia, but if he could have been anywhere else, that would have been it.

After seeing Ashlyn and Eric at lunch the other week, and listening to Rachel rant about them, he imagined whatever tiff they were in had ended; however, he wasn't going to lie, he was ecstatic to see that she was hanging out with her friends instead.

Eliza hovered over her son on the couch for a moment before making her presence known. "It's the brunette isn't it?"

Tripp dropped his phone in shock and turned around. "Geez, mom. Don't scare me like that."

Eliza came around the couch and leaned on the side. "She's cute."

"Yeah, okay."

Eliza laughed, fully knowing that her son didn't want to talk to her about girls. "Can you help grandpa set the table in a few minutes?"

"Yeah. I'm just going to text Deacon back."

Eliza patted Tripp on the head like a child. "No rush."

Tripp: Looks like you guys are having a good time!

Deacon: We would be if Emory would shut up about Ash's break-up or whatever.

Tripp stiffened and read that text what felt like a hundred times. He had a million questions for Deacon but decided against digging for information.

He hadn't text Ashlyn over the spring break and she hadn't text him. It was only Wednesday, but that was five days since he had seen her in class. He told himself not to bother her, to play it cool, but after that text from Deacon, his willpower was shot.

"I'm just saying," Emory stressed. "If you told him that the two of you needed a break that's not the same thing."

Ashlyn groaned and patiently waited for the next game to load up.

"You should have said that you wanted to break *up*, like you're done, for good. Saying you need a break just means that eventually you'll come around," Emory went on.

"I'm not a hundred percent sure what I want. I know I don't like the way he's been acting. I thought that he might change if–"

Emory tossed her controller down and fell into the sofa dramatically. "He's not going to change, and seriously Ash, do you even want him to?"

Ashlyn reached for her phone to check the message that had just come in.

Tripp: Hey! Long time. How's your break going?

Emory shot up and narrowed her eyes. "Who is that?"

"No one," Ashlyn quickly responded.

"Oh yeah? Well for no one, you sure are smiling," Emory teased.

"Agh! I can't take it anymore," Ellis groaned. "Deacon let's go out to the pool."

Emory waited for the two guys to leave. "It's Tripp, isn't it."

"Yes," Ashlyn sighed.

155

"Just so you know, your eyes lit up as soon as you saw the text."

Ashlyn threw her phone down without replying. "We're just friends. He's already been on dates with Rachel and he sat with her at lunch last week."

"First of all, I don't know about these dates you're referring to, but he sat with Ellis and Deacon at lunch because Abby and Rachel kept hounding them at dinner after the game that night. Just ask him if he's seeing her," Emory casually advised.

"I can't do that," Ashlyn gasped. "Then he'll think that I like him, or I'm interested in seeing if he's single."

Emory's brow shot up. "But you do like him, and you want to know if he's single."

"I don't want him to know that, and I need to figure me out first."

Emory respected that. "Enough boy talk. Someone has a birthday party next weekend," Emory squealed.

It was something Ashlyn didn't care to talk about, but her mom had insisted on doing a small get-together. Was seventeen even that big of a deal? Sixteen you could drive. Eighteen you could vote. Seventeen was just stuck there in the middle.

Ashlyn apologized for leaving so early, but if she was going to have three paintings to put in the art show, she needed to buckle down. She was halfway done with the one that Tripp almost saw, and today she felt particularly motivated to finish it.

Ashlyn: Sorry for the delay. I'm home now. Painting.

Tripp: Please send a picture!

Ashlyn smiled. There was no way that Tripp could see the painting, at least not right now. She still had a few weeks until the school's art show. That didn't give her a lot of time to get herself together.

She took her phone and zoomed in so that all Tripp would see is a blur of blue and black.

Tripp: The school colors. Interesting. I guess that's all you're going to give me.

Ashlyn: For now.

While Ashlyn didn't know what her other two paintings would be, she knew this one would be the hardest. If she did submit the full limit, her other two would probably be landscapes; those were generally her specialty.

After days of silence, all the remaining days of spring break, Tripp text Ashlyn. He even sent pictures of his time in Georgia. There was one that he sent of himself and his little brother on the beach. Ashlyn could have done without seeing that one. It kept her awake and restless every night thereafter.

While she wished that Tripp and his family would have remained in Raymere Grove during the break, and perhaps their paths would have crossed, she took pleasure in knowing that he was in an entirely different state, nowhere near Rachel either.

CHAPTER 16

"I feel like I haven't seen you in forever," Tripp said excitedly when he took his seat next to Ashlyn in science.

Ashlyn was a little ticked. After texting Tripp the rest of the break nearly nonstop like they had early on, for a brief moment she had forgotten about Rachel; however, Tripp, Deacon, and Ellis sat with Abby, Rachel, and several other cheerleaders at lunch yet again.

"Yeah," was all she responded.

Tripp watched her carefully. Her lips were tight, and she looked tense. Just as he was about to say something else, the bell rang for class to begin. They wouldn't be able to have a normal conversation, but since they sat at the back of the room, it never kept them from sharing a few whispers here and there.

"Well, I hope everyone had a relaxing spring break," Mrs. Cohen began, taking out her attendance sheet.

"You never told me if you finished your painting," Tripp whispered quietly. He scooted his chair a little closer to Ashlyn, only for her to lean farther away from him. So, he was indeed the problem. He rolled his eyes wondering what it could be now.

"Yes, Tripp," Mrs. Cohen acknowledged as soon as Tripp's hand flew up.

"I'm really not..." he paused and made a gagging noise. "I think I need to go to the nurse."

Ashlyn gave her full attention to Tripp. His voice was unrecognizable from a few minutes prior, and his face looked like he was about to throw up.

Mrs. Cohen paused with the notes she was just about to begin and waved Tripp up, already writing out a nurse's pass.

Ashlyn didn't buy for one second that Tripp was legitimately sick, but whatever he was doing didn't concern her. With him not sitting right next to her, she'd be able to focus and take her notes in peace and quiet.

"Ash," Mrs. Cohen called out. The smirk on Tripp's face when he turned was all Ashlyn needed to know for what was coming next. "See to it that he makes it to the nurse okay...Or restroom. Whatever comes first," she said, not asked, with much concern.

Ashlyn tried to hide her annoyance while walking to the front of the room, but Tripp was well-aware that she wasn't happy about his little stunt.

Tripp chuckled as soon as the door closed behind them and Ashlyn started in the direction to the nurse. She spun around and glared at him, forcing his laughter to fade.

"Forget it. I'm not missing class for this," she scoffed and headed back to their room.

Tripp stepped in front of her and placed a hand on her shoulder. "Yes, you are."

He looked at her with such intensity that made her knees go weak. As much as she knew she should go back to class, her curiosity was too much. She needed to know what this was about.

Ashlyn shook Tripp's hand from her shoulder and turned, back in the direction of the nurse's office. Tripp's steps were slow; he didn't seem to be in a rush. He also wasn't even sick, so there was that.

After watching Ashlyn stroll beside him for a second more, "What's wrong now?"

"Nothing."

"Clearly. That's why you've barely said more than a few words to me." He shook his head. "I don't get it, I had so much fun talking to you over the break, but now in person..."

Ashlyn clenched her eyes and took in a deep breath. "I'm sorry. I just have a lot going on. I didn't mean to be rude."

She could be friends with Tripp. What she *couldn't* do was get jealous of him and another girl. It was easy to tell herself that, but hard when it came to actually doing.

Tripp paused and leaned back against some lockers in one of the more remote hallways. Ashlyn didn't seem to mind that they were taking the scenic route. He didn't say anything, just watched her through hooded eyes as she grew increasingly uncomfortable.

He gave her a nod to his left and she came closer, until she was pressing her back on the locker next to him.

"That's sweet of you to apologize, but I want to know the cause. Why me? You seemed happy and full of laughter at lunch."

Ashlyn let out a snort. "How would you know?" She sucked in a breath and stopped breathing as soon as the words came out. She let her eyes fall to the floor, praying that Tripp was an idiot jock who wouldn't read into that comment, but she knew better.

"Ash," he began. His voice was so low and rough. Something about it sent prickles across her skin. "Are you upset that we didn't sit with you and Emory at lunch?"

Ashlyn tried her best to pretend that his idea was absurd, and possibly change the subject. "No. You guys can sit wherever you want. It's difficult enough for Emory as Ellis' twin. A little space between those two is a good thing."

Tripp wasn't going to let her off easy. "Is it that we sat with those girls?"

It was an uncomfortable topic for Ashlyn. More than anything, she didn't want to come across as jealous, although deep down, she was, but only a little bit. The truth was, when it came to Rachel, she couldn't compete. As hard as it was to try not to look at Tripp right now, one glance and anyone could see that he and Rachel were much better suited.

"Ash," he asked when she took impossibly long to answer.

Ashlyn took Coach Turner's advice to Ellis, so to speak, and broke away from the locker, now facing

Tripp and deciding to be upfront. "You're free to date whoever you want. I just don't understand why you wouldn't tell me that you're seeing her. I mean we're friends, right?"

Tripp's eyes widened like a deer caught in a set of blinding headlights. He needed to correct her. What made sitting with his friends and a group of girls give her the impression that he was dating one of them?

Before he corrected her, now that they were on the topic of dating, "Are you and Eric still together?"

She hadn't said anything to him about her breakup that Deacon had mentioned, and he had to know, because if she confirmed what he needed to hear, then there was no doubt in his mind that he'd pin her against that locker and show her that he was very much not dating any of those other girls.

Ashlyn sighed, noting that Tripp skirted around the topic of Rachel. "Technically…"

Whatever Tripp pretended to feel in the classroom, he legitimately felt with that one word. He held up a hand to silence her from saying anything else. If she had to start her answer like that, then he already knew. It was a yes or no question, and she didn't say no.

"Go back to class," he said with a shrug. "I'm going to head to the nurse, get my pass initialed." He held up the yellow slip in in hand. "Then I'll be back."

Ashlyn wanted to protest, maybe she should have, but the look on Tripp's face that he tried so hard to mask, was like an arrow to her heart.

As she walked back to the classroom, she hated that she couldn't give Tripp the answer that he wanted...that she wanted. If that answer was so important to him, did that mean that maybe he still had feelings for her?

* * *

"Well, that's new," Emory gasped as she and Ashlyn approached Ashlyn's locker at the end of the day.

Ashlyn was taken aback to see Eric leaning against it, flipping through his phone to pass the time.

"I'm going to go find Ellis," Emory groaned. She could not stand to be in Eric's presence.

"Hey, babe," Eric greeted once Ashlyn was a few steps from her locker.

Babe?

"Hi, Eric. What's up?"

Ashlyn went around him to get to her locker and he took a step to the side to give her some room.

"I was wondering if you wanted to go to a movie tonight," he coolly mentioned.

Ashlyn was thankful that the door to her locker masked the shocked and repulsed look that came to her face. "Uh...It's Monday. It's a school night." No. that was the wrong thing to say. She quickly retracted that with, "Besides, we broke up."

He laughed. "We didn't break up. You just needed some time to figure out whatever is wrong with you."

164

Ashlyn closed the door to her locker. In the distance she could see Emory glaring at her. Unfortunately, she was with several of the guys, Tripp included.

"Nothing is wrong with me. You just don't care about me anymore, so I don't know why you're over here asking me on a date."

"Oh, come on, Ash," he groaned. She felt like she had heard that phrase a thousand times before from him. "Sorry if I said your painting was lame." Ashlyn was quite surprised that he even remembered that he insulted her painting. "I tell you what," he began, reaching down to her tote on the ground, and plucking her camera from it. "Why don't you start by showing me some of your pictures." He clicked the camera on and began to thumb through the saved images. "You haven't shown me your photography in..." His words trailed off as he continued to scroll.

Ashlyn adjusted her backpack and picked up her tote, waiting for Eric to get done going through her pictures. She really had no desire to talk to Eric about her pictures because the only reason he was asking was to try to smooth things over, and after seeing the look on Tripp's face earlier in the day, she had no intentions on fixing things with Eric.

He hit the button to scroll past images much harder than Ashlyn would have wanted. "What the hell is this," he growled.

Ashlyn rolled her eyes. There couldn't possibly be anything on her camera to cause him to go into a fit of blinding rage.

Eric shoved the camera in her face so that she could see the screen. "That?!"

Ashlyn was confused. It was one of the many pictures she had from this season's baseball games. "What? That was the most recent game," Ashlyn said. She didn't understand why Eric seemed to be losing his cool.

"You just go to all the games," he proceeded to yell, drawing a great deal of attention.

"Yes. Ever since I started going freshman year to see you play, and then with the paper. It's almost an understanding now that I do that for–"

"To see me play! That's why you went! Who's your excuse now," he screamed at the top of his lungs waving her camera in the air.

* * *

Both Emory and Tripp began to take a step forward. Ellis grabbed his sister by her wrist and Byron was quick to step in front of Tripp and put his hand on Tripp's chest, lightly pushing him back.

"No. You do not want to get involved with that," Byron insisted.

"Yes. I do," Tripp growled.

"No, you don't," Emory sighed, feeling defeated. "He won't physically hurt her, but he'll pummel you to a bloody mess."

"I don't care," Tripp insisted, trying to push past Byron, although now Deacon had stepped in as well.

"The both of you need to stay out of it," Ellis began. He looked his sister straight in the eye. "She can save herself. You'll only end up pissing him off further."

* * *

"Well, who is he?!"

"Eric, stop it," Ashlyn hissed. "You're being ridiculous. That's for the paper."

Eric glared at her, holding the camera above his head. "You know what I think?" He didn't give her a chance to answer.

Ashlyn felt her heart shatter to a million pieces, just like the lens of her camera as it came colliding into the wall of lockers.

"Eric! No!"

She tried to reach for the camera, but he slammed it against the lockers again. Though her vision was already blurring, she could see a group of people rushing over.

"I think." *Slam.* More pieces fell. "That you're nothing." *Slam.* "But a dumb." *Slam.* "Cleat chaser."

The camera then fell to the floor, a shattered and irreparable mess.

Before Eric could say another word, Ellis and Byron had him slammed against the lockers.

"What is your problem," Ellis growled, grabbing Eric by the collar.

Eric laughed maniacally, his face still red with anger.

Emory pushed her way in. "I swear, I will gut you like a fish for that!" She attempted to take a swing, but Deacon protectively wrapped his arm around her waist and lifted her up and out of reach.

"We don't need you getting into trouble too," he whispered as she squirmed for him to put her down.

"Mr. Weaver," a voice boomed through the hallway. It was loud enough that the students still in the school parted like the Red Sea. Mr. Reynolds was generally more on the quite side when it came to teachers in the school, but looking at him right now put fear in all those around. "Principal Willis! Move it! Now!"

The guys released Eric, although rather roughly, giving him a good shove forward.

Emory and Tripp were bending down in hopes of consoling Ashlyn when Mr. Reynolds made his way in, ushering them aside. He looked down at the camera, fully knowing that Ashlyn opted out of using the school cameras for assignments.

"I'm sorry, Ashlyn. I can't tell you not to worry about this, because I know you will. Please come to my room before school tomorrow. We'll get a school issued camera for you for the remainder of the year."

Ashlyn nodded, but that wasn't the point. This was hers. This pile of plastic was once something that was so special to her, and he destroyed it.

"I'm sorry, but I have to go. There's no telling where that boy is headed," Mr. Reynolds sighed, knowing that he needed to make sure that Eric ended up in Willis' office.

After Mr. Reynolds left, Ashlyn looked for the place where the memory card was and slipped it out and into the pocket of her jeans. She began scooping the remains into her bag, knowing that it would only go into the garbage once she got home.

Tripp began reaching for some of the pieces while Emory tried to give Ashlyn a hug. Ashlyn gave up and shoved Emory away as she quickly stood.

"Ash," Emory began.

"No. I don't want to hear it. Not from either one of you," she cried.

She turned and rushed out of the school leaving behind her nothing more than a trail of tears.

CHAPTER 17

"Ash, is everything okay," Poppy asked, poking her head into her daughter's darkened room. "I have breakfast."

"I'm not hungry," Ashlyn mumbled.

Poppy made her way to the window and glanced at the blank canvas on the easel. "Did you finish the one you were working on?" She pulled back the curtains, allowing the early morning light to trickle in.

"Mhmm."

Poppy looked over to Ashlyn, still in bed, buried in the covers. "I take it you're not going to school today," she asked, now sitting at the foot of the bed.

"I'm sorry, mom. I just don't feel good," Ashlyn only partially lied.

"I understand. Sometimes we all need a break, a mental health day."

Ashlyn pulled the covers away. Her eyes burned from the light streaming through her room.

"Is there something you want to talk about?" Poppy knew that something had happened at school the moment she saw Ashlyn the evening prior, but Ashlyn had clammed up and not mentioned a word.

"I just want to stay in my room, forever," Ashlyn sighed, attempting to prop herself up with pillows.

Poppy laughed softly. "I've been there before, especially as a teenager. Just remember, a ship in a harbor is safe, but that's not what a ship is built for."

Ashlyn groaned. "Really, mom? What does that even mean?"

Poppy patted Ashlyn's legs over the covers. "It means, you can sit in this room where it seems safe, but that's not what you're meant to do. That's not what life is about. You can choose to stay in places and situations where you'll feel comfortable, but you'll be missing out on so much."

"Why do I have a feeling that you're talking about something else?"

"Sweetie, I know you're scared of change." Ashlyn nodded in agreement. "But don't sit in the harbor just because it's what you know, what makes you feel comfortable. You might run into storms and rocky waters by venturing out, but it's worth it. At the end of the day, if you're not happy, and you go to bed in tears, then wake up the next morning and change it. You're the only one who can make sure that you're happy."

A brilliant and beautiful picture began to emerge in Ashlyn's head while her mother kept ranting about ships and happiness. She stared at the empty canvas on her easel, and the lines and colors started to paint themselves like something magical.

"Hey, thanks for that mom," Ashlyn interrupted. "But can I stay home where it feels safe, just for today?"

Poppy rose and leaned over, kissing Ashlyn on her forehead. "Absolutely."

Though she hadn't slept well, and she felt exhausted, Ashlyn had an entire day and a great idea. Her last painting, now hidden in her closet, had been from a picture. This one would have to be entirely from the image in her head, and if she didn't do it now, she was afraid everything that she saw might drift away.

With both her parents gone, and Carmen only cleaning on Fridays, it meant that the house was eerily quiet and perfect for concentration. It wasn't until she looked at her silenced phone that she realized just how wrapped up in her creation she had become.

It was nearing lunchtime and she could feel that she had skipped breakfast. While she made herself a quick peanut butter and jelly sandwich, she looked over all the texts she had ignored.

Emory: I don't see your car. Where are you?

Kayla: Emory said you're not here today. Are you okay?

June: We heard about what happened to your camera. I'm so sorry! I hope you're feeling alright.

Emory: Seriously? Can you get back to someone? I'm going to text your mom!

Emory: Your mom said you're home sick. We know that's a lie. Please get back to me.

Tripp: I don't see you at lunch with Emory. I guess you stayed home. How are you doing?

* * *

"I can't believe she isn't texting any of us back," Emory huffed. She stabbed at her plate of food.

"Don't take it out on the pasta," Ellis teased.

"Oh, shut up!"

"I didn't see Eric today. What's the deal there," June asked. Emory had filled her and Kayla in on yesterday afternoon's events.

"Suspended, three days," Deacon added.

"He's this close," Emory began, holding her thumb and forefinger so they were almost touching. "To getting expelled. One more big mistake and he's gone."

Tripp looked at down at his phone halfway through lunch but saw no new messages.

Tripp: Emory and Ellis are about to kill each other over here.

He hoped that the message would at least make Ashlyn smile. When his phone vibrated on the table a second later, he couldn't stop his heart from racing in anticipation.

Emory quickly shot him a glare. "Who is that?"

Tripp flipped the phone over. "Just my mom. Paranoid much?"

"Ugh, sorry. You'd be the last person she'd talk to anyway," Emory sighed.

Tripp tried not to smile, because this time, Emory was completely and totally wrong.

Ashlyn: You're with them?

Tripp: Yes. Everyone misses you.

Ashlyn: Haha. I doubt it, but thanks for trying to make me feel better.

Tripp: I miss you.

Then there was silence.

"I just hope she's in a good mood for Saturday," June grumbled, catching Tripp's attention.

"What's Saturday," he piped up.

The three girls gave each other incredulous looks, but then remembered that as comfortable as it seemed having Tripp around, he was still technically the new guy. There were several things they assumed he knew but didn't.

"Ash's birthday! Her parents are having a simple little thing at their house. We're all invited," Kayla squealed. "Weren't you invited?"

Tripp felt left in the cold. Ashlyn had never told him about a birthday coming up. He knew she was sixteen while most everyone else was seventeen. It was easy to assume that she had a spring or summer birthday, but that was never a question he had asked.

Sensing Tripp's hurt, "Don't worry, Ashlyn doesn't advertise it. Unlike some people who talk about it for a whole month." Emory raised her brow in Ellis' direction. "Also, her mother sent invites like a month ago. She wouldn't have known to send you one."

Tripp shrugged. "It's no big deal." But it was.

Emory continued to quietly poke around at her food, awkward silence now running through the table. A moment later she dropped her fork. "Oh my gosh! You can be my date!"

"What," Ellis, Deacon, and Tripp shouted in unison.

Emory glared at her brother and his best friend, and flipped her hand about like she was shooing them away. "Not like a real date. I'm actually talking to a football player from Halshire." Ellis groaned at the comment, but Emory paid him no attention. "Anyway, you could be like my plus one. I'll tell Ash's mom that I'm bringing a date."

Something about the idea didn't sit well with Tripp. "I don't think that's a good idea," he hesitated. "If Ash would have wanted me to come, I'm sure she would have mentioned something."

"Okay, can we all stop pretending like Tripp doesn't have the biggest crush on Ash," Emory sighed.

"Wait, what?!" Ellis appeared shocked. "What about Rachel?"

Tripp groaned. "What about her?"

"I thought…"

"No. That's between you, Abby, and Rachel." Tripp then remembered his conversation with Ashlyn the day prior. He needed to talk to Rachel and clarify a few things. He directed his words back to Emory. "Ash and I are just friends, that's all," he insisted.

Emory rolled her eyes. "Whatever! You're going to come with me, right?"

"I'd rather–"

"It'll be a nice surprise for her. I promise!"

"I'll think about it," Tripp finally said after seeing that it didn't look like Emory would be letting up anytime soon.

"I'm sure if you just ask Ash if you can come," Deacon began.

"No," Kayla shouted. "That just looks pathetic."

Tripp felt increasingly uncomfortable with the plotting that his friends were doing. The easiest thing to do would be to tell Ashlyn that he had heard about her birthday and let it go from there. After all, they were friends. Wouldn't she at least invite him?

Tripp: Emory can't stop talking about your birthday.

Ashlyn: Ugh. I'd text her and tell her to shut up, but I'm kind of avoiding opening the door for communication.

Tripp: You're texting me though.

176

Ashlyn: You also haven't given me a hard time about yesterday. Don't mess it up.

Tripp: I'm here if you want to talk. I also have my own opinion if you want it. But at the end of the day, it's your life.

Ashlyn: Thank you.

She never mentioned another word about her birthday party, and neither did Tripp. A sick part of him liked Emory's idea. While he knew Ashlyn would be shocked and probably hate the both of them for just a little while, he also had the perfect idea for a gift. He had already thought about buying it just because, but now he definitely had an excuse; all he needed was his dad's permission, or rather, his credit card.

That was one thing that would have to wait. What couldn't wait was Rachel.

"Hey," Tripp said, announcing himself just as Rachel rose from the table to head to class.

Rachel gasped with surprise. "Tripp! Hi! How are you? We missed you and Ellis today." Thinking quickly, she added, "And Deacon."

"Yeah...Umm, I need to talk to you."

"Right now? Lunch is over," Rachel whined.

"On the way to class is fine," he said with a shrug.

"So," Rachel began, just as they walked out of the cafeteria. "You're walking me to class?"

Crap. Tripp hadn't thought much of the act when he suggested it. Now he understood what it must look like to someone like Rachel, someone who already thought they had been on dates.

"I'm walking in the same direction as you so that I can address something," Tripp clarified.

"Wow, so formal," Rachel giggled. She playfully nudged her shoulder into Tripp.

He tensed. He didn't want to be mean to her, but he had to set the record straight, before she got any more ideas about what they were or weren't.

"Yeah, umm–"

Rachel stopped in front of him, a smile so big it had to hurt. "You are so cute! If you're officially asking me out, the answer is yes!"

Tripp could feel his face scrunching up and a headache coming on. He had barely said a handful of words to her and that's what she thought. This was going to be a lot harder than he imagined in his head.

"Actually, Rachel, the opposite."

Her smiled faded and she blinked at him rapidly. She couldn't be hearing him right. "I'm sorry. I don't understand."

"You're a nice girl and all," he started, already knowing he sounded like some poorly written character in a movie. "I'm just not interested in you like that."

"What about our dinners? And sitting with me at lunch?"

Tripp uncomfortably ran his fingers through his hair. There had been girls that he went on a date or two with, but generally he never got seriously involved with them. It was pointless. He never knew when his dad would be transferred to another country. It wasn't fair to lead a girl on like that. Needless to say, the one time he did break up with a girl, it was because he was moving.

This was something out of left field for him. Breaking up with a girl he never dated.

"Those dinners, those two dinners," he felt the need to clarify. "Were with a group of friends. They weren't dates. Also, I sat with you and your friends at lunch at Ellis' request, which was probably at Abby's request, because you–"

Rachel stomped her foot, actually stomped her foot. "Wow! I cannot believe you right now!"

Tripp's jaw dropped. Was she being serious?

"After all that, and now you're walking me to class, you're going to act like we're not kind of together in a sense?"

"We're not together. I don't even have your phone number," Tripp pointed out, instantly regretting it.

"Is that it? You need my number? Here, give me your phone and–"

"I don't want your number." Tripp took a step back, disliking the little bit of attention they were getting in the busy hallway. "There's someone else," Tripp blurted out.

"You're seeing someone else, but asking me for my number? What is wrong with you?!"

"No. I'm not seeing someone else. I just don't want anyone to be under the impression that we're together." He could not believe how exhausting she was.

"You, Tripp Scott, are a freaking jerk," Rachel screamed at the top of her lungs.

Her outburst drew a great deal of attention. Normally Tripp didn't mind the attention, but right now he wanted to crawl in a hole. If he had known that to begin with, there wasn't a chance in hell he would have ever accepted Ellis' invite.

From now on, he'd sit with the guys from the team. Some of them could be a bit strange, but none of them were as crazy as Rachel.

CHAPTER 18

Ronan laughed at his son's request. "You want how much?"

"Yeah, I know. It's really important though," Tripp pled.

Tripp's father pushed his computer aside and motioned to the spare chair inside his home office. "Have a seat."

Tripp groaned, but gave in to his father's request.

"I know you really like this girl," Ronan began, really wishing that Tripp had gone to his mother and asked her for help buying a gift. No doubt she probably would have given in, but at least then he wouldn't have known how much was spent. "You can't buy someone's love."

"Dad, please, stop." Tripp shook his head. He hadn't seen his dad look so awkward in quite some time. "I'm not stupid. I know that. I know that's what it looks like, but it's not. It's her birthday and this is something she'd love."

"What if next week she decides she wants nothing to do with you anymore?"

Tripp didn't want to get into the details of his friendship with Ashlyn. While his dad's comment made him sad to ever think of that being a possibility, he knew if he made one wrong move with her at the moment, it could very much be a reality. Instead of saying all that, he went with, "Then that's up to her and what she wants. I'm not doing this for any reason other than wanting her to have a nice gift for her birthday."

"You said her mom's a therapist and her dad's a lawyer. Couldn't they buy it?"

Tripp hated how when it came to their family, his dad splurged; however, when it came to doing nice things for others, not so much. "It's not that she's poor and can't afford it. That's not the point. This needs to come from me."

Tripp hated begging his dad for money, but he knew the deal. As long as he did well in school and on the team, his father would give him anything he asked for.

Ronan grunted. "Just put it on the Amazon credit card when you order it."

Tripp wanted to hug his dad, but decided against it. He wasn't much for affection. "Thanks, dad. Really."

Tripp stood to leave his father's office, knowing that he was getting antsy to get back to work. Just when he was at the doorway, "Tripp?" He turned back to face his dad. With a somber look on his face, "I just don't want your friends using you. I don't want to see you get hurt."

Tripp laughed. "Trust me, that's not the case with this one." He coolly threw his hands to his side. "Besides, I'm not even invited to her party."

* * *

"You look surprisingly upbeat," Emory pointed out.

She closed the car door and waited with Ashlyn in her car before the bell rang to start heading to classes.

"I started working on a new project. It's something different," Ashlyn announced excitedly.

"Wow! That's great. I'm proud of you. So, you're okay?"

Ashlyn didn't look Emory in the eyes. She still had to talk with Eric. What he did was unfathomable. That camera meant everything to her, and he treated it like garbage. It was garbage now. The best magician couldn't attempt to repair the thing.

"Yeah, I'm okay." It was a lie, but she was holding it together.

Emory quickly changed the subject to Ashlyn's birthday party Saturday. Party was the wrong word. It wouldn't be a wild and out-of-control high school party like the movies led you to believe. It was really just her friends and family coming by to visit and grab a bite to eat. Ashlyn didn't think it was a big deal, and wasn't at all enthused about being the center of attention for one day.

"Guess what I got you," Emory jumped up and down enthusiastically as they began making their way through the parking lot.

Ashlyn couldn't help but smile. "I don't want to guess. I want to be surprised."

"Oh, you'll definitely be surprised." Emory refrained from adding that it wasn't the gift that would surprise Ashlyn.

"Not if you keep mentioning it the rest of the week." Ashlyn patted the pocket of her jeans. "Ugh. Go on ahead. I left my phone on the charger in my car."

"You sure?"

"Yeah, I'll see you at lunch," Ashlyn told Emory, giving her a quick half hug.

She rushed back to her car, despite having plenty of time to make it to her first period. She grabbed her phone and just as she was about to slip it into her pocket, she saw that she had a new text.

Tripp: Hope you're feeling better today! Looking forward to seeing you.

Ashlyn couldn't help but notice that his texts were bordering on bold and flirtatious, but could also be considered thoughtful and friendly. She wasn't entirely sure where he was, and she needed to deal with Eric once and for all before the idea of another relationship crossed her mind.

Just as she passed through another row of cars, "I mean what was he thinking?! Can you believe that?!"

Ashlyn paused and looked in the direction of the overdramatic shouting. It was Rachel and one other girl, Melody. Melody looked terrified by her outburst but went along with it.

"He's such a player. You can do so much better," Melody insisted.

"When he broke up with me, he said he was dating someone else! Who does that?! I don't know where he came from, but he can go back for all I care," Rachel continued, ranting away. It was likely she'd scream about it to anyone who would listen. Unfortunately, that meant that Ashlyn was caught in her web. "Ash," she gasped as soon as she saw Ashlyn a few feet away. "I can't believe you and Emory didn't tell me what a jerk Tripp is!"

Ashlyn's eyes widened in shock. How was this her fault?

"Tripp Scott is nothing but a player. He told me yesterday that we weren't dating, and he was seeing someone else! How can you be friends with someone like that?!"

"Umm, I'm sorry?" Ashlyn didn't know what else to say. Rachel's meltdown was a little concerning. Also, it's not like she and Tripp could have been dating long enough to garner such a strong emotional reaction.

Suddenly Rachel calmed down. "No, I'm sorry," she whined. "I shouldn't be yelling at you. I'm just really upset."

Ashlyn didn't know the correct protocol for this type of meeting. She and Rachel weren't friends. She had no real knowledge of her relationship with Tripp. She had no desire to console her over something that seemed so trivial to her.

"You're going to be fine, Rachel. There are so many other guys out there," Ashlyn finally said.

"He was just so hot." After thinking a moment more. "You know what though, you're right. Ugh! I'm going to be head cheerleader next year. I deserve more than just some baseball player."

Just like that, the pretend tears went away. Ashlyn knew they were pretend because not a spec of Rachel's makeup was out of place.

Ashlyn still had her phone in her hand, on Tripp's message. If she had thought about replying, Rachel did a pretty good job of changing her mind.

As she continued to make her way to first period, she thought about why Rachel had been so upset. Tripp really was something else. Any time that she thought he might be challenging her preconceptions of him, he proved her first thoughts right. The fact that a flirt like Rachel called him a player said something.

A curious part of her wondered about the girl that he had moved on to. Rachel seemed perfect for him, at least as far as looks were concerned. She wasn't exactly the brightest when it came to much outside of cheerleading. Tripp on the other hand was very smart, much better at science than Ashlyn, though she'd never admit that to him. She had to assume that he'd go for someone that he could have a stimulating conversation with.

"Ugh. Snap out of it," she mumbled to herself, hating that she had allowed a single moment of her thoughts to care about Tripp's dating life.

CHAPTER 19

Ashlyn finished off with a little bit of mascara and stood looking at herself in the mirror. She wore more than her usual amount of school makeup. Her hair was fixed in her classic side fishtail braid, barely extending over her shoulder due to the length of her hair.

She had also opted to wear a dress. She rarely went places anymore where she got to wear many of her dresses. Unlike some girls, school wasn't the place for her to wear them. She felt like she had to stay too pretty and neat, which was extremely difficult when it came to art.

"Are you ready," her mother called through her room. Ashlyn popped out of her bathroom to see her mother standing in her doorway. "Aww," Poppy squealed, clasping her hands. "You look so adorable."

Ashlyn tried to hide the look of disgust that came to her face from her mother's comment. Her mother meant well, and it was supposed to be a compliment, but she didn't know of many seventeen-year-old girls who wanted to be referred to as *adorable*.

"Your aunt and uncle are here," Poppy announced.

Ashlyn looked at the time on her phone. 2:28. The party was supposed to be from 3:00 to 7:00. Of course, her aunt and uncle had to be early, probably to get first dibs on the snacks.

"I'll be down in just a second," Ashlyn replied.

Thankfully her friends wouldn't pick on her for how lame the party would probably be. Her parents tried, but this was something she did not want. She would have been happier just going out for pizza with her girlfriends.

She was pleasantly surprised to see that Kayla and June were the first to arrive. She didn't expect any of the guys to show up early; however, she was a little disappointed that Emory hadn't been the very first person at her door.

By half past three her main group of friends, with the exception of Emory, were all present, as well as aunts, uncles, cousins, and neighbors. It was a nice blend of age groups and everyone seemed to be enjoying themselves.

* * *

"You look like a ghost," Emory laughed, attempting to break up the awkward silence in the car.

"I'm a little nervous." Tripp felt strange admitting that. "I don't want to upset her on her birthday, you know?"

Emory flicked her wrist and waved him off. "She should have invited you anyway. You're part of the group."

That felt good to hear. Tripp was thankful that his father had taken a job where he'd be at for years to come. It felt good having friends that he could finish school with, maybe even go to college with, who knew?

"Can you do me a favor," Tripp asked as he parked the car on the very crowded street. He reached into the back seat and handed Emory a fairly decent sized box. "Can you put this with the rest of the gifts?"

Emory looked at him with confusion.

"I'd rather Ashlyn not know it's from me. At least not right away," he said, trying to hide his embarrassment.

"Nope. Sorry. First the flowers, then the texting. You come into school this confident hotshot, and with her you're this scared puddle of mush," Emory pointed out.

"I never intended to take credit for the flowers. The texting, well...I guess she wasn't my biggest fan. The anonymity let me get to know her, without her blocking me the second she knew who I was."

"For the record, I don't think she ever hated you," Emory admitted. "Guys have never been that forward with her, largely in part because she's dated Eric all through high school. I think you took her by surprise. Then every girl in the school was drooling over you, so that didn't help the situation much," Emory scoffed. "Plus, you are a little cocky when it comes to–"

"Okay, I get it," Tripp chuckled. Emory wasn't holding back.

She shoved the box that Tripp extended towards her back to him. "So be that confident and cocky hotshot when it counts," she said with a wink and jumped out of his passenger side door.

* * *

Once Ashlyn was able to get away from a few girls she knew well from her art class, she found Deacon alone, grabbing a soda from one of the coolers.

"Hey, happy birthday," Deacon said when Ashlyn walked up, holding out his hand for a fist bump.

"Glad you could come."

Deacon wasn't a big talker, which made this both difficult and awkward. She should have gone to find Ellis, but he was talking with a couple girls.

"I thought Emory might come with you and Ellis, but I haven't seen her or heard from her," Ashlyn began. She tried to keep cool and not freak out bombarding Deacon with questions as to where her best friend was.

Deacon's expression turned cold. "Yeah, about that," he hesitated, looking more annoyed by the second. "She was waiting on her ride when we left."

Ashlyn was shocked. "What? She didn't tell me she's coming with someone." How could Emory keep something like that from her?

Deacon seemed increasingly uncomfortable with the topic. "You know Emory. Just don't be mad at–"

"Ash," Daniel called from the front door. "Some more of your friends are here."

That had to be Emory! She was the only one that Ashlyn could think of that wasn't present. She gave a quick smile to Deacon and excitedly rushed to the front door.

Whatever bits of good and happy emotions she had running through her instantly disappeared when she rounded the corner and saw her dad ushering in her best friend and her unexpected guest.

Ashlyn felt like the ground was spinning, and at any given moment the world might flip them all upside down.

"Ash! Happy Birthday," Emory squealed and rushed to her for a hug.

"Hey. I'm glad you're finally here," Ashlyn managed.

From over Emory's shoulder Ashlyn watched Tripp casually walk up to the two of them. For a moment, her shock, hurt, and rage took a backseat to admire him. To say he looked incredible was putting it mildly. He looked like he had just come from a photoshoot. His untucked blue button down with the sleeves rolled up to his elbows fit him so perfectly, accentuating broad shoulders and a slim waist. His dark-washed tinted jeans had to have been altered for him and him alone. Then there was his stupid dark blonde hair. She could never look at his hair and not recall that day in the library. He had just enough product in it to give the illusion that it was haphazard and messy, although it probably took a good ten minutes to fix.

"Happy Birthday, Ash," Tripp quietly greeted her, now standing next to Emory.

"I hope you don't mind that I brought a guest," Emory piped up.

Ashlyn felt a foreign feeling rush through her. She loved Emory to death, but for once, she really didn't like her. She couldn't believe what she was feeling. Jealousy. Crap. She was jealous of her best friend.

Ashlyn forced herself to put on her best fake smile. "No, the more the merrier right?" Wrong. So wrong.

"Where's the table for the gifts," Emory asked, pretending that everything was cool. She could slap her friend for being such an idiot sometimes. How could Ash think that after all these years she couldn't read her face?

Before Ashlyn could answer, Emory saw the table and headed towards it.

"The invitation said no gifts," Ashlyn grumbled, a split second forgetting that Tripp was still standing there.

"Then I guess it's a good thing that I didn't get an invitation."

Ashlyn looked up and saw his eyes intensely focused on hers. She hoped that he couldn't tell that she wanted to cry. She had heard what Rachel said earlier in the week; however, Rachel was also crazy dramatic.

Worst of all, Tripp had kissed her. How could he have kissed her, and continued to be so sweet, and show up to her party, uninvited, with her best friend?

Ashlyn looked down at the box and then back up to Tripp. The gift didn't matter. It would have been better had he not gotten her anything, especially now.

"I had no idea that Emory was bringing you. If I would have known I would have told you to come anyway," she said, attempting to be nonchalant about something when inside she was screaming, stomping, throwing things. Inside she was Rachel. Just wonderful.

"But you didn't."

If he was upset with her, he didn't show it. Now she felt twice as crappy. She hadn't given her party much thought. Her mother had sent out the invitations, and at the time her friendship with Tripp was uncertain.

He brushed past her and took the box to the table set up for gifts, all gifts that the invitations said specifically not to bring.

Just then the doorbell rang again. Ashlyn saw her dad look up from the glass patio doors, but she waved him off and made her way to the door a few feet away.

If she thought her day couldn't get any worse, somewhere out there her puppeteer was laughing like a madman.

"Eric. What are you doing here?"

Rather than letting Eric inside, Ashlyn stepped over the threshold and closed the door behind her so that she and Eric were alone on the front porch.

"What? I can't come see *my girl* on her birthday?"

Ashlyn was cautious in whether she should point it out, but she had to, regardless of the demonic way Eric was looking at her. "I'm not your girl. You made that perfectly clear when you destroyed my camera."

"But we didn't break up."

"After the things you've said to me? Eric, I can't be in a relationship like that. It's toxic, and I feel miserable," Ashlyn sighed.

"It's always about you isn't it," he spat, taking a step forward.

Ashlyn grew nervous and was just about to reach back for the handle of the door when Eric stepped to the side and opened it himself.

"I'll just stay for cake." He now stood in the open doorway while Ashlyn remained frozen. "Besides, I have a really nice gift for you. I'll make this right."

Ashlyn didn't see a gift in his hands, but gift or no gift, it would be best if he wasn't there, ever.

"We can see each other later," she lied, hoping to get him to leave.

"Ash," he chuckled. She couldn't tell if he was being sarcastic or actually amused. "Relax. If you want to argue about this...Well, I'd hate to cause a scene on your birthday."

He then made his way inside the house. Ashlyn clenched her fists, attempting to control her fingers that were shaking uncontrollably. Eric had to know after what happened Monday that her friends would be livid to see him there.

So, this was seventeen. That uneventful birthday between sixteen and eighteen.

CHAPTER 20

"Okay, everyone," Poppy shouted over the crowded living room and throughout the patio doors. "We're going to do presents in five minutes."

Ashlyn was dreading that part. She was hoping that her mother would allow her to open them later, in the confines of her own room, where no one could see her reactions. One of her aunts and uncles always gave her something that had no relation to anything that she was interested in. Then she had to pretend what an awesome gift it was.

Poppy came over to Ashlyn. "Your father and I have a very special gift for you!"

"Can't wait." She refrained from telling her mother how much she didn't want to open gifts in front of everyone.

"I can't find your father," Poppy mentioned, looking from side to side.

"Maybe he's on a quick call. I'll check his office," Ashlyn told her. She loved her friends but was thankful to get a moment away.

She had been nervous at first with Eric barging in, but he was at least pretending to be on his best behavior. Emory, Kayla, and June were less than thrilled to have him around, and had even said as much. Surprisingly, the guys were amicable toward him; however, after a few minutes of socializing, Eric hung back in a corner on his phone for the most part.

One person that Ashlyn hadn't spoken to since he arrived was Tripp. It seemed as though he just disappeared. It's not like Ashlyn was extensively looking for him, but she thought their paths would have crossed more. There were barely fifty people throughout the common space and patio and backyard, but not a single one was Tripp.

Ashlyn took her time down the hall toward her dad's office at the end. The door was open, and she could tell that the light on his desk was on because of the unique amber glow pouring through the opening. Sure enough, she heard him talking. She thought his case was wrapping up, but something must have come about last minute. She was just about to turn around and go back to the party when she heard a familiar chuckle. What was Tripp doing in her dad's office?

Ashlyn curiously rushed to the office's doorway. Her father saw her immediately and all conversation stopped. Tripp sat in a chair on the other side of Daniel's desk, directly across from him. He glanced back momentarily to see Ashlyn standing there, shocked and confused.

"Hey, Ash," Daniel greeted with a smile. "Can I help you with something?"

"Uh...yeah. Mom is looking for you. She wants to do presents soon." Her words were spoken to her father, but she couldn't help but watch Tripp.

Daniel clapped his hands and stood; as he did, so did Tripp. "Perfect." He and Tripp then walked toward the doorway. Ashlyn took a step out into the hall, but still watched them carefully. "It was good talking with you Tripp," Daniel said, patting Tripp on the shoulder. "I really hope everything works out for you."

"Thank you, Mr. Jennings," Tripp said shyly.

Daniel closed his office and took off back to the party, leaving Tripp and Ashlyn alone in the hall.

Once her father was out of earshot, "What was that about?"

"Nothing," Tripp said with the most melting smile.

"How long have the two of you been back here? I haven't seen you since you arrived...With Emory," she added.

Tripp raised a brow and took a step closer to Ashlyn. His smile had faded into lips that harbored the faintest of smirks. "Were you looking for me?"

Ashlyn could feel her breathing becoming more difficult with him so close, with him looking at her like a hungry animal. "No. I was just pointing out the obvious."

"I was talking with your dad, as you've *obviously* seen."

"About what," Ashlyn asked once more.

Tripp's eyes dropped from hers down the hall toward the party. "Just baseball stuff."

He was lying. His whole demeanor had shifted.

"I don't believe you."

"Oh, yeah? Then what do you think we were talking about," he asked, unable to look at her.

Ashlyn let out a deep breath. "I haven't a clue, but just forget it. I don't have time for whatever games you're trying to play."

Ashlyn started back down the hall and Tripp fell into step surprisingly close beside her. "Trust me, Ash, I'm not playing any games. You really should work on your patience. Not your strongest virtue," he teased.

Ashlyn paused her steps momentarily to glare at him. "Oh! When it comes to you, you have no idea how patient I am."

His face turned serious and dark. "Likewise." Not allowing her to control the situation, he took a step around her and went back to the common area, leaving her alone in the hallway.

* * *

Ashlyn sat down in a chair her mother had placed near the table of gifts as others stood around, some solely focused on her, others drinking soda and stuffing their faces.

"Alright," Poppy began. "Your father and I want to go first, because I know this is going to be your best gift, and I simply can't hold it in any longer!"

Ashlyn smiled. Her mother's excitement was contagious. She didn't know what she was expecting. Her parents hadn't asked her what she wanted for her birthday, nor had she mentioned anything. She only hoped this wouldn't be one of those gifts where she'd have to pretend that it was the best thing ever.

She was a little surprised and slightly under-whelmed when her father handed her mother the en-velope which she then received. Knowing the practi-cality of her parents, it was probably a trust or maybe something set up for college.

"Thank you," she told her mom once she received it.

"Hurry up, open it," Poppy exclaimed. Daniel placed his hands on her shoulders and whispered in her ear.

Ashlyn put her finger under one of the corners of the envelope and began tearing it open. When she looked inside, she saw something colorful, and as she carefully withdrew it, realized that it was a pamphlet full of picturesque nature scenes. She opened it. There were more pictures, ones of animals, with de-scriptions and statistics that she didn't have time to read as she sat there.

She looked up to see her parents smiling from ear to ear. "I don't under–"

"We're taking you to Africa this summer," Poppy screamed. Several people gasped and clapping en-sued. "There's a reserve that we'll be staying at. You'll get to see so much! We know how much you love to take pictures and we thought this would be a won-derful experience!"

Ashlyn looked back down at the pamphlet. The next page talked about excursions and activities.

Tears came to her eyes, and the only thing she could think of was to tell herself not to cry. As happy as she was, she knew that there was going to be an uncomfortable talk in the future, one where she had to tell her parents what happened to her camera.

She jumped up from her seat and ran into her parents' arms. "Thank you, so much! This is like a dream come true." It was. She'd be able to see things that she had never seen in her life.

"We love you," her father said, and gave her a quick kiss on her forehead, not wanting to embarrass her.

Ashlyn went back to opening the rest of her gifts. She wanted to be quick about it, fully knowing that her friends and family didn't want to stand around quietly watching something so uneventful. Most of her friends got her gift cards. She was grateful for that. They were something that she could either definitely use for herself, or absolutely regift at a later point in time.

She was rather surprised when she opened the gift from the aunt and uncle who were horrible when it came to presents and knowing anything about her. It was an extremely large and heavy coffee table book on various artists, their work, their lives, and their influence in modern day society. Not bad.

Ashlyn had two gifts left. She knew exactly who they were from, Emory and Tripp. Every year, party or not, she purposefully left Emory's for last, knowing that her friend had little patience when it came to gifts. She was surprised that Emory hadn't stormed over to her earlier and insisted that she open it right then and there.

She was terrified to see what Tripp had gotten her. Knowing him, it had to be absurd and ridiculous, or thoughtful and sweet. Wanting to delay that for just a second longer, she reached for Emory's box. Before she could begin opening it, Eric stepped forward.

"Wait, I have something for you."

"Seriously," Emory shouted throughout the room, garnering a few laughs.

"Babe," he began, to which Ashlyn cringed. "I know we've had our ups and downs." Was that what he called smashing her camera and calling her names? "But I want you to know how I feel about you."

He withdrew a small box from the pocket of his ripped jeans. Ashlyn froze. What was he doing? She felt like she was drowning, but then remembered that was probably because somewhere along the way she had stopped breathing.

He handed her the small box. Thank goodness he did so without doing something as stupid or insane as getting down on one knee.

Upon opening it, Ashlyn was slightly relieved to see a silver necklace; however, it wasn't that simple. It was a heart with an engraving that read, *Love Always*.

Ashlyn eyes immediately shot up to Eric. He had the biggest smile on his face, and in the past she would have found that melting; however, something in his eyes was different, and it had been for a long time. She was just about to tell him thanks for the gift and move on to Emory's when his next words knocked the air from her lungs.

"I love you, Ash. And I'm going to make sure that you know that, every day, for the rest of your life."

He had never said those words to her. They had never said those words to each other. It wasn't until then that Ashlyn realized that she had never used the word *love* when it came to talking about her relationship and feelings for Eric.

Emory looked to Ashlyn's parents, hoping her mother would step in and take the gift from Ashlyn and place it with the rest of the opened ones, but everyone seemed stuck in place, waiting to see what Ashlyn would say. This was one time that Emory was certain that Ashlyn needed saving, and if no one else would say something, then she'd take it upon herself to snap everyone from the spell that Eric had cast with the garbage that he poured from his mouth.

Before she could take a step forward, she felt the space next to her, where a towering guy once stood, turn cold and empty. She looked behind her to see Tripp retreating from the room. She could seriously kill Ashlyn right now.

"Yay," Emory exclaimed as she stomped her way up to the table and snatched the box that was hers. "I *love* you too, Ash," she said in a snotty and sarcastic tone, as if it was obvious that everyone loved Ashlyn and Eric wasn't saying anything new. "Here," she demanded. She held out her gift for Ashlyn, who was still holding the box with the necklace. Emory yanked it from Ashlyn and snapped it shut. "Let me get rid of that so you can wrap this up. Some of us haven't made it to the snack table yet," she laughed, but Ashlyn could see that Emory was shooting lasers with her eyes. Emory handed the box to Ashlyn's mom, who then placed it on the table with the rest of the opened gifts. She realized that Eric was still standing there. She looked at him like she was confused and blinked very rapidly, as if to say, *Why are you still standing there*?

"Thank you, Eric," Ashlyn managed as he proceeded to step to the side with other guests.

Emory then bounded back to her group, with Ellis shaking his head and rolling his eyes in disappointment.

"What? I had to," she whispered.

"No. You did not. You just pushed every button there is on Eric Weaver," Ellis told her, showing great concern.

Ashlyn tried to go back to the way she was before Eric's stupid confession. She had dreamed of a guy telling her those words one day, but that's not at all how she pictured it, and that's not at all how she thought she'd feel after hearing it. She didn't feel butterflies and excitement. She didn't want to jump up and down and scream with joy. She wished he never would have said that. More than anything, she just wanted him to leave.

Instead, she put on her happy face and pretended that she was having the best birthday ever.

Emory's package took forever to open, solely because she used more tape on the wrapping paper than needed. When she finally managed to get to the actual box and open it, her eyes widened. She ran her hand over the beautiful pieces. There were various sizes of Kolinsky Sable brushes. Ashlyn knew of them, but had never bought one for herself, knowing just how expensive some of them could be.

Emory was thrilled when she saw the look on Ashlyn's face. For a moment it erased the damage that had been done moments ago.

Poppy soon took the box of brushes away, knowing that Ashlyn could sit there and play with them forever. "And the last one..." She paused and flipped the box around. "There's nothing on it," she whispered to Ashlyn. "I don't know who it's from."

"Then I guess it's a surprise," Ashlyn told her mother. She knew who it was from.

She quickly glanced about, looking for Tripp. She didn't see him, and she didn't want to make finding him a big deal, so instead, like ripping off a bandage, she began opening the box.

She barely tore one of the sides of wrapping off when she felt the bag of bricks drop in her stomach. This was the kind of gift her parents should be buying her. Emory easily spent a couple hundred on her brushes, but this, this couldn't be.

Ashlyn stopped unwrapping it and stared at the image on the side of the box. *Panasonic LUMIX G95*.

"Well, what is it," someone shouted. It was either Kayla or June, but Ashlyn couldn't tell. The voice seemed foreign with the blood pumping through her ears.

She wanted to both hug and punch Tripp Scott.

CHAPTER 21

Tripp pressed his back against the wall of the empty hallway. He honestly didn't know if he wanted to see Ashlyn open his gift or not. More than anything, he was certain that he couldn't stay in that room and listen to Eric's garbage for one more second.

He hadn't thought things through when Emory invited him, and while he wasn't sure what to expect, Eric's presence wasn't even in the realm of possibilities.

He showed up. He told her happy birthday. He gave her the gift he planned to buy her before he even knew about her birthday. He had done his part as a friend. Perhaps it was time to bow out gracefully.

Tripp felt the phone in the pocket of his jeans go off several times. Hesitantly, he reached for it, expecting the worst.

Ashlyn: Where are you?

Ashlyn: Are you still here?

Ashlyn: We need to talk.

Tripp let his head fall back into the wall. Nothing good ever came from those last four words. As much as he wanted to slip out the front door, he couldn't do that to Ashlyn on her birthday.

Tripp: I'm here.

Ashlyn: My room. Now.

Tripp wasn't sure he read that right. It was only three words, but they didn't make one bit of sense to him. He replied immediately and agreed, feeling a combination of anxiousness and uncertainty.

The stairway upon entering was roped off with a whimsical sign that said guests should remain downstairs only. Tripp climbed over it and proceeded up. Though he had only been to Ashlyn's house once before, he knew exactly where he was going.

* * *

Ashlyn picked up the small box from the table and looked around the room and through the glass doors leading outside. She didn't see Eric anywhere. She had two people she desperately needed to talk to, and she preferred to get him out of the way first.

"Ashlyn, darling," Aunt Carol interrupted her, just as she was trying to get away from everyone. "How did you like the book? You don't have it already, do you?"

"It's wonderful, Aunt Carol." She saw her uncle in the distance talking with her father. "No, I don't have that one. Please give my thanks to Uncle Roger as well."

She turned to leave, but Aunt Carol wasn't having it. "Why don't you come tell him," she insisted.

Ashlyn squeezed the box tightly in annoyance. She felt her phone buzz in the pocket of her dress. It was a text from Tripp obviously, and she couldn't help but wonder if he was already waiting for her. When she told him to meet her in her room, she didn't anticipate running in to Aunt Carol. She also didn't anticipate Eric to have now pulled a disappearing act as well.

"I just need to run up to my room real quick," Ashlyn responded, rushing off before Aunt Carol could say another word to her.

She fumbled over the barrier her mother had put on the staircases and bounded up to her room, knowing that Tripp was already there. Her head was all over the place when she told him to meet her there. She wanted to talk to him away from everyone else, and the only place she could think of was upstairs.

Tripp felt lightheaded when he walked into Ashlyn's room. It smelled sweet, clean, and delicate, probably from the lingering of whatever fragrance she had put on earlier in the day.

What caught his attention most was the late afternoon sun pouring through the open curtains, highlighting an uncovered canvas. He slowly walked to the far side of the room toward the easel. Ashlyn couldn't get mad at him this time. He wasn't snooping. She had asked him to come here and she had been the one that left her work uncovered for anyone to see.

It was simple and beautiful. It must have held some sort of meaning to Ashlyn because it wasn't something he could see her painting. He remembered that she had told him she painted from her photographs. There was no way that she took that picture anywhere near Raymere Grove. It was too surreal, like something from a fantasy.

Ashlyn stood at the doorway, watching Tripp and attempting to catch her breath from bolting up the stairs. She couldn't be sure if that's what was causing the rapid and frantic beating in her chest or if it was the person on the other side of the room.

Tripp anxiously turned around the second he heard Ashlyn's bedroom door close. "Hey," was all he could say as she walked across the room toward him.

She looked beautiful, so beautiful that all he could think of was touching her to make sure she was real. He had never seen her in a dress before, but the orange and teal one she had on made her skin glow and her hair seem that much darker and shinier. She looked like she had stepped out of a fairytale.

It wasn't until he saw the box in her hand that his hope faded, and his heart fell to the pit of his stomach.

Ashlyn sat the box down on her desk and continued toward Tripp. She had never felt so nervous in his presence. "You could have waited outside my room," she told him, unsure how to start one of the many things she wanted to talk about.

"Nope. That's not what you said," he teased, sensing that a heavy and devastating conversation was about to take place. "Besides, it took you forever. I got bored."

"And you thought you'd pry?" The glimmer in her illustrious blue eyes told him that she wasn't upset.

Tripp turned back to the unfinished painting. "It's incredible."

Ashlyn stood beside him, already feeling the heat from his arm that was so close to touching hers.

"Why this," he asked. "Knowing you, it has to be something more than just a ship."

Knowing you. She liked that. As much as she could dismiss it, the truth was, Tripp did know a lot about her.

"My mother told me a quote the other day and this is what popped in my head," she admitted, staring at the canvas.

A large ship was the focal point, positioned just a little more to the left than to the right. The background near the stern of the ship was a dark and stormy sky, with murky waters, whereas at the bow, in the direction the ship was headed, contained a magnificent sunset with a sky full of birds and the clearest and bluest waters. The ship itself still needed a bit more work before it was finished.

"What did she tell you," Tripp quickly asked, wanting to know what it was that inspired Ashlyn.

Ashlyn thought for a moment, making sure she got the wording right. "A ship in a harbor is safe, but that's not what a ship is built for."

When Tripp looked over to Ashlyn, their eyes met, and for a moment, everything felt right. Tripp knew it was just his mind playing tricks on him. Ashlyn needed to talk to him about something, and after earlier events, he couldn't imagine it would be in his favor.

Ashlyn looked away. This was going to be so hard. She was horrible with putting her heart and feelings out there. Tripp must have sensed that she was having difficulty getting started.

"Just say it," he sighed, stepping away from the easel and into the center of the room, creating a vast amount of space between them.

"There's so many things I have to say. I just don't know where to start," Ashlyn said. She grabbed at her forehead and shook her head.

"Look, I don't want you to be upset or aggravated on your birthday. We can talk another time. I figured that coming might not be a–"

"You came with my best friend," Ashlyn blurted out with more emotion than intended.

"I didn't exactly have an invitation," Tripp pointed out. He didn't want to get angry, and he wouldn't throw it in Ashlyn's face, but how could she have not invited him but still had that idiot.

"They were sent out a long time ago, before..." she paused. She wasn't sure how to end her statement.

"Forget it. It's no big deal."

It was. They both knew it was. Ashlyn knew it was a horrible mistake on her part. Just another to add to the list of many, and she had a feeling that in the coming moments that list would only grow.

Once she expressed her concern, Tripp would know that she felt something for him, and that terrified her.

"Did you seriously break up with Rachel for Emory," she blurted out.

Tripp's jaw dropped. That was not at all what he was expecting as one of the many things she claimed that she had to say. "What," was all he could say.

Ashlyn toyed with her side braid, the shorter pieces on the opposite side already making their way out. "Ugh. I feel so stupid bringing it up. Earlier in the week, Rachel flipped out, calling you a player. She was upset about you breaking up with her and dating someone else." Ashlyn couldn't even look at Tripp anymore. Regardless how hurt she was, she wasn't going to cry. "I just can't believe that neither of you told me, that I find out on my birthday."

"Stop," Tripp insisted. He didn't know where to begin with straightening everything out. He walked up to Ashlyn so that they were less than a foot apart, forcing her to look at him. "First of all, I told you that Rachel and I weren't dating. She's nuts, and if you believe anything she says, I might be forced to re-think your mental state as well."

Ashlyn's brows clenched and her jaw dropped at the insult.

"It's a joke," Tripp chuckled. He knew that he'd have to be serious. This was obviously a big deal to Ashlyn.

"What about Emory?"

"I thought she would have made it clear that we came as friends. However…" He hesitated, thinking carefully about his next words. "I'm glad she didn't."

"Oh yeah, and why is that," Ashlyn scoffed, annoyed with the situation or lack thereof.

"Because right now, you're telling me a lot without saying anything."

Ashlyn swallowed heavily, fully aware what Tripp was insinuating. She was just about to change the subject and bring up the camera when his next words hit her like an anvil in one of those old cartoons.

"What I can't understand," he began. His eyes that were often so golden now turned dark. "Why is it that you care so much about who I am or am not dating? Especially after that lovely little show from Eric."

"Please don't. I don't want to talk about that." Thinking about what Eric said made her feel sick to her stomach.

"Why not? Is that why you didn't invite me, because he would be here? We all know that he can't control his temper, but I can and–"

"I didn't invite him," Ashlyn coldly interrupted, her stern eyes firing daggers at Tripp. "He showed up, and…"

When she paused for longer than he would have liked, "And?"

"He threatened me." Ashlyn saw a look come across Tripp's face that frightened her. "Wait. No. Not like that. Ugh. Let me explain." She took a deep breath and started over. "I asked him to leave. I really did. He said he'd only stay for a bit and if I wanted to argue about it, that he'd cause a scene. So...I just let it be."

Tripp ran his hand through his hair. He wanted to scream, but he knew that's not at all what Ashlyn needed.

"Then what was that down there?"

"It's taken me a long time to come to terms with it, but it's just another one of his ways to keep me around. He's never said that before. I guess he thinks–"

Tripp couldn't help but interrupting her. "You've dated him for two years and he's never said that?!"

Ashlyn shook her head, feeling a little embarrassed. "The amount of time is insignificant." Her mother had told her as much. "It never felt right, but at the same time, being in a relationship with him after a while felt...comfortable." She left it at that, refraining from pointing out that he wasn't always like the way he was currently.

"What about now?"

"No." Ashlyn didn't bother elaborating once she saw the relief in Tripp's eyes.

Tripp glanced to Ashlyn's desk and the jewelry box sitting on top of it.

Ashlyn saw where his eyes went, and before he could say anything, "I planned to give it back to him, but then I realized that you were waiting on me."

A playful glimmer came back to Tripp's face. "I have a feeling that you didn't ask to talk to me privately just to talk about Rachel and Emory."

Ashlyn quickly took a couple steps forward and wrapped her arms around Tripp. He sucked in his breath in shock and stopped breathing. She was hugging him.

"Thank you," she mumbled softly into his chest.

He brought his hand up to touch the back of her head, but before he could respond to the embrace, she stepped back and swatted at his chest.

"But what were you thinking?! I can't accept that."

He blinked a few times, letting the last few seconds sink in. Realizing what she was talking about. "Oh, the camera." He shrugged. "It's no big deal. I was going to get you one anyway."

"Why?"

He looked at her like she had grown a second head. "Because you needed one." His words were phrased more like an uncertain question than an actual statement.

"It was my fault it got broken. It wasn't your responsibility–"

"I'm going to stop you right there. It absolutely wasn't your fault. I also know that I didn't need to or have to, but I wanted to," he stressed.

"It's too much. You can't try to buy my affection."

Tripp laughed, not his usual chuckle or even like he found something humorous, but a full on deep and hearty laugh. Ashlyn didn't know how to respond or why that comment was funny.

He brought himself impossibly close to her. She thought she might pass out from how intoxicating he smelled. It wasn't until he spoke, and his warm breath danced across her skin that she realized how much she desperately wanted him to kiss her.

"I don't need to *buy* your affection, Ash," he said with a sinister smirk. "And we both know why. I just wish you'd say it."

He already had it.

She had practically made that clear when she asked him about Rachel and Emory.

Something in that moment made her decide to give him what he wanted.

"Fine. I might have a small...faint...tiny...crush on you," she told him, holding back. She couldn't show all her cards.

"I'll take it," he whispered with a smile. He drew back from her and headed toward the door, allowing whatever moment between them to come to an end. "Let's get you back to your party."

Ashlyn could feel her hands shaking and a tsunami stirring in her stomach. "Wait."

Tripp stopped just short of the door and turned back around, realizing that Ashlyn wasn't right behind him. He couldn't imagine what else she still wanted to talk about, but she walked toward him with such purpose and certainty.

She didn't stop until she was nearly on top of him. She grabbed either side of his collar, and pulled him down toward her, which he willingly allowed.

Before Tripp could respond to the warm set of lips tightly plastered against his, Ashlyn pulled away, her eyes wide with fear.

She clasped her hands on her forehead, trying to hide her embarrassment. "I'm so sorry," she exclaimed. "I don't know what came over me. That wasn't me. I'm not that bold and reckless. I don't know what I was thinking. Can we pretend that didn't just happen," she asked, now beginning to ramble.

Tripp lightly grabbed her wrists and pulled them from her head, forcing her to look up at him. "No."

She opened her mouth, no doubt to protest, and Tripp swung her around until she collided into the wall next to the door. He dropped her wrists and placed his hands on either side of her head, and dropped his forehead so that it was nearly touching Ashlyn's.

"I want you to be as bold and reckless with me as you want." His voice was deep and rough, sending chills down Ashlyn's spine. Then he asked the strangest and sweetest question, sending her back to the first time they kissed. "I want to kiss you so badly, but I don't want you to think it's a mistake, so I'm asking you right now, can I?"

Ashlyn bit her lip and looked into his eyes. He was serious. He was really asking her for permission. Her heart thundered throughout her chest. It was so loud that Tripp had to hear it too. The longer she waited, the more concerned his face became.

Every second of silence, even though it was only about three before she gave him an answer, felt like eternity to Tripp. When she nodded and softly told him yes, it took every bit of restraint in him to make it deep and meaningful, despite wanting to slam her into the wall like a ravenous barbarian.

Their lips had barely touched when a soft moan escaped from Ashlyn. Tripp brought one hand to her cheek, his thumb gently caressing her before moving his hand to the back of her neck and pulling her into him. His other hand found its way to her waist and around to the small of her back.

Her hands went to the back of his neck just as her lips parted. Tripp couldn't stop the growl that came from deep inside when their tongues touched and began fighting for dominance like they were fighting for air.

She tasted like sweet icing and smelled like a field of flowers. It was invigorating and as her body continued to melt perfectly into his, only one word came to mind. More.

Ashlyn didn't know what had come over either one of them. She also didn't know just how much she both needed and wanted this kiss. She felt like she was floating on air with clouds beneath her feet. She tried to gain her footing and only then realized that Tripp was holding her up with a single arm. The kiss was nothing short of pure magic.

Tripp eventually placed her down, though she could barely stand with how weak her knees felt from the kiss. They slightly broke contact, untangling themselves from the mess of passion and hormones they had become. Tripp placed his forehead against Ashlyn's, both of them breathing heavily onto the other.

"Wow," he managed, partly because he was breathless, partly because there weren't words to describe what just happened.

At that moment, looking so closely into his eyes, Ashlyn saw it. Though she was terrified of something new and different, Tripp was the beautiful adventure in front of her.

Tripp pulled away like someone threw boiling water on him and Ashlyn shook with fear at the banging on the door next to them. Then an all too familiar voice came through.

"Hey, Ash. Can we talk?"

CHAPTER 22

Ashlyn stepped outside her room, quickly closing the door behind her.

"Uh, maybe we can go inside," Eric suggested.

Ashlyn held on tightly to the handle behind her back. There was absolutely nothing that he could say that would make her let him in her room. If he saw who was in there, Tripp was dead.

"I don't think that's a good idea."

Eric ran a hand across Ashlyn's cheek, and she couldn't help but flinch a little.

"Five minutes? Just to talk?"

"I have some paintings in there. I wanted to keep them a surprise until the art show," Ashlyn only partially lied.

Eric rolled his eyes and crossed his arms. "Seriously? Nobody cares about your stupid paintings. It's not like I'm going to steal your idea," he scoffed.

Ashlyn didn't want to have a conversation with Eric. All he did was ruin her birthday ever since he showed up.

"Fine, whatever. We can talk here."

Ashlyn stayed quiet. She could see Eric's cool and calm demeanor changing into irritation and anger.

"How could you do that down there?"

"What are you talking about," Ashlyn asked, although she already knew.

"I gave you that awesome gift and I told you all that crap and you didn't say anything back! You even allowed your stupid friend to come up and throw me to the side."

"You know I can't control her," Ashlyn began. She tried her best to skirt around the first part of what he said.

"You could have at least said it back!"

"I think we need to talk," Ashlyn said slowly and carefully.

"Duh, Ash! That's what we're doing."

Ashlyn knew once she said what she was about to, Eric would explode. Remembering the necklace, she quickly excused herself and darted back in her room, locking the door behind her. She ignored Tripp's presence and rushed to her desk to grab the tiny box.

On her way back to the door, Tripp stepped in front of her and mouthed the words, "Are you okay?" Ashlyn nodded and tried to put on her best smile and hope that Tripp couldn't see how nervous she was.

She waited for him to take several steps from the door until she went back out.

"What was that about," Eric immediately asked.

Ashlyn held out the box he had given her. "I need to give this back."

He narrowed his eyes and took a step forward. "And why is that?"

Ashlyn took a deep breath and made herself look him in the eyes. There were so many times over the last two years that she should have tried to end things, but she had never broken up with a boy, and Eric seemed to be the only one who had ever showed any interest in her. She thought that had to mean something.

"I don't want just a break. I want to break up. For good." Her words were rushed, but Eric heard them loud and clear.

"Why," he growled.

She had thought for days about how the conversation would go, and she was prepared for the *why*. "Because you're not the same person you were when we started dating. You get kicked out of school. You broke my camera. You never say anything nice to me. You–"

"I just told you that I loved you," Eric screamed.

Ashlyn shook her head and gathered her thoughts. "You didn't mean it. You and I both know you didn't."

"Is this because your friends are all in your head? I know Emory hates me and hates you with me."

"No. It's that they don't like how you treat me, but this has nothing to do with them. This has to do with me."

Eric took a step forward and Ashlyn pressed her back to the door. For once, she was definitely scared of him.

"Is there someone else?"

Ashlyn could feel her eyes widen and she tried to hide any telling reaction. "No. I just can't go through the ups and downs with you anymore. This has nothing to do with anyone else."

"Good," he said with a sinister grin spreading across his face. "I like to hear that." Before Ashlyn could ask him what he meant by that, he snatched the box from her hand. "See you around."

Ashlyn felt the oxygen return as soon as Eric began to descend the stairs. Something about that interaction didn't feel right. Breaking up with him felt like a weight had been lifted from her, but there was something else. She couldn't quite place it; however, the knots in her stomach told her that it couldn't be that easy.

* * *

Ellis' screams later confirmed to Ashlyn that Eric was not going to take the breakup well.

She waited until a tow truck took Ellis and Emory's car and they, along with Deacon, got a ride home with Tripp. Then, before she even looked through her presents, she text Eric.

Ashlyn: Really? You slashed all the tires on Ellis and Emory's car?

Eric: I have no idea what you're talking about.

She knew he wouldn't admit to it on text; after all, her dad was a lawyer.

Say it, forget it. Write it, regret it.

223

Ashlyn: They share that car! I thought Ellis was your friend.

Eric: First of all, stop accusing me. Secondly, none of them are my friends.

Ashlyn wasn't going to bother responding to him after that. She was certain he did it. Once she told Emory about their conversation outside her room, Emory was even more certain.

Ashlyn's heart thundered in her chest when Eric didn't leave it at that, and another message came in.

Eric: I hope you weren't lying.

Ashlyn: About what?

Eric: There not being someone else. Anyway, I'll see you at school.

Just like that, he was back in her head. She didn't know what kind of games he was playing, but his text was far too ominous. She didn't expect for him to clarify on text.

Ashlyn had to wonder, if he hated Emory so much to do that to the car she shared with her brother, what would he do if she did start dating someone?

CHAPTER 23

"I didn't see you with your friends at lunch today," Eric said, announcing his presence at Ashlyn's locker.

She had successfully both avoided him and Tripp for the entire day. She still had Tripp in science, but thankfully there was a test.

"I had to meet with a senior for an interview for the paper," Ashlyn responded.

"Oh, a senior. Anyone I know?"

Ashlyn shut her locker and glared at Eric. "Yeah. Kyler West."

She saw Eric's eyes widen in surprise. It's not like she stood a chance with the star quarterback. Not only was he a year ahead of her, but he was also head over heels with the valedictorian. An atomic bomb wouldn't separate the two of them. She didn't know if Eric knew that, but what she did know was that if Kyler had been her new love interest, Eric wouldn't dare touch him.

"What's so special about him," Eric asked, trying to play off his jealousy.

"He got a full ride to Cartwright University."

"Whatever. We still sucked last season," Eric said with a shrug.

Ashlyn was just about to mention how they'd be unstoppable in the fall when Ellis would be quarterback and Deacon would be wide receiver. As best friends, they read each other like a book and were a force to be reckoned with on the field.

Then Ashlyn remembered who she was talking to.

Changing the subject, "What do you want, Eric. We're broken up. Or did you forget that?"

He chuckled and leaned into the lockers. "I see the Parkers got some new wheels."

"Did you just come here to gloat? Don't worry, they have more important things than trying to sue you for damages."

"I actually came here to reinforce a point." His voice turned deep and quiet. "I know Emory filled your head with garbage, so I wanted to teach her a lesson."

Ashlyn had to refrain from rolling her eyes, knowing it would only make him angrier.

"So, you can imagine what I'd do if I see you with someone else."

"You're saying I'm not allowed to move on," she hesitated.

Now he laughed, a dark and irritating laugh. "I just think it would be a little ironic if you break up with me and in a matter of days or weeks start seeing someone else. Especially if that someone else has already been in the picture."

Ashlyn wondered if he knew about Tripp. He couldn't. The only public place where she and Tripp had ever shown affection was the library, but there's no way Eric knew about that.

He pushed off the lockers. "Trust me, slashed tires would be the least of your worries."

Ashlyn didn't say anything. She needed him to have the last word and walk away. She understood exactly what he was saying. He had insinuated it in his messages, but she never thought he'd come out and directly say it like that.

Without a doubt, she knew she had to stay away from Tripp, at least until Eric found someone else to torture.

* * *

Tripp watched Ashlyn carefully at lunch. Though they had conversations through text since Saturday, he had yet to say more than a few words to her in person.

"Can't wait for the game tonight. I am so pumped," Byron exclaimed, slamming his fist on the table, startling Ashlyn, who had been in a daze.

Ellis nodded toward Tripp. "How many hits, or should I say, home runs do you think you'll get tonight?"

Tripp only laughed and shook his head.

"Don't be modest. You've gotten a home run at least once in every game," June chimed in.

"How about a bet," Ellis began. "Lunch tomorrow if you get a home run tonight."

Tripp laughed. "Sure. Deal."

"Great. So, if you get a home run, you buy me lunch."

Tripp shook his head and let the others go about their conversations. He was a little disappointed to be so far from Ashlyn. She had flanked herself with Emory and Kayla and was farther down the table from him. The few times they did make eye contact, something seemed off.

Since they had the same class after lunch, Tripp made it a point to wait around for Ashlyn to say goodbye to her friends and walk alongside her.

"I have an idea for a bet," Tripp stated, surprising Ashlyn in the busy hall.

She didn't want to come off as cold and rude. After all, she could still be friends with Tripp, that is, until he softly whispered his next words.

"A kiss if I get a home run. Deal?"

Ashlyn's face lost all expression and she stopped in the middle of the hallway. Students continued to flow around them as they stood, staring at each other.

Tripp didn't give her the chance to say anything. "I know that look. Let me guess, *we need to talk*?"

"Can you meet me after school somewhere?"

Tripp shook his head. "Just say what you need to say now."

Ashlyn glanced around the hall. To unsuspecting eyes, it would look like they were having a lover's quarrel if their conversation continued.

"Tripp..."

"Fine. Back of the library, after school."

Tripp hated that his gut told him that Ashlyn probably wanted to put a screeching halt on whatever was happening between them. After her party, he couldn't imagine why. Things had escalated between the two of them, and above all, she gave Eric the necklace back and broke up with him for good. At least, as of Saturday, they were broken up. Maybe he had missed something in the last few days.

Needless to say, the rest of the day sucked for Tripp.

* * *

Tripp quickly showered at the end of eighth period so that he could be at the library right away, both dreading and anticipating what in the world Ashlyn would have to say.

Obviously, she had still managed to beat him to the far reaches of the library. It was secluded enough so that no one else would be privy to whatever heartbreak Ashlyn was sure to deal out.

"Hey," she spoke just as Tripp came into view.

She was leaning against a shelf skimming through a book that didn't hold her interest.

"Hi," was all that Tripp could manage. He suddenly felt lightheaded and sick.

Ashlyn tried her best to hide the forlorn expression plastered across her face; however, Tripp saw right through it. He had watched her enough to know how much she tried to fake her emotions, covering what were her true thoughts.

"I'll make this quick. I'm sure you have—"

"Take your time," Tripp insisted.

Ashlyn wanted to throw up just from looking at his face. He looked so sweet and innocent...and hurt. She really didn't want to hurt him. She gripped on to the shelf behind her, needing to find something to do with her trembling hands.

Breaking up with Eric had been easier than she thought, but he deserved it, and she knew what to expect from him. Breaking up with Tripp, or whatever this was, that was going to be something else entirely, especially because it was hurting her more than she'd ever admit.

"Is everything okay," Tripp asked. He drew himself opposite Ashlyn and leaned into the shelf behind him, matching her. He shook his head. "That was stupid. Obviously, we wouldn't be here if everything was okay."

"Tripp, you're a great guy and all," Ashlyn began.

"Whoa." Tripp couldn't help but chuckle a little, although the situation was far from humorous. "Don't do that. I know I'm a great guy."

Ashlyn's eyes widened. She didn't know what kind of reaction she expected from Tripp, but his cockiness wasn't it.

"Just tell me point blank what the problem is. You're not going to crush my ego," he continued.

"I think we should be friends," Ashlyn finally replied. Tripp had somehow managed to catch her off guard, and everything she had planned to say suddenly floated away.

He gave her the most melting grin. "We are friends."

"You know what I mean. I think we should stay just that. *Just* friends." As hard as it was to say, she felt relieved that she had managed to do so, especially with looking into his glowing eyes.

"Why?"

Crap. She had prepared herself for the why with Eric, but with Tripp standing right there in front of her, what was her why? Oh, right. Eric was crazy and she didn't want Tripp to end up like Ellis and Emory's car. That, however, could not be her response.

Tripp laughed when Ashlyn took more than a few seconds to answer him. "For this conversation being your idea, you're having a really hard time navigating through it."

Ashlyn let out a breath she didn't realize she had been holding in. "It's just for the best." Then it clicked, and she couldn't believe how stupid she was. "I just got out of a very long relationship, and I'm not ready to get involved with anyone."

Tripp's eyes were skeptically narrowed, intensely watching her. Her statement was partially true, but she had to wonder if he could see more.

"Fine. That I believe."

More relief flooded over Ashlyn. "Great, so we're just friends."

"No."

Ashlyn fell farther into the shelf as Tripp pushed off his and stood inches in front of her.

His voice was low and deep, far too sexy for a seventeen-year-old. "I can be friends with you, but it will never be *just* friends for me. After what happened in your bedroom, I know you feel the same way."

"It was just a kiss," Ashlyn interrupted.

Tripp raised a brow. "Nothing about that was *just* a kiss."

Ashlyn could feel her cheeks heating. Now that the kiss had been mentioned, all she could think of was trying that again.

"Meet me after the game tonight."

Ashlyn's eyes widened in horror. "I came here to end things."

Tripp shook his head and a bigger smile came to his face. Ashlyn couldn't stand how much he smiled. It was a *coup de grâce* for all girls.

"Look, Ash. If you would have yelled at me, told me what a horrible person I am, how repulsed you were by me, how you couldn't bear the thought of so much as touching me..." He reached for her hand when he said that, and not to his surprise, she didn't pull away. "Then I would have believed that you wanted to just be friends."

"Can I start over," Ashlyn huffed.

Tripp shook his head. With his closeness, Ashlyn could smell whatever masculine and invigorating shampoo he had just used. It was only one more thing that made trying to walk away from him so difficult.

"I feel like there's something you're not telling me, and that's fine for now, but don't lie to me."

"I'm not lying about anything," Ashlyn insisted.

Tripp suddenly turned dark, not in the way that Eric turned when he got angry, but in a serious and passionate way. "Fine. Tell me you don't have any feelings for me, whatsoever...or meet me tonight after the game."

Ashlyn felt like a boulder just landed on her chest. This wasn't supposed to be how the conversation went. She was supposed to tell Tripp that they needed to stay strictly friends, and while he might be a little bummed, he would eventually agree. This, however, this was too intense for her. Everything he was saying made her feel like the heroine in some ridiculously romantic high school drama.

She knew what she needed to say. She needed to lie. More than ever, she needed to lie. She hadn't realized it until that moment just how much her feelings had grown for Tripp.

Tripp wouldn't allow himself to take his eyes from her. He watched as hers fell from his and darted from side to side. He desperately wanted to know what she was struggling with. He wanted to put her on the spot, but the truth was, if she told him the worst thing in the world right now, he knew she'd be lying.

Ashlyn swallowed heavily. "I'm sorry, Tripp."

Tripp immediately dropped her hand and she felt like her heart might have just dropped along with it.

"All I feel for you is friendship." That was the best way she could say it. She was certain that Tripp would know that she was lying, however, when she looked up, she wasn't prepared for the hurt plastered across his face.

Tripp expected her to fumble, but he never thought that the end result would be that. Now he knew how the losers of swordfights felt.

He so desperately wanted to call her out on it, but he couldn't argue with her. Every fiber in his body told him that it wasn't the truth, but that's something she'd have to come to terms with. For whatever reason she was telling him that, she'd have to deal with it. He couldn't push her. It wasn't fair to either of them.

CHAPTER 24

"Oh, don't you look cute," Poppy squealed as Ashlyn hit the bottom of the stairs.

She was in a blue dress with black leggings and dainty combat boots. She told herself that it was because those were the school colors. The truth of it, she had been bawling her eyes out on her bed ever since she got home after her conversation with Tripp, and she really wanted to look like she wasn't just smashed into with a garbage truck. She even had more makeup on than usual, not to impress anyone, but because her skin was so blotchy and her eyes so swollen.

It wasn't until she thought she might die from a dry throat that she came to a horrific realization. Eric still had control over her.

"Thanks, mom."

"Going to the game with Emory and Ellis?"

"Yes." Ashlyn hesitated. "I might go out to eat with them."

Her mother smiled sweetly. For some reason she looked more tired than usual, but Ashlyn refrained from pointing that out. "I'll put a plate in the refrigerator just in case. Is your homework done?"

"Yes, mom."

Poppy laughed. "Then be home by eleven. Lights out by 11:30."

Ashlyn gave her mom a hug and headed out to the front steps to wait for the Parker twins.

* * *

He wouldn't say it was the worst game of his life, after all, once he lied to his coach and played with a sprained wrist.

Maybe he was being dramatic. Suddenly everything felt like the worst.

He had managed to get a couple hits, but after they finished two more innings, it would be the first game in a long time when he wasn't able to get a home run.

The team still won the game, so everyone was in high spirits; however, the last thing Tripp felt like doing was going out to eat or hanging out with anyone really.

Just as he, Deacon, and a couple other guys made their way out from the locker room and into the parking lot, Tripp felt his chest tighten and he forgot how to breathe.

He knew she'd probably be there to take pictures, but he didn't imagine seeing her standing beside Ellis and Emory. She couldn't possibly think of going out to eat with the team, especially after everything that happened only a few hours prior.

Though a guy of few words, "Sorry, man." Deacon slowed his steps beside Tripp. "I didn't know that she'd stick around."

Tripp didn't gossip much, but after the first couple innings, Deacon had sensed that something was off. Rather than lie about it, Tripp ripped it off like a bandage and confided in him.

"Don't worry about it," Tripp grumbled. He shuffled his bag around over his shoulder. "I plan on going straight home."

Rather than say something to change his mind on the matter, all Deacon did was grunt in acknowledgement. Tripp liked him. He was someone that was completely drama free.

Tripp didn't intend to hang around in the parking lot making plans and deciding who went where and which car who was going in. So instead, he gave a quick goodbye to the guys around him and headed to his vehicle. He intentionally parked it in a less populated area so as to avoid idiot teenagers.

He threw his bag into the backseat and slammed the door in frustration.

"Hey," a soft voice called from behind.

Tripp instantly spun around.

Ashlyn appeared to be slightly out of breath, like she had debated whether or not to follow him and decided to right before he could leave.

"Hi." When Ashlyn attempted to say something but closed her mouth to think it over, Tripp spoke. "What do you need?"

He saw the surprise and hurt look on her face, and he couldn't help but feel satisfied and sickeningly guilty at the same time. Despite what she did to him earlier, he really didn't want to intentionally hurt her. That didn't mean that he wasn't a little irritated.

He never expected her next words. They were so quiet that he couldn't help but give her a look, suggesting that she repeat herself.

Ashlyn's eyes fell to the ground and she cleared her throat. "You told me to meet you after the game."

Tripp had to tell himself to close his mouth because he was pretty sure he was gawking at her like she was a made-up monster from a childhood nightmare.

When Tripp didn't answer, Ashlyn turned back around. Sure enough, Emory stood at her car, arms crossed, and only pretending to be involved in a conversation with some of the guys.

"It's okay if you changed your mind. Emory said they'd wait to–"

"I didn't," Tripp quickly interrupted. It was only then that he wanted to kick himself for sounding so eager. She basically stomped on his heart. He couldn't make it that easy. "I just thought after this afternoon, that was out of the question."

Ashlyn shuffled on her feet uncomfortably. "I thought about it."

"And?"

"And, I was curious." Redness slowly crept to her cheeks.

Though eager to spend time with her, Tripp still remembered how he felt in the library. "Should we replay the rest of that conversation?"

"I know what I said," Ashlyn answered coldly. Tripp wasn't making it easy. "Everything I said, I meant."

"Then I really don't know why you're here."

Ashlyn bit her bottom lip. It had been a bad idea. When she thought about what she had told Tripp in the library, she was ashamed that she thought for a moment that she could begin to repair things between them, especially in such a short amount of time.

"I'm sorry." Then, trying to save a little bit of her dignity, and sounding as upbeat as possible. "I'll see you tomorrow."

Fifty different thoughts ran through Tripp's head when Ashlyn turned to leave. The best thing for the both of them, especially for him, would be for that to be the end. He should have just gone home, and she should go about her evening, whether that meant going home, hanging out with Emory, or going out with the team. Unfortunately for him, despite how shallow it might seem, she looked incredible, and the narcissist in him desperately wanted for her to have dressed up for something other than a baseball game.

Even though his ego was shredded from earlier, the fact that she had come to him said enough.

"Wait," Tripp sighed. The little voice inside his head was groaning and telling him what an idiot he had become, a glutton for punishment.

Ashlyn slowly turned, her expression something along the lines of hope and fear.

"Are you hungry?"

Ashlyn clasped her bag with her camera tightly. Without answering his question, "Were you planning on joining the–"

"No," Tripp quickly interrupted.

Ashlyn took in a deep breath realizing what that meant. If she went with Tripp, it would end up being just the two of them. She fully thought he'd just give her a ride to Flip's Grill, or maybe a ride home.

That was a lie. She really didn't know what she expected. All she knew was that after crying half the afternoon, after seeing him play, after he walked away in the parking lot, she had to make a decision. It just so happened that it led her to the very spot she now stood.

His next words were a bitter pill to swallow. "Just a friendly bite to eat. That's all," he said. He coolly held his hands up in a surrendering fashion.

"No. I mean, yeah. Of course. Yeah. That's fine," Ashlyn fumbled.

Tripp's brows rose, silently asking her if she was okay and she felt her cheeks heating.

She had to get a grip. She was the one who told him there were no feelings. She was the one who said they could only be friends. So, she could not be the one to become flustered at the idea of being alone with the guy.

Tripp nodded to his vehicle and they walked around to the passenger side, much to Ashlyn's surprise. Then he had to chip away at her just a little more by opening the door for her.

It's not a date. It's not a date. It's not a date.

She repeated the words over and over. She couldn't give Tripp the wrong idea, not while Eric was still very present in her life.

From the moment they got in the vehicle together, everything was awkward. The banter they used to have was gone.

Tripp couldn't take the weirdness between them. This wasn't what he intended for the night to be when he asked Ashlyn to meet him; however, he was still going to go with what he initially planned on doing. It wasn't a grand gesture, but it was also already after eight on a school night.

"I'll be back in just a second," Tripp told her once he parked at the Ghiaccio Nero Pizzeria, leaving Ashlyn slightly confused.

Ashlyn: This is so weird. I never should have done this.

Emory: Ugh! Whatever! Just know, if you really want to keep it strictly platonic, you probably shouldn't kiss him, AGAIN!

Ashlyn: Not helping.

Emory: Just be nice to the guy. No one here can believe that he messed up his home run streak.

Ashlyn had noticed that Tripp's head didn't seem to be in the game the way it had been in the past. A sick feeling came to her when she thought about what she said to him in the library and if that could have had any effect.

Before she could respond any further to Emory, she saw Tripp coming from the doors of the pizzeria. For just jeans and a black t-shirt, he still looked incredible.

Tripp opened the door to the backseat and put the boxes in. It wasn't until he got in the driver's seat and buckled up that he met the pair of inquisitive and confused eyes. He could almost see the wheels in her head turning.

"What," he laughed, suddenly feeling at ease with her.

"You never said what your plans were, so I'm a little lost here," Ashlyn admitted.

Tripp still held a deathly gorgeous smile. "No plans. Just a bite to eat between friends, just like I said."

Despite being exactly what she wanted, Ashlyn couldn't help but wonder how many times they were going to keep pointing out the just friends thing.

Tripp watched from the corner of his eye as Ashlyn perked up and glanced around once they turned down her street.

"Relax." He veered to the side of the street beneath an oak tree that blocked the blinding streetlight from streaming into the car. "So you don't miss your curfew," he pointed out.

Tripp proceeded to getting out of his vehicle and opening the driver's passenger side door where his bag was. He dug around for a moment and retrieved an iPad. He then threw his bag from the passenger seats toward the back. He came back to the driver's seat, but didn't get in, only rolled the windows down about four inches each.

"You can go ahead and get in the back," he casually said as though it was completely obvious to Ashlyn what was going on.

She undid her seatbelt and did as suggested, already queueing a million questions in her head.

When Tripp was content with the windows, he closed the door and hopped into the backseat as well, the box of pizza with the most enticing smell separating him from Ashlyn.

He toyed around on the iPad, but could feel the tension radiating from Ashlyn. From the light of the screen, he knew that she could see the smile on his face.

"What's going on," she huffed.

"Well," Tripp began, placing the iPad between the two seats in front of them. "For the sake of time, since it's a school night, dinner and a movie."

"Uh huh," Ashlyn hesitated. "And we're in the backseat of your car like a block down from my house."

Tripp took a smaller box off the large one and place it on the floor. He handed Ashlyn some napkins from a stack. "Well, if we went out to dinner, just the two of us, it might give off the wrong impression. We could have gone to my house and done the same thing, we actually have a home theatre," he pointed out. "However, I have a nosey brother and meddling mom. I'm still a little new so I wasn't sure of any spots that didn't include a lot of traffic, and I wasn't going to go to some random parking lot. If you want to continue this, I suppose we could just go the extra block or so to your house?"

"No, this is fine," Ashlyn quickly answered.

"Don't want to bring me home for something other than homework?"

Ashlyn had to be honest with him. "Something like that."

Tripp quickly changed the subject. "I have a couple movies downloaded. Action or romance?"

Ashlyn choked on her spit.

"Right. Action then."

"Wait, what," she gasped. "You didn't let me answer."

"I just figured that your response meant that you couldn't do romance right now."

Ashlyn let out a frustrated breath. "I can do romance." Quickly realizing how that sounded, she tried to clarify. "I like both genres. I was just surprised that you had any romantic movies."

"So…"

"I don't care. You pick," she grumbled.

"Nope. Ladies choice," he insisted, motioning to the loaded screen of movies.

Tripp easily assumed that Ashlyn would pick one of the action movies. Who would want to watch a romantic movie alone with a guy they were just friends with? However, she surprised him when she settled on a romantic comedy.

"I never asked you what all you liked on your pizza, so I played it safe," he told her when he opened the box.

Ashlyn felt her stomach rumble as she looked at the gigantic cheesy and greasy pepperoni pizza between them. "This is perfect!"

Just as Ashlyn reached for a slice, the movie started. They both sank back into their seats and could not have been farther apart. Several minutes later, Tripp ended up sprawling across the seat and digging for something in the back.

He handed Ashlyn an icy cold bottle of water while he had an orange sports drink.

"You keep a cooler in your car."

"Only on game days," he said quietly and pointed back to the movie.

Tripp pretended to pay attention to the movie, just in case Ashlyn was one of those girls that would quiz him to see if he was actually paying attention or ask him his thoughts on it.

He would have much rather preferred a quiet restaurant with nice conversation, but he felt like he was still walking on eggshells with Ashlyn, and oftentimes, conversation is what got them in trouble.

It was painful to focus with her being so close. Had their conversation in the library gone differently, she'd be cuddled in his arms right now, not leaning into her door.

Once the pizza was finished, Tripp cleared the space and put the box in the back with his bag and cooler. "I hope you're not full."

Ashlyn laughed and grabbed at her stomach. "Are you kidding me? That thing was huge!"

He reached for the smaller box he had placed on the floor much earlier. "Yeah, but I ate like two-thirds."

Ashlyn eyed the box, fully knowing that she could not eat another bite of whatever greasy goodness it contained.

A smile came to Tripp's face when Ashlyn's eyes widened upon him opening the box.

"Cannoli?"

She reached for the box and Tripp pulled it away. "I thought you were full?"

Ashlyn rolled her eyes and scooted from where she was plastered against the door closer to the center. "Don't be ridiculous."

Tripp couldn't help but bring himself closer to the middle as well. He took one out and handed the box with the other to Ashlyn.

He thought he might lose it when a small moan escaped from her lips after taking a bite.

"Sorry," she mumbled with a full mouth. After swallowing, "Are these strawberry?" She held hers closer to the screen of the iPad for light. "Wow, they are. They're amazing."

"Glad you approve."

Just then Ashlyn's phone went off. Tripp tried not to be curious, but her body immediately tensed. While he couldn't read the message at first, from the corner of his eye, he saw the name at the top of the screen. He was relieved to see it was only Emory.

Emory: Eric's was at Flip's picking up food. He asked where you were.

Ashlyn: What did you say?

Emory: That you bailed so you could get an article written.

Ashlyn: Thank you.

Emory: That's not the strange thing. Then he asked where Tripp was, and why he wasn't out with us celebrating another win.

Ashlyn swallowed heavily, not liking the sound of that. Another message came in which gave her a sense of relief; however, she couldn't help but think that Eric knew something, and more than anything, she didn't want him bringing any harm to Tripp.

Emory: Look, I don't know what the deal is. Deacon actually covered for Tripp, said he sucked at the game and didn't look well, probably went home.

"Remind me to both thank and insult Deacon for that," Tripp said, pushing his shoulder into Ashlyn.

It was then that Ashlyn realized that they were sitting only a few inches from each other now. She pretended to be offended and pushed him back. "Ugh. Personal space."

Tripp paused the movie and turned, placing one leg beneath him, so that he was directly facing Ashlyn. "Is everything okay with him," he asked with great seriousness.

Ashlyn played dumb. "Yeah. Why wouldn't it be?"

"He's asking about you, and now me."

There was no way that Ashlyn was going to tell Tripp about Eric's threat. "Well, that's probably because we're the only two not there."

"Does he think anything is going on between us?"

She hoped not. "No, and that's because nothing is going on between us."

Ashlyn's phone went off again, only this time she laughed and held it up to Tripp.

Dad: How was the game? How did the Scott boy do?

"That is so weird," Ashlyn sighed, and quickly responded.

Tripp wished that she would have showed him her response. "Why?"

"I don't know what you said to my dad, but he's a fan."

Tripp grew quiet and uneasy. "Nothing."

Ashlyn watched him carefully. "No. Tell me. What were you and my dad talking about at my party?"

"I told you, baseball."

"Come on, tell me. Are you in trouble? Were you asking for his legal expertise," Ashlyn teased.

Ashlyn sucked in a breath when Tripp leaned in impossibly close to her. His expression a mix of seriousness and playfulness, his eyes exceptionally dark in the dim lighting.

"If you're so curious," he began soft and low in a deep voice that sent tingles down Ashlyn's spine. "Why don't you ask him?"

Ashlyn took a moment to compose herself from the scent of Tripp's cologne that the night breeze happened to catch. It was intoxicating and it filled her head with thoughts that she shouldn't be having, given what she told him many hours earlier.

"So, it wasn't just baseball? Why won't you tell me?"

Tripp's eyes moved slowly from her eyes to her lips and back. "Not the time."

In just that moment he knew what crap the library had been. He wanted to pull his hair out in frustration. He saw with his own eyes the effect he had on her, so why would she insist that she didn't have feelings for him?

249

From the moment he met her, every instinct told him to back off, to go after a girl that was much easier. Rachel would have been easier. He wouldn't have to try so hard. Something about the girl before him was just too different to pass up.

Finally, he broke the spell and leaned against his door, his feet on the long seat and his knees drawn up. Ashlyn took off her shoes and did the same, their toes only inches from one another.

It was already after ten. Her house was only two minutes away, she could just go home, but something about Tripp Scott suddenly intrigued her more than before.

"Where was your favorite place to live," Ashlyn asked.

Tripp's eyes widened in surprise. It wasn't even in the realm of possible things that he expected her to say. "Why?"

Ashlyn's eyes fell, becoming embarrassed. "Well, when you were texting me, you knew who I was, and I told you everything, but you were always vague and didn't talk much about yourself. I know now that's because you didn't want me to know it was you." Treading lightly with what she was about to bring up, "I guess we would have continued like that had that whole library thing not happened."

Library thing?

Tripp tried to hide his amusement with how nervous she was bringing up their first kiss.

He shrugged. "Sorry about that. I just really wanted to get to know you." He saw an uncomfortableness in Ashlyn's body language. Did she really want to only be friends? He had never met a more confusing girl. "Anyway, my favorite place. I guess I'd have to say Georgia." Ashlyn's eyes shot up, her brow drawn together with curiosity. "I don't remember too much, but that's where I was born and lived until all the traveling started."

"Oh, right! Your grandparents still live there," Ashlyn added, remembering that's where Tripp and his family went for spring break.

Tripp's eyes brightened at the fact that she had tucked away that small piece of information. "Yeah..."

CHAPTER 25

Tripp pulled into Ashlyn's driveway. "I'm so sorry about that."

"No. It's my fault. I lost track of time," she sheepishly admitted.

They never did end up finishing the movie. It really didn't matter. It was one of those predictable ones where the couple has a miscommunication but ultimately ends up getting together in the end.

Tripp put the vehicle in park and Ashlyn undid her seatbelt.

"Wait," he insisted.

Ashlyn bit her lip and tried to calm her nerves as Tripp quickly exited the driver's side and ran around to her door. He opened it for her and held out his hand to help her out. Once she stepped down, she turned back to grab her camera bag off the floor, taking a moment to reflect. This was not at all how tonight was supposed to go. More than anything, this was not supposed to feel like a date.

"You don't have to walk me up."

Tripp closed the door and motioned to her front steps. "I know."

"Then why are you," Ashlyn asked teasingly as Tripp walked beside her.

"Because I'm a gentleman."

Despite that she missed curfew by fifteen minutes, she couldn't help but realize how slow their pace was to her front door. Was Tripp going slow and she following suit, or was it the other way around?

Ashlyn pressed her back into the front door, not knowing how this was supposed to end. When Tripp took one too many steps forward, Ashlyn sucked in a sharp breath.

Tripp immediately saw the look of terror on her face. Little did she know, his only intention was walking her to the door.

"I'm not going to try to kiss you," Tripp laughed.

Ashlyn tried to hide her surprise, and maybe a little bit of disappointment. She couldn't let him see either. "I'm glad you realize that can't happen anymore if we intend for this friendship to survive." Ashlyn cringed when she said that. What the hell did she just say? Who says that? She couldn't believe something so stupid just flew out of her mouth.

Tripp stepped just a little closer so that he could see the blue sparkles of Ashlyn's eyes beneath the porch light. He wasn't going to miss such a great opportunity to mess with her.

"Oh, Ash," he began, shaking his head. "That's not at all why." He stopped, taking a moment to watch her overthink, knowing that she'd have to ask.

"If not that, then what?"

He took another step forward and thought Ashlyn might break down the door with how tightly pressed against it she was. They were only inches apart, he could have touched her face, gauged her reaction, and finally kissed her, but this would be so much better in the long run.

"I told you, I'm a gentleman." He watched as Ashlyn glared into his eyes, waiting for him to elaborate. "I don't kiss on a first date."

Just like that he swiftly stepped away and smiled when he heard her let out a deep breath. He was already down the steps when she called out to him.

"Tripp! You know this wasn't a date!"

"Uh huh," he acknowledged.

"I mean it! This wasn't a first date!"

He didn't turn to face her until he was back at his vehicle. She looked absolutely adorable standing on the porch yelling at him. "I had fun," he said, now getting inside.

Ashlyn continued to fume. "Don't you dare for one single minute think this was anything close to a date!"

* * *

Ashlyn was still irritated when she got out of the shower. Tripp was unbelievable. He just loved to get under her skin, and he knew that comment would do it.

After quickly drying her hair and brushing her teeth, she immediately went to hop into bed. Upon plugging her phone in, she saw that she had a new message. There was only one person who would be texting her, knowing that she was still awake.

Tripp: When can I see you again?

That one question should not have made her stomach flip the way it did.

Did Tripp not at all listen to a word she said in the library? No, of course he did. The hurt look on his face was still plastered in her mind. She, however, had completely obliterated everything that was said the moment she sought him after the game.

And after tonight, she was falling for Tripp more than anything. This was bad, so bad.

Tripp laughed when Ashlyn's text came through moments later. She really wasn't going to make it easy for him. It didn't matter. After their evening, he knew there was something deeper as to why she said what she did in the library.

Ashlyn: Tomorrow. Unless you've recently received a concussion, you sit beside me in science.

Knowing how much he had gotten to her on her front porch, he decided to take it one step further, already foreseeing that she would not be responding to his message.

Ashlyn slammed her phone down on the nightstand. Why did he have to go and do that? It's like he knew exactly what to say and exactly how to push her buttons, and as much as she wanted to forget that simple text, when she closed her eyes, the words flashed in the blackness.

Tripp: Goodnight, beautiful.

CHAPTER 26

"Hey, man," Eric announced, casually greeting Tripp the next afternoon in the locker room.

Though he wasn't on the baseball team, he still had athletics eighth period.

Tripp glanced over to Deacon and Byron nearby and both gave him skeptical looks.

"Hey," was all he said as he closed his locker and took his shoes to a nearby bench to finish changing out.

Most of the guys were already on the practice field, so the locker room was fairly quiet. It was so quiet that Tripp could hear Eric's footsteps behind him. He pretended not to notice the shadow hovering over him as he continued lacing his shoe.

"Heard you guys won last night," Eric said. He put one leg over the bench next to Tripp and straddled it.

"Yeah."

Eric didn't seem satisfied with Tripp not pressing forward for conversation. "I didn't see you out celebrating with the team."

"Homework."

Eric laughed sarcastically. "I also heard you played pretty lousy."

Tripp tried his best to stay calm and not make any cocky statements that would surely rile Eric. "Had an off day."

Bringing the subject back to dinner, "You know who else I didn't see at Flip's?" Eric didn't give Tripp the chance to answer. "My girlfriend."

Tripp clenched his teeth together so tightly he was sure they would crack.

"You do know my girlfriend, right?"

From the corner of his eye, Tripp saw Deacon making his way over. "Can't say that I do."

"Ashlyn Jennings. I met you at her house, so I'd say you know her."

Attempting to downplay any relations with Ashlyn, "Oh, yeah. She's my partner in science, friend of Ellis and his sister."

"Ugh. Don't even mention that braindead cheer idiot." Just then, Eric saw Deacon approach, and a sinister smile spread across his face. "Right, Deacon?"

"Leave Emory out of whatever this is," Deacon growled. Unlike Tripp, he wasn't light and bubbly. He didn't smile and laugh. Though he was gentle and kind under his rough exterior, and chose to remain out of the business of others, if Eric were to say the right thing, he wouldn't hesitate putting him in his place.

"Whatever. Nobody cares about her."

Tripp rose from the bench and Eric quickly stood from his. "Anyway, nice talking to you," Tripp said with his most upbeat voice, as though nothing was wrong. "But Deacon and I are late for practice."

Eric took a step forward. "Yeah, good talking to you too," Eric said, beginning to leave. He patted Tripp on the shoulder, perhaps a little rougher than necessary.

"It's not my business," Deacon began as they headed out. "But you should be careful with Ashlyn."

"We're just friends."

Deacon made a noise that was as close to a laugh as Tripp ever heard from him. "You two left the game together. You were with her last night, yeah?"

"We just went for dinner."

"Like a date?"

Tripp shook his head and couldn't help but smile at the memory of leaving Ashlyn the night before. "She made it very clear that it wasn't a date."

"Regardless, be careful. Eric is nuts. If he's still calling her his girlfriend, I'd be a little concerned."

Of all the things that Eric could have said, that had bothered Tripp the most. "Do you think that's why Ash is keeping me at arm's length?"

Deacon turned and looked Tripp over. "You're completely different than Eric. If she was into him, then you're probably not her type." His voice was dry, but Tripp had learned to read his eyes. He was definitely messing with him.

Tripp nudged Deacon toward the field. "Thanks for that," he laughed.

"What can I say, at least one girl at this school isn't into you," Deacon continued as he jogged forward.

"You can stop now!"

Ashlyn was tweaking the bow of her ship when she heard her phone nearby. She quickly wiped her hands on her apron and reached for it, unable to contain the smile that came to her face when she saw the name.

Tripp: Done with practice and heading home. Do you want to get together and work on the science packet?

Ashlyn began and deleted several messages. After last night, it would be best to put the brakes on anything with Tripp outside of school; yet, here she was, desperately wanting to see him.

Tripp: If you feel like playing twenty questions, you can come over to my house.

Before Ashlyn could overthink it, she sent the message. Adrenaline raced through her as she tore off her apron and headed for the mirror. No sooner than she took out her messy bun and began to make two pigtails, Tripp's message containing his address came in.

She didn't want to appear too eager, so she simply told him that she'd try to be over soon. She also didn't go overboard with her attire. Tripp was used to seeing her at school. Sometimes she wore dresses, sometimes overalls or jeans. If he was asking her to come over after everything she continued to put him through, even though it was just for studying, obviously he didn't care too much about her clothes.

Ashlyn made her way down the stairs and headed into the living room. Strangely, both her parents were home early, and even stranger, her mother was on the couch watching a movie.

"Hey, mom. Is it okay if I go study with a friend?"

Poppy paused the movie and her attention flew to her daughter, a playful glimmer in her eyes. "Girl friend or boy friend?"

Ashlyn shifted her weight from side to side. "Ugh. Boy. If it helps, his mother and little brother are home."

"Depends. Do you plan on missing curfew?"

Ashlyn's eyes widened. Both her parents had been asleep when she got in the night before, and neither had said anything about it all day. "It was only fifteen minutes." Then her mother laughed. "How did you know?"

"Sweetie...The doorbell picked up movement." She shook her head. "That poor boy."

Ashlyn's face turned red from mortification. "It recorded everything..." It wasn't a question, simply a statement.

"And it was obviously a date."

Ashlyn couldn't meet her mother's eyes. She was completely horrified that she had seen that. "Just stop. Please."

Poppy laughed so hard that tears came to her eyes.

"I'll even be home for dinner," Ashlyn stressed.

"It's fine, really. Before you go, I think your father wanted to speak with you. He's in his office."

Without bothering to entertain her mother any further with her embarrassment over last night, Ashlyn headed to her father's office. He rarely called her in for a talk, and neither of her parents were big disciplinarians, so she couldn't imagine what kind of trouble she might be in.

Though Daniel's office door was open, Ashlyn still knocked.

"Hey, dad. You wanted to see me?"

"Yeah. It won't take long," he said with half a smile.

Ashlyn cautiously made her way in. "Am I in trouble about curfew?"

He gave her a perplexed look. "Your mother said it was only by fifteen minutes."

Ashlyn couldn't help but laugh on the inside. Her father probably didn't think anything of it since he was generally always running late.

"Anyway, no. Forget the curfew thing." He sighed, and the now serious look on his face concerned Ashlyn. "You know my Mickey Mantle ball?"

Ashlyn rolled her eyes. Of course she knew that thing. He won it at an auction years earlier and Ashlyn was pretty sure that if their house was robbed, he'd trade her before letting them take that ball.

"What about it?"

"It's been missing since your party." Daniel watched an uncomfortable expression come to his daughter's face. "I don't want to accuse any of your friends. I didn't want to say anything until I talk to Carmen. Maybe she was cleaning and moved it somewhere."

Ashlyn knew her dad was just being too nice. Carmen wouldn't dare touch that stupid ball.

"We both know Carmen won't know anything," Ashlyn sighed. She began thinking about her party and a sickening feeling came over her. "You were talking to Tripp in here, you don't think..."

Her father couldn't help but chuckle and rub his forehead. "Trust me, that boy wouldn't have it in him to steal something."

Not liking how easy it was for her father to dismiss the possibility, "But he likes baseball, and if he was in here with you, he obviously saw it. I'm going to study with him, I can ask–"

"So, the two of you," he interrupted but paused, finding certain topics with his daughter to be quite difficult. "Dating?"

"What? No!"

Daniel appeared shocked. "Sorry, I just thought...You know what, never mind."

Suddenly remembering her conversation with Tripp the night before, "Dad, why was he in here with you during my party."

Daniel smiled sweetly. "I think that's something he needs–"

"Oh my gosh! Are you kidding me?! The two of you are both saying the same thing. All I can think is that he needs your legal expertise for something."

Seeing how flustered Ashlyn became, Daniel blurted it out. "He asked me for permission to date you."

Ashlyn felt lightheaded. "What?!"

Her father only nodded in confirmation.

Ashlyn honestly felt like she was getting off the worst roller coaster in her life. Was Tripp serious? Who does that anymore?

"Look, forget I said anything about the ball. I'm sure it will turn up somewhere," Daniel told her, interrupting the thousands of thoughts running through her head.

Ashlyn was still in a daze when she left her father's office and grabbed her backpack near the front door. It seemed so outlandish. Tripp had said he was a gentleman, but not like something from the 1800s. Boys her age didn't ask fathers for permission to date their daughters. The idea of even talking to her parents about dating was uncomfortable, and yet, Tripp talked about it with a virtual stranger. She had to give it to him, he had confidence.

CHAPTER 27

Tripp diligently worked on his homework across the table from Ashlyn. His mom busied herself in the kitchen, while his little brother sat on the couch reading a book. His mother severely limited screen time.

He looked up to Ashlyn. Her brows were scrunched together, and she was biting at the corner of her lip.

"Stuck?"

"Yeah," she sighed. "This matching section. I'm messing up somewhere..."

Tripp leaned forward across the table trying to see where she was at on the packet. "Oh, the one about faults."

He extended his hand to try to point to which answer needed to be where. He wasn't sure if Ashlyn heard his mother clear her throat in the kitchen, but it was one of her not so subtle ways to gain attention. When he looked up, Eliza had narrowed eyes and flicked her finger from side to side. Thankfully Ashlyn couldn't see his mother's gesture behind her.

"Umm, here. Hold on."

Tripp slid his work across the table to the spot next to Ashlyn and went around to sit beside her.

Though it was comfortable being next to her, and where he wanted to be the entire time, he could feel Eliza's eyes searing through his back expecting him to mess something up.

"Switch these two around and you should be good," he told her, motioning to her paper.

Ashlyn looked up at him and only then realized how close they were. Oddly, Tripp wasn't laying on the charm or being flirtatious. He was simply sitting next to her and helping her with a problem. His closeness and the smell of his cologne still didn't stop her heart from racing.

Tripp saw his brother carefully watching as he made his way into the kitchen. He glared at him and shook his head. All he needed was for Cason's mouth to run away and tell some embarrassing story, true or not. Though young, he had a knack for storytelling, and Tripp could see him making up something ridiculous.

During spring break there had been a set of twins at the beach who thought Cason was adorable; however, when it was clear that they were using him to get a chance to talk with Tripp, Cason informed them that the night prior Tripp wet the bed. He went into more details than Tripp could ever imagine at his age.

"Mom. Can I have a snack?"

"Dinner will be ready after your father gets home," Eliza informed him. "He's running just a little late."

Cason groaned and stomped off; however, much to Tripp's surprise, he didn't go back to the couch and his book. Instead, Cason pulled out a seat directly across from Ashlyn.

Tripp shot him a set of eyes that told him to go away, but all that did was cause an adorably sinister grin on his brother's face.

"Ashlyn," Cason began, pleased when she looked up from her worksheets and at him.

She smiled sweetly at the little boy. He was dangerously adorable. There was no doubt in her mind that he and Tripp shared the same lucky genetics.

"We're all wondering, mostly me and my mom, but probably my brother too..."

"Don't you have a book to read," Tripp asked with a stern authoritative voice.

Ashlyn nudged him and shook her head. "It's fine."

"Are you my brother's girlfriend?"

Ashlyn's eyes widened and her mouth went dry. "Wow. You don't mind being blunt."

"Cason," Eliza screamed from the kitchen. "Book. Now."

"She didn't answer," he yelled back. "I thought you wanted to know too," he pretended to whine.

"Cason, you're really testing me."

"Ugh, fine." Cason got up from his chair and pushed it in but didn't immediately leave.

Ashlyn and Tripp watched him carefully. He glanced over at Tripp and then shrugged.

"I think you can do better," he said, directing his words to Ashlyn.

Tripp swatted at Cason from across the table, knowing that he couldn't touch him. Cason let out a squeal and ran laughing from the room.

"Sorry about that," Tripp grumbled in a low voice.

"It's not a big deal," Ashlyn assured him. She was thankful that the conversation played out in a way that she didn't have to answer. It was an obvious no, but for some reason she didn't want to have to say that aloud. She scrunched her face at the thought. "I think I should be going anyway."

"You can stay for dinner if you want."

"I would, but I told my mom I would be home for hers. After all, I don't want to push it too much tonight after missing curfew last night," she said quietly, hoping that his mother and brother didn't know about their evening.

Tripp could feel his cheeks reddening at the thought of the night before. That was something that never happened to him. He didn't get embarrassed and blush.

Ashlyn actually expected the afternoon to go much worse after Eliza's overly pleasant greeting. She hated how his mother looked at her, with so much hope. She didn't think she'd ever ask Tripp, but she had to wonder how many girls he had brought home over the years. From the surprise on his mother's face, it didn't seem like many, which contradicted what she thought, especially with Tripp's personality.

"Thanks for hanging out," Tripp told Ashlyn just as he closed the front door behind him.

"Sorry if they gave you a hard time."

They were now at her car, but Ashlyn wasn't really in a rush to leave. Tripp stood next to her with his back pressed into the cold exterior.

As if to answer Ashlyn's unspoken question, "If you couldn't tell, I don't invite many girls over."

Ashlyn found herself curious. "Why not?"

"I don't know. It's not just girls, people in general," he clarified. "We never really lived in places long enough and I just never wanted to get too attached."

"So, why now?"

"I like being around you, Ash," he sighed.

She could feel butterflies spring to life in her stomach. Unfortunately, there was a nagging thought in the back of her mind. She dreaded bringing it up, but if she didn't, she'd never feel right around him.

Ashlyn step forward and turned so that she was facing Tripp and not beside him. "I have something I need to ask you."

Tripp knew from just the tone in her voice that it wasn't going to be good. "Shoot."

She didn't know how to begin such a question and borderline accusation, but beating around the bush with Tripp wasn't the way to go. "My dad had a Mickey Mantle signed ball in his office..."

"Yeah, I know. We talked about it briefly." Sensing her uncertainty, Tripp replayed her words. "Wait, *had?*"

Ashlyn uncomfortably shifted her weight and brought her eyes to look into Tripp's. She knew she'd be able to read his eyes. "It went missing around the time of my party."

Tripp took a deep breath and his nostrils flared. He wasn't an idiot; he didn't need for Ashlyn to continue what she was about to say. He crossed his arms and glared at her. "And you think I took it?"

"No...I don't know. I had to ask because–"

"Do you want to know what your dad and I were talking about?" His voice was annoyed, almost angry.

"No," Ashlyn quickly blurted out. She couldn't go into that discussion with Tripp. "Look, I'm sorry. I shouldn't have–"

Tripp shrugged aggressively. "You don't trust me. I get it." He stepped forward and Ashlyn could see red in his golden eyes, or maybe she was just imagining that with how angry he was. "You want to know something," he asked, although they both knew it was rhetorical. "And you can think I'm as full of myself or as cocky as you want." He ran his hand through his dirty blonde hair. "My dad will give me anything I want. I only have to do three things." He lifted a finger for each item he listed. "Play baseball. Make good grades. Stay out of trouble." He shook his head. "How do you think I got that camera for you. I sure as hell didn't steal it."

Ashlyn felt horrible. Though she hadn't known Tripp long, she shouldn't have thought he would have done something like steal from her father. Her father had even laughed at the idea, and he was a very good judge of character.

"Tripp, I'm sorry. I just had to mention it, because you were in there with him, and you knew about it, and–"

"Newsflash, Ash. There were a lot of other people at that party, ones with not so wonderful reputations," he growled. He refrained from pointing out the obvious at first. "It's not like it was under lock and key. It was on the first floor. Anyone could have gone into that room." Not being able to contain himself on mentioning Eric. "Maybe you should ask your *boyfriend*." He brushed past her and headed back to his front door.

"Excuse me?!" Now it was her turn to get offended.

Tripp turned for just a moment, loathing how the day had gotten ruined in a matter of seconds. "Yeah, at least that's what he called himself when he decided to give me and Deacon crap in the locker room."

Ashlyn swallowed heavily. This was exactly why being around Tripp was a bad idea. If he thought a few words from Eric was bad, he had no idea what dating her would mean.

* * *

Ashlyn wiped away a few tears as soon as she reached the first four-way stop after Tripp's house. She hated how hurt and angry he looked. He basically admitted that he was a spoiled brat and could get anything he wanted from his daddy. It's not like the ball was even that valuable; it wasn't in the most pristine condition. The camera he got for her was probably more.

She should have gone about it a better way, one that didn't make it look like she was accusing him.

The worst part, she really enjoyed studying with him. He didn't try anything stupid; he was just a good friend. She could only hope that he was as forgiving as he seemed, because she felt like she really set their friendship back.

Ashlyn was so busy thinking about Tripp that she completely missed the car parked on the street near her driveway. It wasn't until she was pulling in that she saw the gloomy figure dressed in all black sitting on the steps to the front door.

Eric.

With the way she felt, he was the last person on earth that she wanted to deal with.

"Whoa, have you been crying," were the first words to come out of Eric's mouth as he bounded toward her car.

"No."

He rolled his eyes. "Yes, you have. I've made you cry enough times to know."

Ash let out an exasperated breath. "Something which you sound rather proud of."

"Anyway, where were you? I've been waiting here for half an hour."

Ashlyn wanted to tell him that it was none of his business, but his attitude would only end up going into a tailspin. "I was at the library. You could have text to let me know you were coming over," she quickly told him, hoping that he wouldn't try to pry further into her whereabouts. "Also, did you even ring the doorbell." She glanced inside the open garage. "Both of my parents are home," she pointed out.

"Yeah, but your mom is nuts, your dad hates me, and heaven forbid that maid is here. I don't know what her fixation is with my shoes," he scoffed.

Ashlyn glanced down at his muddy boots but said nothing on the matter. "I'm late for dinner. Is there something you needed?"

"Yeah. Since we're *broken up*," he began, using air quotes, but before he could finish, Ashlyn interrupted him.

"Don't do that. Don't pretend like I'm mad and this is something I'll get over."

Eric clenched his jaw in anger. "Whatever. I need my stuff back."

"Your stuff?"

"Yeah. I know you have one of my hoodies, and a t-shirt, video games, DVDs–"

Ashlyn couldn't believe him right now, but it was fine. She wanted every part of him gone from her life. What a wasted two years. "Fine, Eric. I'll get it together soon and drop it off."

"Cool."

Ashlyn widened her eyes and gave him a questioning look, waiting for him to either leave or say something else. Unfortunately, he had something else to say.

"So, are you seeing anyone?"

She gasped in shock. "Seriously?!" She threw her hands in the air, completely done with him. "No, Eric," she scoffed. "I'm not seeing anyone."

"Good," he said, appearing to be pleased.

"No. You don't get to care if or when I start dating."
She didn't mean for her anger to get the best of her,
and perhaps she shouldn't have brought it up, but
her day was already going downhill, why not add to
it. "And you know what? Why were you giving Deacon
crap today?" She intentionally said Deacon, a mutual
friend, and made it a point to leave Tripp out.

Eric narrowed his eyes, and Ashlyn pretended not
to have a reaction that he might know something he
shouldn't. "First of all," he began with a growl. "I was
giving Tripp crap. Deacon inserted himself where he
shouldn't be."

"Whatever. Just don't. You know you're in enough
trouble with the school. You don't need harassment
up there," she added, pretending to care.

"So, you and Deacon?"

Ashlyn's eyes bulged out of her head. "What?! No!"

Eric chuckled. "Yeah, I think we all know where
he stands. What about Tripp?"

Pretending to have the same reaction as she did
when he mentioned Deacon's name, "No! Ugh, you're
unbelievable!"

Eric watched her carefully and she fought with all
her might not to lose her composure, pretending to
be irritated at his suggestions. After a few moments,
he seemed to be satisfied.

"Anyway, try to get me my things soon." He started
down the driveway toward his car parked on the
street. "See you around school, babe."

Ashlyn wished she had a rock to throw at him. She
hated that so-called term of endearment.

It wasn't until she made her way inside and put her bag down, that she realized how he had dominated their conversation. She should have asked him about the Mickey Mantle ball.

CHAPTER 28

Ashlyn: Hey, I know it's late. I just wanted to apologize again. It all came out wrong.

Tripp: You wouldn't have mentioned it if you didn't think I had something to do with it.

Ashlyn: I'm really sorry.

Tripp: It's fine. I'm sorry too.

Ashlyn sank back into her pillow. She was supposed to be the one who felt horrible for assuming, and here Tripp was the one now apologizing.

Tripp: I guess I thought you knew me better. Looking back, I can see how I would be a good suspect. Anyway, sorry if I lost my cool with you.

Tripp wasn't sure how Ashlyn felt, but he felt the worst. He hated that she thought he'd do something like that, but he hated how he reacted even more. He never meant to raise his voice or storm off like he had, especially after they had such a nice and normal evening together.

Tripp: So, we're cool? Friends?

Ashlyn: Yeah, friends.

Ashlyn turned her phone to silent and threw it on the nightstand. She hated that she ever had to say the things she did, and she wondered if Tripp really was only going to pursue a friendship with her because of that. He had called their night after the game a date...She shook her head at the thought. She had told him several times how it wasn't. Then there was his text that night. It was completely different from the one now.

Maybe Eric said more to Tripp and Deacon than Tripp was telling her? Could that have anything to do with the fact that she just spent all that time with him and there wasn't one bit of flirtation on his part? He did sit beside her, but that was about as intense as it got.

She rolled over and groaned into her pillow. The only thing she needed right now was sleep.

* * *

Tripp tuned out of the conversation Ellis, Deacon, and Byron were having at Ellis' locker the next morning. They still had a good ten minutes before the bell signaling to head to first period would ring, and he had hoped to see Ashlyn before lunch or science.

As if the heavens heard that thought, far down the hall he saw Ashlyn along with her best friend.

Ashlyn's locker was only a few down from where they stood at Ellis', so he'd at least get to see her for a second.

Just as they made eye contact and she gave him a sweet smile like nothing had ever been amiss between them, two girls sashayed up to their group.

"Hey, guys," the redhead greeted.

While Tripp didn't know them, he knew of them. The redhead's name was Grace, and from the little he did know, she was on the paper with Ashlyn. The other one, with the jet-black hair and dark brown eyes was Melody. He had English with her, but other than that, knew very little.

"Hey, Grace, Melody," Ellis spoke up.

"We just came over to invite you guys to a party we're having Saturday," Melody quickly blurted out without so much as an introduction.

"Ellis, I need the keys," Emory insisted, squeezing herself through everyone, along with Ashlyn. "I left my second period notebook in there."

Ellis groaned but handed his sister the keys. Emory whispered to Ashlyn to stay there, that she was going to run out really fast, and just like that, she dashed off through the hall.

"So, party," Ellis asked after being interrupted by his sister.

Tripp watched Ashlyn, but she wouldn't meet his eyes. Maybe she was still embarrassed and shy about the day before. For him, it was all water under the bridge. After thinking about it from her perspective, he could see how she'd want to at the very least mention it to him and see his reaction.

Rather than meeting his gaze, Ashlyn appeared generally interested in the details of whatever party the two girls were talking about. Before they could even finish, Emory was back, chunking the keys at Ellis.

"Wow, that was fast," Ashlyn whispered.

"Athleticism runs in our genes," Emory joked.

Tripp was taken aback when a cool and dainty hand was placed on his forearm. He tore his eyes from the girl who refused to look at him and to the one touching him with such ease.

"I really hope you can make it Saturday," Grace told him sweetly, perhaps batting her eyes just a few times too many.

"And you too, Deacon," Melody added. After seeing the strange looks from the others, "Well, all of you."

Ashlyn couldn't help but notice Deacon tense at Melody's words; however, she was even more surprised with Tripp.

Tripp took a step backwards, breaking the uncomfortable contact with Grace. "Actually, I'm out. Sorry."

Grace appeared shocked and disappointed. "Really? Is there a game? The party is–"

"No. No game. I have a date."

Grace's jaw nearly fell to the floor. She shot a quick glare to Melody. "I thought you and Rachel broke up?"

Ashlyn and Emory looked at each other rather un-comfortably. Byron took the opportunity to slip away. It appeared that Deacon wanted to as well, but maybe he was thinking over Melody's special invitation to him.

"We were *never* dating," Tripp insisted.

"Oh, well–"

Just then the bell rang, muffling any further pro-test from Grace. Everyone shot out in different direc-tions. Tripp was so annoyed that Grace and Melody had taken up those few precious minutes before the start of the day. The only thing he was slightly thank-ful for was the fact that his and Ashlyn's classes were in the same direction.

Tripp jogged to catch up with Ashlyn, eager to get in just a few words before he'd go hours without see-ing her.

"Hey, how's it going?"

Ashlyn barely took the time to glance at Tripp when he caught up to her. She couldn't believe that one minute he's trying to do a movie night with her, and the next he's already got a date with someone else. Now she knew why there was nothing more than a friendly homework session between them the day before.

"Good."

"Really? You look pissed," Tripp blurted out.

"Just trying to get to class."

Tripp softly grabbed her wrist in hopes of getting her attention. It worked, as she slowed her steps and glanced up at him, unfortunately for him, she also wiggled her arm from him and pretended like the straps on her backpack needed her attention.

"I thought we were alright?"

Ashlyn took a deep breath and paused. Tripp turned so that he was standing in front of her. She couldn't ignore the concern in his eyes.

She tried to put on the best smile she could. "We're fine. We're still friends."

Tripp didn't buy it. It wasn't the same smile she had given him when she first walked into school that day, but he didn't want to go in circles with her. "I actually needed to talk to you about something."

A tinge of pink graced his cheeks and suddenly he had a difficult time making eye contact with Ashlyn.

"I can't be late for class." Ashlyn stepped around Tripp and went on her way to her classroom.

Before Tripp could insist any further, she was already inside her room. He stared at the door to the journalism classroom wondering what in the world had just happened.

He fired off a text and slowly went in the direction to his classroom. Ashlyn didn't stand a chance of being late. They still had three minutes until the tardy bell.

Tripp: I need to talk to you. It's about this weekend.

Ashlyn read the text and put her phone away without responding. Whether or not Tripp intended for her to hear his excuse to Grace, she heard it.

She glanced over to see Grace going at it on her phone before class. She was sure that Grace was probably ranting to Melody about Tripp. Seriously, did every girl in school have a crush on the guy?

Ashlyn tried to get Tripp out of her mind as she grabbed her notebook and the memory card from her camera and booted up the computer at her station. However, the thought of him going on an actual date with someone else sent a feeling through her that she wasn't prepared to deal with. It was even worse now, worse than when she saw him at her birthday party with her best friend.

* * *

Tripp arrived to science early, and took his place at the table he shared with Ashlyn. She hadn't been at lunch. Her friends said she had told them that she was working on a project. At least he knew her phone was working. She could text them nonstop, but she had yet to reply to him. Maybe he should have gone to the library to see if she was just trying to avoid him.

Ashlyn entered right when the bell rang, and Mrs. Cohen immediately began taking roll.

"Alright, today's assignment will be a movie." Student's began whispering with excitement. "Not so fast." Mrs. Cohen went to her desk, grabbed a stack of papers, and began passing them to the students in the front, informing them to take one and pass them back. "Just so I know you're paying attention, you'll need to listen carefully and fill in answers along the way." She smiled when there were several groans throughout the room.

Tripp reached for the papers handed in his direction and slid one to Ashlyn. She mumbled her thanks, but so far that was the most she had said to him.

No sooner than they wrote their names on the papers, Mrs. Cohen dimmed the lights to a little less than half their brightness and began the documentary.

Tripp glanced over the questions. Some he could answer just on his knowledge from of the topic.

He scooted his chair closer to Ashlyn, which she pretended to ignore.

"You weren't at lunch today," he whispered.

Maybe it was his closeness and what that did to her now, but shivers ran down her spine. "I was busy."

"You never responded to my message," he pointed out.

Pretending like this morning hadn't bothered her, "Oh, yeah. Sorry. What did you want?"

Tripp picked up on it. Her eyes and the tone in her voice said so much. He thought about when she first arrived at her locker to where she attempted to avoid him in the hall. A satisfied smirk came to his face. Was Ashlyn, the one who was adamant about a friendship only relationship, jealous?

"I was going to ask you what your plans were for Saturday."

Without missing a beat, "Well, they don't include Grace's party." She shut her eyes and bit down on her lip. She couldn't believe how snotty and catty that came out.

"That's good to know," Tripp softly chuckled.

Ashlyn didn't like that he was amused by that. "Just watch the movie."

He would have liked to have told her that he'd rather watch her squirm. Instead, he went for something a little less intense. "If not the party, what?"

Ashlyn sighed and looked away from the movie. She wished she wouldn't have. Tripp's face was so close to hers, and his hooded eyes darted from her eyes to her lips. All she could think of was kissing him, almost forgetting what he asked.

She quickly looked away and wrote down the next answer that she had vaguely heard mentioned in the background. "I just have plans. Don't worry about it."

"Can I be a part of them?"

Tripp tried his best to keep a straight face and hold in any laughter, all the while knowing that he was getting to her, and knowing that she was going to kick herself for so easily showing her cards.

Ashlyn stopped writing and looked at him with wide eyes. *Don't say it. Don't say it.* "I thought you had a date." Apparently, curiosity always won.

"Oh, you heard that," he asked, feigning innocence.

Ashlyn scoffed. "Everyone heard that."

Tripp shrugged. "Nothing is set in stone yet."

Ashlyn was livid, but thankfully his comment didn't require further response from her. Who did he think he was? Even if it was Rachel, Ashlyn felt bad for the girl, being strung along until Tripp found something better to occupy his time.

As much as he wanted to, Tripp couldn't mess with her anymore. "Remember when we were messaging, and you didn't know who I was?"

"Mhmm," Ashlyn said in acknowledgement.

"And I told you that I'd tell you who I was if you agreed to spend a day with me?"

"To which I never agreed."

Tripp nudged her playfully and leaned in so that his breath prickled the skin on her neck. "So, agree."

Ashlyn snapped her head in his direction. They were so close their noses could have touched. "I don't understand. I thought…What about–"

"You should stop assuming. I thought it was obvious that the only person I want to be on a date with is you."

Ashlyn was thankful for the little bit of darkness in the room. She felt like her face was on fire and her heart thundered in her chest.

"You're such a jerk," she mumbled with embarrassment.

"And you were so jealous," Tripp pointed out.

"I'm sure that's just what you want. For all these girls to fall head over heels for you," Ashlyn spat.

Hoping to calm Ashlyn before her voice rose over the movie, Tripp grabbed her free hand and pulled it beneath the table. She sucked in a breath and tensed but didn't pull away.

He had missed contact with her the day before, and now that he had her small hand in his, he didn't want to let go. He entangled their fingers while his thumb drew soft circles on the back of her hand. Slowly he felt the tension ease from her body.

"There's only one girl I want falling for me," he whispered, attempting to quell any and all doubts Ashlyn might have.

Occasionally Tripp let go of her hand to write in an answer, but she always allowed him to take it back. They only separated for good when the documentary ended and the lights came back on.

"We barely made that," Mrs. Cohen announced from the front of the room. "Please pass your papers forward, the bell will soon be–"

Her words were cut off by the ringing of the bell from the speaker in the ceiling.

"Okay," Ashlyn said confidently as she rose from her seat.

Tripp's brows rose in confusion, not sure what she was responding to. They hadn't said anything to each other for a good fifteen minutes.

After seeing the look on his face, Ashlyn tried again, this time using her words and speaking quiet enough so that students nearby wouldn't hear. "We can hang out Saturday."

Then, as if embarrassed by what had just happened in class, Ashlyn grabbed her bags and darted through the students shuffling about. Tripp wanted to ask her if he could walk her to class, but perhaps that would have been too much too soon.

What he felt was incomparable to anything he had felt before. He only wished that Ashlyn would finally crack and admit that the whole *just friends* thing was crap.

CHAPTER 29

The remainder of the week went on quite uneventfully. Much to Ashlyn's surprise and relief, she hadn't heard another peep from Eric. She had also put off going through her room and finding whatever junk of his she might still have.

With another baseball game and a project looming over Tripp's head, he didn't get much time to see Ashlyn outside of class. Normally he would have been bummed about that, but it only made the anticipation of spending Saturday with her that much greater, despite Ashlyn being a little skeptical when he told her to be ready by ten.

"When you said the day, I didn't expect this," Ashlyn said, putting on her seatbelt.

"When you agreed to the day, I had to make the most of it."

He had told her to dress casual, and she didn't disappoint. For some strange reason, he loved when she wore her overalls and pigtails. There was something so carefree and different about it. Most of the girls he knew wouldn't dare style their hair in such a childish way or wear something deemed as unflattering.

Tripp reached in the cupholder and withdrew one of the large cups and handed it to Ashlyn. "I wasn't sure how you took your coffee. If you don't like it, we can find you something else along the way."

Before saying anything, Ashlyn took a sip. It was sweeter than she probably would have ordered for herself, but it had a hint of vanilla that she loved.

"It's great. Thank you."

Then he reached toward the back and brought out a bag. "Donuts," he informed her as he handed it to her.

Ashlyn had breakfast a couple hours earlier. She may have woken up at an ungodly hour after being unable to sleep with anticipation. She wasn't hungry, but she wasn't about to pass up a donut.

"I take it we're not going anywhere for lunch then."

Tripp pulled out of her driveway. "Nope."

He watched as relief came to Ashlyn's face. He had figured that she wouldn't want to be seen around Raymere Grove with him. He'd have to bring it up later and tell her that he was fine with everything, but he didn't want to venture into that right now. Right now he wanted everything light and fun between them.

Ashlyn got a little concerned when Tripp headed outside of Raymere Grove and got onto the highway. "Where exactly are we going?" She had asked that several times ever since she agreed to spend the day with him, but now she really needed an answer.

"There's a place in the city I wanted to take you. It's about an hour or so away."

"Do you plan on telling me…"

Tripp briefly glanced in her direction before pulling his eyes back to the road. "You've waited this long."

Though they talked about random bits and pieces of their lives throughout the drive, whenever there was a moment of silence, Ashlyn was deep in her thoughts. All she could think about was how right it felt with Tripp.

She knew he was going overboard with trying to woo her. After all, Eric had been sweet and caring at first too. She only wished that she had a magic ball that could see into the future.

She didn't think that Tripp would ever treat her and talk to her like Eric. He had already proven to be different after she found out about his discussion with her father. However, she was still concerned. Every girl in school had a crush on Tripp. What would happen if she let things progress, only for him to find her boring and want to move on to the next shiny toy?

"We're here," he told her, awakening her from her insecurities.

"The botanical gardens," Ashlyn gasped, seeing the entryway ahead.

Tripp smiled with success. "Most of their spring stuff is very prominent right now. I thought you could get some good pictures, and since I've never been…Well, why not?"

Ashlyn, full of excitement, reached for her camera. She strangely expected Tripp to take her somewhere, to something, that was about him and what he liked.

That wasn't to say that he wouldn't appreciate the gardens, but he had obviously put her first when he made arrangements for their day together.

When Tripp headed to the entryway, "Oh, we'll need tickets to get in." Ashlyn nodded toward an enclosed booth.

Tripp reached in his pocket and held up a folded piece of paper. "Bought online." Ashlyn was about to protest but Tripp cut her off. "I just thought it would be easier in case it was busy. Just because I paid for you doesn't mean you have to consider this a date if you don't want to."

Ashlyn's cheeks reddened. She didn't want to tell him that, but that was one word that she was hoping wouldn't be brought up. The worst of it, she was beginning to change her mind on what it was or wasn't called, and the word *date* was suddenly growing on her.

* * *

Ashlyn sat on a bench and looked through the pictures on her camera while Tripp headed inside the main center to use the restroom. When he finally returned and joined her, she couldn't help but notice the strange change in his earlier calmness. He looked giddy, but also very secretive.

"Get a lot of good ones," he asked.

"Yes. I was planning on using some of my action shots of the games for the photos I can display, but I'm thinking that I may do a floral collection."

"Sounds awesome."

Ashlyn looked away from her camera to Tripp. He was fidgety, tapping one of his feet, and had the most awkward smile.

"What," she asked, drawing the word out.

"Nothing," he said a little too quickly. "Are you ready to head out?"

"Okay, you're being weird," Ashlyn pointed out.

Tripp took a deep breath and tried to calm his nerves. "I may have something else planned."

It was only a little before three. Ashlyn knew they weren't going to go straight home. "Of course you do."

"Are you hungry," Tripp asked as they headed back to his vehicle.

Ashlyn didn't want to say anything, but breakfast and the donuts had worn off some time ago.

"Yeah," she finally admitted.

Tripp opened her door and waited for her to step in. A calculating smirk crept to his lips. "Good."

"I suppose you're not going to tell me anything else about this whole outing," Ashlyn pointlessly asked when Tripp got in the driver's seat.

Tripp did that melting chuckle of his. "Nope."

From time to time he glanced over to her. If she thought he was taking her to some fancy restaurant, she was hugely mistaken. A restaurant outside of Raymere Grove would have been the normal thing to do, but he wanted to be alone with her. He had things he needed to tell her, and he couldn't hold them in any longer.

Ashlyn was confused. "We're almost back home."

"Don't worry. I'm not taking you to some diner in town."

Ashlyn moved about uncomfortably in her seat.

"I'm also not taking you back to my house."

"You're telling me everything you're not going to do. It would be easier for you to just say where we *are* going."

Tripp made a turn before they reached the outer part of Raymere Grove, and headed down a road leading to nothing.

Ashlyn took in her surroundings, the landscape, the countryside. She didn't know of much being out in the direction they were headed.

Tripp sensed her uncertainty. "There's a little lake out here...And this spot," he began, fumbling for words.

He parked his Mercedes-Benz in a field that seemed to stretch for miles. Before Ashlyn could ask him just what was going on, he excitedly hopped out and she quickly did the same before he'd run around to open her door. Strangely, he didn't come to her side, he went to the back.

Ashlyn grabbed her camera, just in case there were pictures worth taking. When she went to meet Tripp at the back of his SUV, her heart stopped. She should have known that only he would come up with something like this.

Tripp bunched the folded blanket up in his arms and picked up the cooler from the ground.

Ashlyn crossed her arms and drew her lips together. "I thought you didn't know the area, yet you found a perfect spot for a picnic?"

He nodded in the direction for her to go. "Research."

Ashlyn shook her head but couldn't help smiling as they walked toward a beautiful oak tree near a crystal blue lake. Tripp flopped out the blanket and Ashlyn grabbed two of the corners, helping him spread it out.

"Do you do such extensive research for all your dates?"

Tripp froze and their eyes met. Ashlyn quickly realized her mistake and attempted to correct it.

"Not saying that this is a date...I just meant–"

"Stop," Tripp insisted, interrupting her.

After seeing the look on Tripp's face, Ashlyn stopped talking. He had been amazing all day, all week. If she thought about it, ever since she met him, he had been amazing to her in his own unique way, and all she ever gave in return was to push him away. She couldn't believe that after everything, he'd still want to be around her. She concluded at that moment that if Tripp were to call it a date at any point in the future, she wouldn't correct him.

Tripp began popping the lids off the containers and placing them neatly on the blanket until it was filled with various meats, cheeses, crackers, and fruits.

"Did you do all this yourself?"

Tripp's face clenched up. "No. My mom may have helped a little, gave me a few pointers."

Ashlyn's eyes widened in surprise. "Oh. So, your mom...She knows that–"

"That I'm trying my hardest to win over a girl who refuses to admit that she's on a date with me? Yeah."

Ashlyn grew quiet. She wanted the conversation to go back to being light and fun, which is why she didn't bother correcting Tripp and telling him that he had already succeeded.

Thankfully Tripp began a normal conversation that didn't focus on what they were or weren't. Neither had realized just how hungry they were until the entire spread was nearly gone.

"He seems sweet," Ashlyn said of Cason after Tripp got done telling a story.

"He can be so annoying."

"At least you have a sibling. It can be even more annoying to be all by yourself," she pointed out.

Tripp thought for a moment. "I remember when we first started texting and you told me you were an only child, but not by choice."

Without Tripp needing to ask, "My parents tried to have children after me." She shrugged. "I guess it just wasn't in the cards for them."

Tripp hated to hear that. Though she didn't always show it to him, Ashlyn had a sweet nature about her, and he knew she would have made a great big sister.

"Speaking of your parents, whatever happened with the Mickey Mantle ball?"

That was something in the back of her mind that went unsolved. "No idea," Ashlyn sighed.

"I can check online," Tripp began. "Maybe find him another one?"

Ashlyn laughed. "You don't have to do that. My dad likes you enough as it is."

Tripp felt the heat creeping in his cheeks, and he let out a breath of air. "He told you?"

"Yeah."

"Well, this isn't awkward," Tripp grumbled.

He began throwing the empty containers back in the cooler. Ashlyn refrained from mentioning his talk with her father after seeing how embarrassed he became.

"This was fun."

Tripp closed the cooler and shoved it to the side. There was still a lot he wanted to get out when it came to Ashlyn. He hesitated asking, but did anyway. "Are you ready to leave?"

Ashlyn could see in those honey colored eyes from the sun's descent that Tripp wasn't ready. "Maybe in a little bit."

She spread her legs forward, facing the lake, and leaned back on her outstretched arms.

Tripp sat beside her, a war of words waging in his head. He didn't know where to begin, how to lead in. Words failed him, and he just blurted it out.

"I like you, Ash. A lot."

His heart pounded in his chest, growing more frantic by each passing second that she didn't respond. When she finally did, her words shocked him.

"I don't know why." She heard Tripp take in a deep breath. She didn't need for him to protest, to list all the reasons why he'd say that. "I haven't been the nicest or most welcoming toward you. I'm an insecure and indecisive mess from my last relationship."

She looked from the lake to Tripp. His eyes were burning into hers. He reached behind himself until his hand clasped over hers and Ashlyn sucked in a breath.

Tripp smiled, his eyes never leaving hers. "I know you feel something too. Every time I touch you, it feels electric."

Ashlyn swallowed heavily. He was right.

"It's fine. I think I get it."

Ashlyn didn't say anything, her questioning eyes told him to continue.

"You just got out of a relationship. You don't want people thinking that you're rebounding or that we had something going on prior to your breakup."

Ashlyn liked what Tripp was saying. Was he seriously helping her with an excuse for not dating him? If so, it was a believable one. It was way better than her telling him how oddly possessive and crazy Eric had become. It was definitely better than telling him that she was afraid of what Eric might do if he found out that she and Tripp did have more than friendship between the two of them. This was good. Hopefully what Tripp was saying would buy her enough time for Eric to move on.

Just to make sure, "What are you saying?"

"I don't know," he laughed. "I guess I just want you to know that I kind of understand why you wouldn't want to jump into something with someone else. All I ask though, if you feel something, which I know you do," he confidently pointed out. "Don't ever say what you said to me in the library just to push me away."

Ashlyn let out an annoyed sigh. "Fine. Yes, Tripp. I have feelings for you that extend beyond friendship. There. Happy?"

Tripp wrinkled his nose and pretended to be deep in thought. "How far beyond friendship," he asked, unable to pass up a moment to tease Ashlyn.

"You're so impossible."

They sat in silence. The sun was still some time away from setting, but it was much lower on the horizon, giving everything a warm glow.

Tripp looked over curiously when he heard her camera click a few times. She quickly turned it off and put it down.

"Did you take a picture of the lake?"

"Something like that."

* * *

"Please, don't walk me to the door," Ashlyn insisted when Tripp opened her door and helped her from his SUV.

Tripp noticed the way her face reddened. "Why?"

She reached back in and grabbed her bag before closing the door and leaning into it. "We have one of those recording doorbells," she began, embarrassed to admit what she was about to say. "And it kind of picked up the last time."

Ashlyn rolled her eyes when Tripp nearly doubled over in laughter. She playfully kicked at him.

"Sorry," he managed trying to catch his breath. It was difficult not to laugh, realizing that her parents saw that exchange at the front door. "Anyway, thanks for spending the day with me."

Ashlyn gave a small smile, but it quickly faded when Tripp reached in his pocket and withdrew a small box.

"I got you something to remember it."

Ashlyn didn't need anything. This was one of the best days she had in a long time. She hesitantly took the white box and looked it over. Her eyes shot up to meet Tripp's when she saw the logo for the botanical gardens etched on the box.

He took a step forward and lowered his voice. "I may have stopped in the gift center."

Ashlyn opened the box and revealed a gorgeous pair of butterfly earrings. Colors of blue, pink, and yellow, sparkled in the soft evening light.

"Tripp," she gasped. "They're so pretty."

Tripp thought he might come undone when she looked up at him. That was the look he wanted by the end of the day. He would have done anything to keep that look of happiness on her face.

"I noticed that you don't wear much jewelry besides earrings."

Ashlyn bit her lip. Of course he did, because he noticed all the little things. She closed the box and tucked it inside her bag. She pressed herself farther into the vehicle behind her.

"I have a question now," she began, surprising Tripp. She could feel her hands getting sweaty from nerves. She couldn't believe she was nervous now. "You said that you don't kiss on a first date. What about on the second?"

Tripp could feel his head begin to spin as his heart nearly beat out of his chest with what he began assuming. "Depends." He shrugged and took a step forward.

"On?"

Tripp's eyes briefly fell to Ashlyn's lips. He placed his hands on his SUV, at both sides of Ashlyn's head, enclosing her, and leaned in, so they were only a breath away. "On if this is a second date."

"Yes."

Before she could get indecisive on him, he pressed his lips to hers. Her bag slipped to the ground and her hands flew around his neck pulling him in deeper. It had been something the both of them wanted all day.

Tripp took the opportunity to deepen the kiss and it nearly sent him over the edge into oblivion. The kiss in the library was good. The one in her bedroom, even better. This kiss was something different, and he knew that without a doubt she wouldn't freak out or call it a mistake.

He pressed his chest into hers, wondering if she could feel the insanely erratic pounding of his heart.

Playfully he bit at her bottom lip and the softest of moans from Ashlyn rippled through him.

Tripp pulled back slightly, barely separating their lips, just enough to say something. "You really need to head inside."

Ashlyn shook her head and pulled him in for another deep kiss. Though she had kissed him twice before, she wasn't prepared for how it would feel again. All she knew was that she wasn't ready for it to end.

Tripp smiled and pulled back again. "If you don't go in now, I don't know if I'll be able to leave."

"And we do need him to eventually leave," Poppy shouted from the bottom of the porch steps.

Ashlyn and Tripp sprang from each other like each was acid.

"Mom!"

"I saw the vehicle pull up and I was going to ask if your *friend*, and I use that term loosely, would like to stay for dinner," Poppy mentioned quite casually.

Ashlyn couldn't speak. If you could die from embarrassment, she was certain that the coroner was on his way.

Despite being anything but calm, Tripp played it off rather nicely. He ran a hand through his hair and took a step forward. He didn't have a problem when it came to talking to adults. "Thank you for the offer Mrs. Jennings, but I need to be heading home."

Poppy smiled sweetly. "Maybe another time."

"Definitely."

Poppy blinked rapidly and started back up the stairs. With her back facing them, "Try to refrain from putting on too much of a show for the neighbors."

CHAPTER 30

"Hey, Emory," Grace cooed, not bothering to greet Ashlyn. "We have a couple questions for you."

Ashlyn closed her locker to see Melody standing next to Grace. She rolled her eyes. None of those girls cared about Emory. The only reason most girls talked to Emory was because Emory was one of the guys.

"What?"

"You go first," Grace told a brightly lit up Melody.

"So, Deacon," she began.

Emory rolled her nose up in disgust. "What about him?"

"He came to the party with your brother, and we had some nice moments. I guess I was just wondering, what's his deal? He didn't even ask for my number."

Emory sighed. "Deacon doesn't do serious relationships. He hangs out with girls but that's about it. If you think he's going to make the first move, you're mistaken."

"So, you're saying that I should ask him out," Melody asked excitedly.

"Sure. I guess." Emory shrugged.

"Okay, now me," Grace squealed.

"Are you guys serious," Ashlyn huffed.

Grace narrowed her eyes but dismissed the comment. "Tripp didn't come. I know he said he had a date, but I've asked around. No one knows of any girls that he's been out with that go to this school. Do you have the inside scoop?"

Emory glanced up to Ashlyn. Ashlyn tried to keep cool. Things with Tripp were still a little fuzzy. They liked each other, but they hadn't really established what things were between the two of them. She couldn't have a strong reaction to Grace's questioning.

"Oh, they just got here," Emory said as she nodded a few yards away. "You can ask him."

Several lockers down, Tripp and the guys stood at Ellis' locker. Maybe something had changed since Saturday. Ashlyn always thought that Tripp looked good, but as he stood there in a pair of designer dark washed jeans and a casual t-shirt tucked only slightly in the front, all she could think about was slamming him into the lockers and revisiting the end of their date that was sadly interrupted.

The four girls stared at the guys for a moment before Grace quietly whispered, "I can't do that."

"Fine." Emory rolled her eyes. "Hey, Tripp," Emory loudly called out, gaining both his attention and her brother's.

"We're standing right here! Shut up," Ellis yelled back.

Tripp laughed. "What?" Perhaps he should have walked over, but something about the group ahead made him a little doubtful.

"Grace wants to know if you're seeing anyone?"

Grace slammed her elbow into Emory, but it didn't bother Emory. She suffered worse from her brother and his friends.

"Yeah," Tripp answered calmly.

Ashlyn was anything but calm with the exchange. Surely Tripp wouldn't say something stupid.

Grace sighed and softly whispered, "Well, can you ask if it's that serious?"

Emory groaned. The only reason she was doing this in the first place was because she didn't care for Grace and if Grace wanted to be humiliated, so be it. "Is it serious," she yelled, much more loudly than needed. Ellis shot her a look of annoyance.

This time Tripp couldn't refrain from looking to Ashlyn. Even with the distance separating them, he could tell that she was holding her breath, her eyes set on his. She was probably anticipating his answer much more than Grace. "Without a doubt, absolutely."

Ashlyn dropped her gaze and she lowered her head, hoping that no one would notice the fire beaming from her cheeks. If the pounding in her chest had anything to say about it, the day was already proving to be too much.

Thankfully, Grace and Melody left, and so did the guys, leaving just Emory and Ashlyn with a few minutes before the first period bell.

Ashlyn could feel Emory's eyes on her, carefully watching like a hawk, waiting to attack. She needed to say something first.

"Do you think you should have told Melody that," Ashlyn quickly asked before Emory could mention Tripp.

Emory appeared stunned, not quite following.

"The stuff about Deacon," Ashlyn clarified.

Emory waved her hand dismissing it. "Deacon doesn't really date. She'll be lucky if she can get a movie out of him."

"Oh! There's the bell," Ashlyn exclaimed and darted off.

She could hear her friend's shouts behind her. "That was low! You know you owe me details!"

* * *

Tripp knew he should have been on the field by now, but when he heard her name mentioned at the lockers on the opposite side, he had to listen in, already knowing the sick voice behind it.

"I don't get what's the big deal," an unknown voice went on. "I mean, she's cute, but you said yourself, she's never even stayed the night at your place."

Tripp cringed when he heard that comment, but was quickly filled with relief at the realization.

"Yeah, she's a good girl. That's why I have Crystal though," Eric replied.

"Stick with her then. Don't waste your time on Ash."

"I've put too much time into Ash. Plus, she has rich parents, and her dad is a lawyer. I've got too many things looming over my head that he could–"

"Maybe if you'd stay out of trouble," the unknown voice interrupted.

"Dude. Shut up." There was a pause, and Tripp thought they might be done. "Do you know I asked her for my stuff back? You know, just stuff that I've left there over the years."

"And?"

"She hasn't given it back yet. She's sentimental and all. She's holding on to it because she knows we're going to get back together. We've had little spats, but she knows that I'm the only one who's going to love her."

The unknown person groaned. "I still can't believe you told her that!"

Eric laughed. "Girls want to hear that. I still can't believe she broke up with me after that. It's those stupid friends of hers. We have an understanding though."

Tripp didn't care to listen any further. Eric was scum. Ashlyn had to see through whatever garbage he threw at her. Just as Tripp began to quietly slip out of the locker room, Eric's last statement sent a chill down his spine.

"Don't worry. I've got a plan to get her back. It's as easy as snapping my fingers."

CHAPTER 31

"Hey, babe," Eric announced, sliding in next to Ashlyn at lunch.

She wanted to scream. Of all the times he could have talked to her, he had to do it now, when Tripp and the guys were eating lunch with them.

"I got your text last night."

Ashlyn wanted to vomit with how he said those words. All her text said was that she found all his crap and she'd be dropping it off soon.

"When are you coming by," he asked seductively, whispering in her ear.

Ashlyn scooted over, closer to Kayla. "When I get time."

The sooner she gave him his stuff back, the sooner she'd never have to speak to him again.

Ashlyn glanced up at Tripp. They hadn't been affectionate toward each other all week, at least not in public. There were times in science that he pulled her hand beneath the table just to hold for a moment, and he did go out of his way to casually walk her to some of her classes, not to raise suspicion by making a habit of it.

Now he wouldn't even look at her, and she knew why. None of her friends should have to be subjected to Eric.

Ashlyn abruptly stood. "Can we talk in the hall a moment?" Normally she'd ask him to step into the courtyard, but she didn't even want anyone seeing them from the line of windows.

"Sure thing, babe."

Tripp didn't allow himself to get jealous as they left. He knew Ashlyn, or at least he thought he did. Everything he overheard in the locker room had to be Eric's sick mind imagining that Ashlyn would be dumb enough to take him back.

The look on Ashlyn's face as she stood from the table didn't look like someone who was still smitten by her ex. It looked like someone who wanted to take an axe to her ex.

* * *

"Stop calling me that," Ashlyn poked at Eric's chest as soon as they were out of the cafeteria and away from her friends. She didn't need her friends for her to tell Eric to shove it.

"I always call you that."

"When we were dating! And you know what, I hated it," she screamed. "Look, I've got everything of yours from over the years and I'll drop it off. Then I want you to leave me and my friends alone."

"I know I haven't been the best boyfriend, but I'm going to change that."

Ashlyn wanted to pull her hair out. He was infuriating. Without thinking about repercussions, "I've moved on."

The playful and flirtatious look on Eric's face changed in an instant. Ashlyn knew that he was seeing red. She shouldn't have lost her cool and let that slip out.

"Who," Eric growled.

Feeling bold, "None of your business."

Eric gave an evil laugh and took a step forward. He reached out to touch her face but she stepped away and crossed her arms. "If it concerns you, it's my business."

They were startled by a female nearby clearing her throat.

Ashlyn looked up to see Crystal. She obviously wasn't too happy. After a moment more, and seeing the shiny piece of jewelry hanging from her neck, above an exceedingly lowcut blouse, Ashlyn knew why.

"Can we talk," Crystal spat, glaring at Eric.

"Give me a minute." When Crystal didn't leave, only purse her bright red lips, "I said give me a minute," Eric repeated.

Crystal's confidence faltered and she stomped away like a whipped puppy.

"Now, where were we," Eric sighed.

"Oh, let it go! I saw the necklace."

Eric's lips tilted on one corner in a smirk. "You didn't want it."

"Obviously, you've moved on too, so please leave me alone."

Strangely Eric didn't say anything when she walked away. It was an ominous feeling for Ashlyn. She was more than happy that Eric was with Crystal, but if that were the case, why couldn't he let her go?

* * *

"Sorry about that," Ashlyn told Tripp when she took her seat next to him in science.

"It's alright."

Ashlyn knew it wasn't, but she also didn't want to talk about Eric anymore. When Tripp went quiet, Ashlyn nervously began picking at some dried paint on her arm.

Tripp felt the need to say something. Ashlyn couldn't control a psycho's actions. "Where did all the paint come from?"

Ashlyn blushed. "I woke up early to finish my last piece."

"Ah, for the art exhibit tomorrow." Not wanting Ashlyn to think that he was bothered by lunch in the least, he took her hand and played with her fingers beneath the table. "Are you still not going to tell me about the other two."

"Nope. You don't get special privileges just because you're my boyfriend."

Ashlyn felt Tripp's hand still in hers. They hadn't used those words.

Tripp hated that she had just said that. He had planned to officially ask her out after her art exhibit that Saturday. Although, if he were being completely honest, he was far beyond a silly title when it came to feelings for Ashlyn.

Ashlyn pulled her hand from his and busied herself with getting her space set up to take notes.

"Well, you kind of ruined it now," Tripp whispered softly.

Ashlyn cringed. "I'm sorry. I know we never talked about that. It just slipped out. I don't expect–"

Tripp interrupted her by grabbing her hand and squeezing it tightly. "Ash, will you be my girlfriend?"

For a moment, Ashlyn forgot all about Eric and what might happen if she should start seeing someone new.

With a smile plastered to her face, "Absolutely."

Tripp squeezed her hand once more. He bit at his bottom lip and shook his head, letting out a deep breath. "This sucks."

"What? Why?"

"You have no idea how badly I want to kiss you now," he softly chuckled.

Little butterflies exploded in a frenzy within Ashlyn. They were in a crowded classroom, not the best time or place for those thoughts.

Ashlyn looked around to see everyone beginning to follow Mrs. Cohen's rapid notes on the whiteboard. Her back was facing the class as she began to ramble about something that Ashlyn couldn't focus on.

They were in the back of the class, and though it was risky, Ashlyn was too elated to care. Adrenaline rushed through her. She didn't allow herself to contemplate any further.

Tripp froze for a moment when Ashlyn pulled him toward her. Before he could process that her lips were on his in the middle of science class, they were gone.

"Seriously," he breathed.

Ashlyn glanced up to see the dangerous look in his eyes.

"You could have warned me. I wasn't ready," he teased.

"If I would have told you, we'd probably be on our way to Willis' office by now."

Tripp smiled and ran his hand down her arm, watching as little goosebumps appeared from his touch. "You're right, because that wasn't nearly the kiss that I had in mind."

"We're behind on the notes," Ashlyn scolded.

Tripp shrugged. "It was worth it."

CHAPTER 32

Lunch and science class had cemented a lot for Ashlyn. For starters, she needed Eric's stuff gone, immediately. Therefore, after dropping her paintings and prints off at the school that evening, she had a detour to make before going home.

"Ash," Eric's mother gasped when she opened the door. "It feels like forever since I've seen you," she said as she took a step out and embraced Ashlyn.

Even though it felt strange hugging her ex-boyfriend's mother, she went along with it. Eric's mother had plenty of problems since her washed-up rock star husband left their family for a woman half his age. She didn't deserve for Ashlyn to be cold and rude toward her.

"Is Eric home? I have a few things I need to return."

Eric's mother's smile faded. "Oh. He said the two of you were having trouble."

Ashlyn could tell that Eric's mother had probably taken some of her candy as she called it. Therefore, Ashlyn treaded lightly.

"Is he here," she repeated.

"No, sweetie. You can drop it off in his room if you'd like." She held the door open for Ashlyn to pass through. "I really do hope the two of you can work things out. You're good for him."

Before Mrs. Weaver could say another word, or heaven forbid, have a mental breakdown, Ashlyn darted towards Eric's room. She might have been good for Eric, but he wasn't good for her or to her.

Ashlyn hadn't been to Eric's house since before Christmas break. In those months, his room had changed greatly. It was a mess. Bottles and cans littered the floor. Several easily recognizable small orange bottles with white lids sat on his desk. The room smelled of smoke and just breathing the air seized at her lungs.

She tossed the two bags of junk on the unmade bed, and in that moment felt like a weight had lifted from her.

Just to feed her curiosity, she continued to glance around a moment more. Long gone were the happy pictures of them together that he kept on his nightstand. Where a frame once stood was now replaced with a tumbler, red lipstick on the empty glass. A few months ago, seeing that would have left her devastated, but now it did nothing. Even when she saw Crystal wearing the necklace Eric had gotten her for her birthday, she felt nothing. If anything, she felt free.

No longer being able to withstand the stench of smoke and other repulsive smells, Ashlyn turned to leave. Upon looking down, watching her steps through the mess, she saw it. Eric could have done a million things to try to hurt her, but seeing that piece of paper was the worst.

She grabbed the slip of paper, and swallowed heavily. *Halshire Pawn Shoppe* was in big bold letters across the top. Raymere Grove didn't have a pawn shop, but the next town over did.

Her eyes fell to the middle where the item was listed, a Mickey Mantle baseball, three hundred dollars. Then at the bottom was a signature she recognized.

She hated him. After all the rotten and demeaning things he had said to her, for some reason this affected her more than anything. He stole from her father!

Ashlyn tore out of Eric's room and through the house. She didn't know where his mother had gone, but she didn't want to stick around, only to hear his mother talk about how great they were together. Eric wasn't great. Eric wasn't even good. There was a time when she would have fought for him, stood up for him, but that was so far out of the realm of possibilities now. If she would have had to see his mother again, she would have told her what a demon her son had become.

* * *

"Daddy," Ashlyn screamed when she walked into the house.

A moment later Daniel rushed from his office. Ashlyn rarely called him *daddy* anymore. Usually it was *dad* or *ugh, what.* It only meant one thing. She was upset.

As soon as he rounded the corner, Ashlyn burst into tears.

"I'm sorry. I'm so sorry."

This was one of those parenting moments that he wasn't prepared for. "Ash, sweetie, calm down. What's wrong?"

She held up the slip of paper and Daniel took it. Ashlyn forced herself to look at him and she couldn't bear the look of disappointment that came to his face.

"I'm so sorry," she began again. "I don't know how he–"

"You have nothing to be sorry for," Daniel interrupted. "If anything, he should feel sorry for getting screwed on that price."

Ashlyn stopped crying for a moment. "Wait, what? You're not mad?"

"Oh, I'm mad. I'm livid. We invited someone into our home, only for them to steal from us. Mad is putting it mildly. However, you don't need to see me blow up right now, and above all, I need you to know that this is not your fault," he insisted.

"Yes, it is. If I never would have–"

"There are always unknowns. No matter how long we know a person, we can never truly know what they're capable of in times of desperation."

Ashlyn knew that her father would never blame it on her, but a part of her would always feel responsible. She should have let Eric throw a fit and ruin her party. She never should have let him inside.

Daniel folded the paper up and put it in his pocket. He'd call the shop and see what he could work out. He then held out his arms and wrapped them around his daughter.

"Don't cry. It's just a stupid baseball. No reason for you to have puffy eyes for your big show tomorrow," he teased.

"Ugh, dad," Ashlyn scoffed.

He wouldn't tell her, but he missed hearing *daddy*.

"It's not my show. Any art students that wanted to show their work will have it there," she continued.

Daniel shrugged. "I still like to think of it as your show."

* * *

Tripp: Not to make things awkward...

Ashlyn: When I get that for a message, it's a little scary.

Tripp: I mentioned the art show at dinner tonight.

Ashlyn: And?

Tripp: My parents are planning to check it out.

Tripp groaned as he flung back on his bed. He figured his mom would want to come. She adored Ashlyn. Never did he think his father would bother making time to tag along.

Ashlyn: So, I'm meeting your parents.

Tripp: You've already met my mom.

Ashlyn: This is different. I'd be meeting them as your girlfriend.

Tripp: I can tell them not to come!

Ashlyn: Wow. This is all so much. You're not planning on proposing, are you?

Tripp: Ha. Ha. I'm glad you think it's funny.

Ashlyn: Sorry. It's cute. I don't mind at all.

She did mind a little, but she wouldn't tell Tripp that. She was pretty sure that he was more stressed about it than she was.

She hovered over the screen, debating if she should tell him about Eric. Now wasn't the time. Everything was good between them. Besides, knowing Tripp, he'd probably be on his way to the pawn shop as soon as she told him.

Tripp: Goodnight, beautiful.

Tripp's hands shook. There was more that he wanted to add, but he wasn't that stupid. He couldn't say more in a text. It was insane that he was thinking it to begin with, but Ashlyn made him feel so much.

CHAPTER 33

Tripp went ahead of his parents to the art showing at the school's commons. The doors opened to the artists at two, but to everyone else at three. Needless to say, he was in the parking lot at 2:55.

Tripp already knew what her photography choices were, as she had sent him digital copies. He had also seen most of the ship painting; however, he had yet to have any hint on the other two, aside from the zoomed in picture of blue and black that Ashlyn sent over spring break.

When he finally got inside and scanned for the ship painting, looking for her section, he became mesmerized with just how good some of the art students were. He didn't know many of them, but they were as talented with a brush as he was with a bat.

He rounded another corner of panels that were set up as makeshift walls. He couldn't help but freeze in his tracks. He saw the small prints of the flowers surrounding the three paintings. What he didn't expect were the paintings.

Ashlyn had done a wonderful job with the details of the ship, and he loved the blending of the two different backgrounds, going from stormy skies to sunlight and birds. It was one of those that had a deeper meaning. He knew because she told him. The other two however...

He couldn't help but smile, knowing that one was painted before spring break, before anything aside from a kiss had taken place between them. This was the painting that was covered in her room that day they worked on the science project. No wonder she freaked at the idea of him seeing it.

Of all the action shots he knew she had of the baseball team, she had chosen one of him sliding into home. He hated to say it, but she almost made him look better on canvas than in real life.

He turned to the third painting and his heart began to beat faster. It was an image that would forever be stuck in his mind. Their feet were so close together on the blanket, and if he looked closely enough, it almost looked like the grass between them and the lake was blowing in the spring breeze. So that's what was captured when he heard the click of her camera.

He couldn't believe how much of him was in her work. It only cemented what he needed to tell her.

"Were you waiting at the doors to be let in," a soft voice called from behind, startling Tripp.

He spun around and his stomach dropped. She was always beautiful, but after seeing her paintings and looking at her now, she was an entirely different kind of beautiful.

Tripp uncomfortably rubbed at the back of his neck. "Wow. You look..."

"Thanks," Ashlyn quickly interrupted him, seeing as he was at a loss for words.

She wasn't dressed overly extravagant, but she was wearing a new dress and shoes with only the slightest of heels. She was already decently tall, which is why she wasn't a fan of high heels. She felt uncomfortable standing near the freshman boys who hadn't hit a growth spurt yet.

Tripp stepped forward and gave Ashlyn a side hug and a quick peck on the cheek. He didn't want to draw any attention with over-the-top gestures of public displays of affection.

They only had the shortest of conversations before Ashlyn was called away by a teacher that Tripp was unfamiliar with.

Tripp wandered about until he found the refreshment tables, as well as people his own age.

"Wow, Emory. You look nice," Tripp greeted.

She glared at him and sipped on her soda. "I wear dresses you know! I have dresses! I am a girl! Hell, I'm a cheerleader," she ranted, throwing her arms up in defeat.

Tripp's eyes widened and he quickly wondered if he was suddenly speaking a different language. "Uh..."

Deacon paused his conversation with Ellis. "I told her the same thing," Deacon huffed.

Emory snapped back to Deacon. "No. It's the way you said it."

"Fine! I won't tell you that you look good."

"Eww. Please don't," Ellis groaned.

"You know what," Emory began, waving a finger at her brother. "Shut up." She then proceeded to stomping away, grumbling something about finding girl friends.

"Did I say something wrong," Tripp asked, completely confused by Emory's behavior.

"No. She's just nuts," Ellis scoffed.

Tripp's attention immediately went to Deacon, seeing how Emory really seemed to be annoyed with him. Deacon didn't meet his gaze, only bit his lip and shook his head. That was his normal and quiet Deacon fashion.

* * *

Halfway through the exhibition, Ashlyn was ready to leave. She had barely gotten to speak with Emory, Kayla, and June. Aside from the very beginning, she didn't even see Tripp anymore. Worst of all her feet were killing her.

She was headed to the refreshment station. Her display happened to be on the way, and as she passed by, an older gentleman, in a suit, about her father's age, stopped her.

"These are yours, correct."

Ashlyn was so thirsty from talking to teachers and people that her teachers wanted her to talk to. "Yes. Did you have any questions about my work?"

"How much would you sell that one for," he asked, pointing to the one of Tripp.

That took Ashlyn by surprise. This was just a showcase for the students, nothing was expected to be sold.

It took a minute for his question to truly register to Ashlyn. "Umm...I was actually planning on giving it to a friend of mine."

The man's eyes narrowed skeptically. "A friend?"

"Yes. It's actually of him," she clarified. "He's a great guy."

"He is. Often too great to the wrong people."

Ashlyn felt the air sucked out of her. Fumbling, "You're Tripp's dad?"

The man extended a hand. "Ronan Scott."

Ashlyn nervously took it, internally cursing Tripp for not telling her that his parents had arrived.

"And you must be the girl that has taken up so much of my son's time," he assumed with a smirk.

Though he appeared to mean it in a joking way, that wasn't the vibe that Ashlyn got from him.

"Well, like I said, he's a great guy," she emphasized. "And he's been wonderful to me."

Whatever smile Ronan had quickly faded, and Ashlyn could feel his eyes scrutinizing her every word and every action.

"Yes. He's a bit naïve when it comes to choosing friends." Ronan glanced behind Ashlyn to his wife holding up a bottle of water in the distance. "If you will excuse me."

When Tripp's father left, Ashlyn felt like crumbling to the floor. He was rude. Right? Wasn't that rudeness? His words were such a surprise to her that she was still having a hard time processing.

Suddenly she didn't feel thirsty. More than anything, she felt like she needed air, and space. She didn't see anyone she knew in her vicinity, so she made a break for the outside, brushing past numerous amounts of people still coming in.

* * *

Tripp began looking everywhere for Ashlyn after realizing that his father had already met her. He specifically wanted to introduce them, but his father had to go and do it on his terms.

He ran in to Kayla along the way, but she seemed oblivious to Ashlyn's whereabouts. He saw Emory stuffing her face with hors d'oeuvres and complaining about something to June. He was tempted to ask her, but feared that he'd only get his head bitten off.

Instead, Tripp continued to go up and down the panels of artwork in the school's commons. He went to Ashlyn's first, but she hadn't been there. After looking everywhere else, he decided to check again, not knowing how much he'd regret that.

"You," Eric growled at Tripp right before Tripp had the chance to veer into a different direction.

Playing it cool, "Hey, man."

"What the hell is this about," Eric said, the volume of his voice garnering a few extra eyes.

Tripp didn't answer. He only looked to the paintings behind Eric and pretended to be in deep thought about them.

"Why is my girlfriend painting a picture of you," Eric went on.

Tripp clenched his teeth. He badly wanted to put Eric in his place, but at that moment, where they stood, wasn't the right time. He knew Eric had a colossal temper, and being the sane one of the two, his best option was to deescalate the situation and get far away from him.

Tripp narrowed his eyes at the painting that Eric was pointing to. "Is that...Huh...Number twenty-seven. Yeah, I guess that is me."

"Cut the crap Scott."

Apparently that hadn't been the best thing to say. "Look, I have no idea why she chose that photo for inspiration, but overall, I think she did a pretty good job, on all of her stuff."

Eric took a step closer. Tripp wanted to back away, but he was tired of Eric. The last thing he wanted was for Eric to think that he was afraid of him and could be easily pushed around.

"Are you messing with my girl," Eric quietly hissed.

Tripp could smell alcohol and smoke on his breath. That was just great. Not only was Eric having a mood swing, but he had the effects of alcohol on his psychotic side as well. That should have been enough to tell Tripp to shut up, but he couldn't help the words that finally fell from his lips.

"What in the world makes you think that she's yours anymore?"

He'd have to say, of all the injuries he had sustained over the years with sports, nothing could prepare him for a fist to the face.

CHAPTER 34

Ashlyn thought she felt bad when she exited the school, but she couldn't even describe how she felt when she scanned the parking lot and saw an all too familiar car that should not have been there.

She cursed under her breath and quickly headed back to the entry doors. Under no circumstances could Eric see her paintings. He would never understand.

Just as Ashlyn reached for the right-side door, the one on her left flung open and Eric stormed out. He didn't notice her at first, and though she heard a great deal of commotion inside, she let the door slip from her hand, and she ran after Eric.

"What did you do," Ashlyn screamed, causing Eric to pause halfway through the parking lot.

He whipped around and all Ashlyn saw was red. Red in his eyes. Red on his face. Worst of all, there was red, actual blood red on the knuckles of his right hand.

"Oh my god," she whispered. She covered her mouth with her hand and shook her head rapidly.

"He'll be fine," Eric growled, taking a step toward Ashlyn.

She tried to hold back her tears, but all she could think about was what happened to Tripp. "What is wrong with you?!"

"Me?! I came here to be supportive, only to find out that you've been seeing someone behind my back! So yeah, I gave him what he deserved for trying to mess with my girl."

Ashlyn blinked, trying to process his words, but she simply couldn't. "Are you nuts? Do you hear yourself?! You're seeing Crystal! We. Broke. Up."

"We never really break up," he said, his voice strangely dropping a few levels.

Off to the side, on the other end of the parking lot, several people were rushing to a car. When Ashlyn glanced over, she knew that one of those people was Tripp.

"What a wuss," Eric scoffed.

"Stop it," Ashlyn growled. "Get it through your head. We are over."

Eric took another step forward and clenched his fist.

"Do it." Her words must have caught him off guard, as his eyes widened in surprise. "Go ahead. Hit me like you hit him, because I swear, if you lay one finger on me, I'll have my dad go after you so hard. You can forget juvie!"

Eric took a step back and shook his head. Chuckling, "You know I'd never hit you."

Without so much as a pause, "No. I don't know that. I never thought you'd ruin the sign. I never thought you'd fail a drug test. I never thought you'd hit a guy over something he had no knowledge of," she stressed, referring to the painting. "And most of all, I never thought that you'd steal from my parents."

Ashlyn forced herself to watch his reaction. There wasn't one ounce of remorse on his face. All she saw in Eric's eyes was shock. He was shocked that she knew what he had done.

"I don't know–"

Ashlyn quickly interrupted him before he could deny or come up with an excuse. "I found the pawn shop receipt on your floor when I took your things over." He opened his mouth to explain. "Stop. Nothing you can say will help you."

"Look, Ashlyn," he began, feigning innocence. "I love you."

"Hearing that from you honestly makes me want to vomit."

That seemed to enrage him, as he slammed his fist on the hood of his car. There was once a time where Ashlyn was positive Eric would never think of hurting her, but that time was long gone.

"You need to leave," Ashlyn insisted, taking several steps backward.

"You're going to regret this," Eric hissed, shoving a finger in Ashlyn's face.

As Ashlyn watched Eric speed out of the parking lot, she had no doubt in her mind that if given enough time, he would end up finding a way to make her pay for it.

❋ ❋ ❋

Ashlyn glanced at her phone yet again when she pulled into her driveway. She had called and messaged Tripp numerous times to no avail. All her friends had told her was that his parents took him to the hospital in case he needed stitches.

Maybe she should have gone to the hospital and tried to find him, despite the fact that running into his dad again was downright terrifying.

As soon as Ashlyn walked through her front door, she was thankful that her mother and father had left the show early. The house smelled heavenly from whatever was coming from the kitchen.

Ashlyn expected her father to be in his office, but was pleasantly surprised to find him in the kitchen washing dishes while her mom cooked.

"Hey, sweetie," Poppy squealed when Ashlyn walked in.

"Uh...Hi. Wow. You didn't have to do all this for me. It's not like I won the Nobel Prize or anything," Ashlyn laughed.

Her mother turned to her father and mouthed something. He then turned off the running water and dried his hands on a nearby dishtowel. Poppy removed whatever was cooking from the stove.

Ashlyn was just about to ask them what was going on. For a second she thought that maybe they had heard about what happened after they left the school, but they were too happy. There was never a conversation that the three of them had about Eric where they were smiling.

"Let's go to the living room for just a second," Daniel said, nodding for Ashlyn to go ahead.

Ashlyn swallowed the lump in her throat. She seriously hoped that whatever they were about to tell her was going to be better than what she needed to tell them.

Once they were all seated, Daniel in an accent chair, and Ashlyn and her mother on the couch, Poppy handed over a bag that she had brought in with her.

Ashlyn rolled her eyes in embarrassment. "You guys didn't have to get me a gift."

Ashlyn looked at the pink bag. It wasn't too heavy. From what she knew over the years as it pertained to gifts, more than likely there was some sort of fabric inside. Neither one of her parents said anything as she carefully took the blue tissue paper from the bag.

When she reached inside, she couldn't help but softly laugh. It was a t-shirt.

She unfolded the green material and forgot how to breathe for a moment.

~~Only Child~~.
Big Sister.

"Surprise," Poppy shouted.

Ashlyn looked from her mother to her father, not fully understanding. "Are we getting a puppy?" She cringed when the words came out, fully aware how stupid that sounded, but there was no other explanation. Her parents never talked of adoption. If they were adopting a kid, it would have been something far out of left field for her.

"I hope you have that sense of humor when you're helping change diapers," Daniel chuckled.

"I'm confused..."

With an intense amount of excitement, "Ash, I'm pregnant."

Ashlyn's jaw dropped. That couldn't be possible. "How?"

Her parents looked at her skeptically. Daniel cleared his throat. "I thought you would have learned these things in–"

"Stop," Ashlyn huffed. She couldn't be bothered with jokes right now. "I thought you couldn't have kids all these years, and no offense, but you're forty."

Poppy laughed, not at all offended. "I guess a higher being thought right now was the time. I've been so busy working that I didn't even think of that as an option."

Understanding what her mother was saying, "How far are you?"

"Not quite three months."

Ashlyn immediately looked down at her mother's stomach. If she were being honest, maybe her mom looked like she had eaten a big meal. Her stomach wasn't super flat, but it wasn't growing so much that Ashlyn had noticed anything over the last two or so months.

She couldn't believe it. She was going to be a big sister.

After seeing the looks on her parents' faces and the excitement in the air, there was no way that she was going to spoil the evening telling them what happened at school after they left.

She wanted to enjoy the evening and talk about all the changes coming to their futures.

One more thing happened that night that she didn't expect. She didn't hear a single word from Tripp.

CHAPTER 35

The first thing Ashlyn did the next morning was speak with her father. She didn't want to upset her mother by telling her about Eric's insanely psychotic outburst.

While she couldn't be sure, there was already gossip going around on social media that this was the last strike for Eric. He'd be expelled indefinitely from Raymere Grove High School. Ashlyn didn't like to believe rumors. She'd have to wait until Monday to see for herself.

By the time she finished a very adult and serious conversation with her father, it was nearing ten in the morning. Tripp hadn't responded to any of her texts or calls from the day before. Rather than attempting any further, and thinking that something must be wrong, she decided to head over to his house. Chances were that someone would be home. She didn't want to downplay what happened, but she couldn't imagine that he'd still be in the hospital.

Excitement and relief rushed through Ashlyn when she heard footsteps coming to the front door; however, that quickly faded when she saw the two people upon the opening of the door.

Mr. Scott and Grace.

Grace appeared shocked to see Ashlyn standing there, and her face scrunched up in annoyance. She was just about to say something before Tripp's father interrupted her.

"Thank you again for the pie, Grace. We look forward to seeing you soon."

Ashlyn's stomach felt like someone had ripped her open and stuffed her with stones, preparing to throw her overboard into a bottomless ocean, where all she'd do is sink for all eternity.

"No problem, Ronan. I had to do something after hearing what happened. Thankfully that jerk will be gone for good now," Grace huffed, glaring at Ashlyn.

"It was a very kind gesture. I'll have Tripp get in touch with you, perhaps invite you to dinner as thanks."

"That would be wonderful," Grace squealed. "Goodbye!" She then bounded off the steps like a puppy after a new toy.

Ashlyn tried to remain optimistic, although her thoughts were interrupting her surroundings, screaming at her. *What the hell just happened?*

It was then that Ronan turned his attention to Ashlyn, and all the warmth he had when he was talking to Grace, disappeared.

Ashlyn decided to speak first. "Good morning, Ronan. I was wondering–"

"Mr. Scott, please," he interrupted her.

Ashlyn knew in that moment that she had read Tripp's father right from the start. He wasn't fond of her. She was floored as to why not. She had never met the man, and when she had first spoken to him the evening before, she was nice. At least, she thought she was nice.

Ignoring his interruption, "I was wondering if I could talk to Tripp."

"He needs his rest," Ronan said coldly.

From the looks of it, Ashlyn didn't expect for him to invite her inside, which only tore at her heart a little more. Maybe if she would have brought a pie it would have been a little different.

"I understand," Ashlyn said as sweetly as possible; however, talking to the man before her was anything but. "I just wanted to check on him and make sure he's doing okay."

"He's fine."

Ashlyn didn't know what else she could say, and she didn't want to argue with Mr. Scott. "That's good. If you could, just tell him–"

"Ash," a voice asked incredulously from behind Mr. Scott.

"She was just leaving," Mr. Scott grunted.

Tripp stepped around Ronan. "Dad, just give me a minute."

Neither said anything, simply stared at each other for a few seconds until finally Ronan nodded and went back inside, closing the door behind him.

Tripp glanced over his shoulder with uncertainty, wondering if his dad planned on listening to their conversation. Rather than find out later, he nodded to the side, motioning for Ashlyn to follow him away from the door and toward a tree on the lawn.

Ashlyn tried not to stare. It wasn't that bad. The left side of Tripp's face was a bit on the rough side, but aside from a black eye, and bandages covering a spot above his eye, he didn't look so bad.

"Why are you here," he bluntly asked, finally turning to face her.

"I wanted to see you, to see how you were."

He laughed as though her words were the dumbest thing he had heard.

Ashlyn could see in his eyes that he was cold and distant. Something was wrong between them.

"I think you should leave."

Ashlyn's eyes widened in surprise. Was she dreaming? What kind of nightmare had she stepped into? The boy before her wasn't Tripp. Tripp would never have asked her to leave so rudely.

"Tripp, I–"

"Stop, Ash. I really don't have time for it anymore." He shook his head and tried to remain cool, but on the inside there was a combination brewing that wanted to both scream and cry right now. "Your boyfriend taking a shot at me is one thing." He stepped closer and Ashlyn could see the darkness in eyes that were often so wonderfully golden. "But you, you running after him like a whipped puppy, not caring what happened to me, not–"

Ashlyn couldn't take hearing what he was saying. "First of all, I thought you were my boyfriend," she spat.

Tripp scoffed and ran a hand through his hair. "I can't be, not when you're still hung up on him."

Ashlyn desperately wanted to ask him what he was insinuating, but the idea terrified her. "Secondly, I did care about you."

"Oh, come on, Ash! Everyone saw you two in the parking lot!"

"Yeah, because I needed to say something to him," she yelled back.

"Let me guess, he came to the event to try to make things better with you, to show his support in you?" When Ashlyn didn't say anything, only drop her eyes to the ground, Tripp knew he was right. "Newsflash, I've always supported you and cared about your interests."

Ashlyn felt horrible. This wasn't at all how she imagined visiting Tripp would be like.

"I knew that I'd never see him again, and I had some things I needed to make clear."

"If that doesn't sound like some tragic love story then I don't know–"

Ashlyn was growing furious with Tripp's assumptions. "Stop it! I messaged you all evening! You couldn't even let me know how you were! I didn't know where you were, if you were okay..." She stopped. She could feel tears threatening to pour out at any moment.

Tripp's voice grew quiet. "I didn't have my phone when I was getting stitches," he said, pointing to the bandaged spot above his left eye. "When I checked this morning, I didn't have a single message from you."

Enraged, Ashlyn whipped out her phone and scrolled through a dozen unanswered messages to Tripp. She was only further hurt when he shrugged and shook his head.

"Then," she began, knowing that she was definitely about to cry like an infatuated idiot. "I come over here, only to see Grace at your house?!"

Tripp's eyes widened in anger. "Don't even!"

"Your dad invited her to dinner! In front of me!"

"I can't control my dad or Grace, just like you can't control your *boyfriend*. I don't even understand why you're so jealous, it's not like you're the one..."

Tripp's eyes widened in horror when he realized what he was about to say. He shook his head and attempted to walk away. The conversation was done.

Ashlyn was sick of him referring to Eric as her boyfriend, but decided not to go back down that road again. "I'm not the one what?"

"Nothing," Tripp quietly said as he brushed past Ashlyn.

Ashlyn softly grabbed his forearm and thankfully he turned around. "I'm not the one what," she repeated.

Tripp already thought this might be one of the last times he'd talk to Ashlyn, especially how things exploded since the beginning of her arrival. He didn't owe her anything. He definitely didn't need to say what he knew was about to come to the surface.

"You're not the one so hopelessly in love with someone to deserve to be jealous."

He watched as Ashlyn's hand fell from his arm. Her beautiful blue eyes grew in size as her mouth opened and closed, unsure what to say, and gasping for air at the same time.

He had wanted to tell her that the night before, albeit in a nicer way, but it seemed that plans never worked out between them.

"What did you...You don't mean..." She couldn't string together a sentence to save her life.

Tripp stepped closer, so that they were only a breath apart. A piece of him wanted to kiss her, while another piece wanted to never speak to her.

"Yeah, Ash," he spat. "You heard me, and I do mean that. From the moment I met you, I was interested. In the last two months, getting to know you, I've fallen for you. And it sucks."

When Ashlyn didn't say anything in response, Tripp headed back toward his front door.

By the time Ashlyn recovered from that blow, Tripp was only a few feet from his door, but she tried anyway. "Wait, can we talk?"

Tripp didn't turn to face her. As hurt and angry as he was, he knew that if he looked into those blue waves that seemed to crash into him every time he met her gaze, he'd give her anything she asked for, including a chance to explain. For once, he didn't want to hear her explanation.

"Not today, Ash. Goodbye."

He quickly slipped inside before she could say another word or before his heart could force him to change his mind.

* * *

Tripp looked over his messages with Ashlyn throughout the day. It had only been hours, and even though he was still mad about her abandoning him to *talk* to Eric, he desperately missed her.

He groaned and threw his phone aside as he fell into his bed, only to stare up at an impossibly white ceiling.

"Everything okay, son?"

Tripp shot up to see his dad standing in the doorway to his room. He had to at least pretend to be alright. His dad wasn't the one who would want to hear about feelings, especially ones that pertained to romance.

"I'm fine. Thanks."

An eerie feeling came over Tripp when he remembered something from his encounter with Ashlyn earlier in the day.

"Hey, dad?"

"Yes?"

"When I was with the doctors last night..." He needed to find a way to ask his father without making it sound accusatory, but such a way didn't come to him. "Did Ashlyn text me?"

His father narrowed his eyes in confusion.

"It's just, she said she did, and she showed me the messages on her phone." Tripp knew how bad it was starting to sound, especially given that his father held on to his belongings, while his mother came into the room with him. "I mean, I guess there might have been bad reception in there...But I have messages from other–"

Ronan couldn't take it. "Yes." He hated the pained look on Tripp's eyes ever since that girl had stopped by.

Tripp bit his lip, not fully understanding, and hoping that the conclusions he was jumping to would prove to be false. "I don't have any though."

"Tripp," Ronan sighed. "You have a good head on your shoulders. You have a lot going for you, both academically and with sports. That girl isn't worth it."

Tripp scoffed. "So, what? You deleted her messages, so I'd think..." Tripp's words drifted off when he saw his father slightly wince. He couldn't believe it. "You don't like her?"

"I don't like how you've become because of her."

"I haven't changed! My grades are still good. This is the best season I've ever played!" Tripp still couldn't believe that his father had deleted Ashlyn's messages.

"Look, you still have one more year of school. Once you get into college and start getting looked at by the major league, then you can worry about girls," Ronan sighed.

Tripp didn't bother telling his father that he had no intention of playing professional ball. As much as he loved it, over the years it had become more like a chore and less like fun.

"And by then, all those girls will only want me for fame and money," Tripp scoffed, disgusted with what his father was saying.

"I just don't think that you need to focus so much of your time on that girl right now, and–"

"Stop it," Tripp screamed. He rarely ever had heated confrontations with his father, but he was running off adrenaline. "Stop calling her *that girl*. I love *that girl*."

Ronan rubbed his temples. "You're young. There are plenty of other girls."

Another realization hit Tripp. "Is that why you invited Grace to dinner in front of Ashlyn?"

"The opportunity presented itself," Ronan said with a shrug.

Tripp knew that it was going to take a long time to forgive his dad for the boundaries that he had overstepped.

Worst of all, he was still torn about Ashlyn. His father didn't make her run after Eric; however, it wasn't as though she had completely written him off either. She did try to get in touch with him.

His head was such a mess. He didn't know what to think or who to believe anymore. His head still hurt from the blows he had taken from Eric, that was more than enough for the day.

CHAPTER 36

As expected in high school, by Monday morning, rumors were swirling.

Ashlyn was at least thankful that Eric would be gone from her life, for good, or she hoped. With his immediate expulsion, she felt she could finally walk the school without looking over her shoulder, wondering which one of her friends he'd go after next.

"Thanks a lot, loser," Rachel hissed at Ashlyn that morning in front of her locker.

"Good morning to you too," Ashlyn grumbled back.

Rachel flipped her hair. "Our baseball team was doing so well, much better than our football team in the fall."

Ashlyn sighed and rolled her eyes, wondering if Rachel had a point. Up until now Rachel had been annoying, but never quite so hostile in her demeanor.

"Now, thanks to you, and that trash you call a boyfriend...Ugh...Thank goodness he's expelled. Anyway, I heard Tripp also took a beating, and I don't mean the one from Eric."

Not following, "What are you talking about?"

"Hello! Do you see him here?"

Ashlyn glanced around. It was still early. First period hadn't even started.

"He's been suspended. There's no telling how many games he'll have to miss," Rachel blabbered.

"Where did you hear that," Ashlyn asked cautiously. There was no way that Tripp would be suspended. He was the one attacked; he never even fought back.

Rachel waved her hand as if it was common knowledge. "And all because of you. I knew there was someone else, but you?" Rachel shook her head. "I thought we were friends. I can't believe you went behind my back and stole my boyfriend."

Ashlyn was seconds away from slamming her head into her own locker. Rachel was over the top dramatic and it was too early in the morning.

While Ashlyn didn't want to believe what Rachel told her that morning, she became a little anxious when she didn't see Tripp at lunch.

Emory couldn't help but take notice.

"He's not here."

That got Ashlyn's attention. "Where is he?"

Emory shrugged. "No clue. I guess at home."

"Is he suspended," Ashlyn immediately asked. That had been the rumor she heard in every single class so far.

"I honestly don't know. I get most of my information from Deacon, but ever since he started dating Melody," Emory huffed, and tipped her head in the direction of Deacon and Melody at a table with several others. "He's been a total jerk to me," she concluded.

Ashlyn bit her lip in frustration. Of all people, Deacon or Ellis would know the truth. Considering that Ellis was with Abby, right across from Rachel, Ashlyn took her chances with the gruff and quiet Deacon.

"Deacon," Ashlyn began, announcing her presence. Once he turned to face her, "Can I talk to you a minute?"

"Oh, I guess you want to steal my boyfriend too," Melody snapped.

Ashlyn pinched the bridge of her nose. Generally Melody was somewhat pleasant, but it seemed that recent events had everyone stirred up.

Ignoring Melody, "I just need to ask you about Tripp."

Deacon's eyes narrowed in suspicion. Ashlyn also knew this to mean for her to continue.

"Is he suspended? Will he get to play tomorrow?"

Ashlyn was extremely concerned about the game. She honestly didn't care if they won or lost, but she had heard through the grapevine, that was the hallways of the school, that scouts would be present. Without a doubt, Tripp had to play.

Despite knowing that he himself was playing a dangerous one, Deacon wasn't much for games. As much as he liked Ashlyn, he knew that she made things hard on Tripp. He didn't want to stir the pot of high school drama, but that didn't mean he needed to tell Ashlyn everything he knew.

"You don't see him here, do you," Deacon asked, avoiding both of her questions.

Ashlyn felt the panic running through her. She hoped that she could make things right with Tripp, but she couldn't imagine how angry he'd be with suspension and not playing, especially in front of scouts.

Awkwardness ensued as Deacon watched Ashlyn think quietly to herself. After a few more moments, her eyes widened as if a lightbulb went off.

"Thanks, Deacon," was all she said before rushing from the cafeteria.

Deacon wasn't exactly sure what just happened, but something told him that Ashlyn was probably going to do something stupid.

Melody nudged him, getting his attention.

"What?"

"You'd never leave me for another girl, right," Melody asked with the softest and yet most insecure voice.

"No," Deacon quickly answered.

He knew dating Melody was going to turn out to be a disaster. After only one week, she was insanely clingy and possessive.

* * *

Ashlyn couldn't believe how the tables had turned, and an eerie sense of déjà vu came over her as she headed to Principal Willis. She smiled as she remembered that it was this same path that led her to meet Tripp.

There was a difference now. Now she knew where her loyalties were.

"Hi, Miss Dora," Ashlyn sweetly greeted the woman at the office desk.

Dora eyed her, already knowing that the girl before her had a problem. She always had a problem when she came by.

"He's busy."

Ashlyn grit her teeth. "I understand, but this is important."

"Isn't it always," she scoffed.

"I'll only be a minute. I swear," Ashlyn pleaded.

Dora sighed and shook her head. Before she could protest any further, Ashlyn darted around the desk to Principal Willis' door.

"Come in," Principal Willis groaned upon hearing the incessant rapping at his door. When he saw the girl who walked through, "Ah, Miss Jennings. If you're here for why I think you're here, let me save you the trouble."

"You don't understand Principal Willis," Ashlyn stressed. "I know what happened at the art showing was inexcusable, but you have to understand–"

"Expulsion was the only option after that. I'm sorry. Our school holds a much stricter policy when it comes to fighting."

Ashlyn's jaw dropped. She could feel tears coming to her eyes. It was worse than she thought. Above all, it was her fault.

"Please, it wasn't his fault. You cannot expel him. He didn't even fight back. He knew the consequences. He's a great student, and more than anything he deserves to get to play tomorrow. He was only there because of me and–"

Principal Willis held up his hand, abruptly silencing Ashlyn. He scratched at his brow with his forefinger and a small grin made its way to his face.

"I think I'm a little confused as to who *he* is," Willis ventured.

"Tripp. Tripp Scott."

Principal Willis let out a deep and hearty laugh, completely shocking Ashlyn. Why was that funny? If anything, she thought it was quite rude.

"Miss Jennings," he began. He put his elbows on his desk and folded his hands together. "I'm recalling a similar conversation a couple months ago, so you can see my confusion."

Ashlyn could feel her cheeks heating.

"I take it you're not here to protest Mr. Weaver's expulsion from the school?"

All Ashlyn could do was shake her head, suddenly feeling her throat close up.

"Let me shut down the rumor mill at this school. Whenever I have to make a decision terminating a student's place here, you can be certain that I do my due diligence. I'm well-aware as to who the aggressor was, which is why Mr. Weaver, and Mr. Weaver alone, is no longer at this school."

"But...I don't understand. Is Tripp still suspended?"

"If you're such good friends with him, perhaps you should have gone to him first, before storming in here," Principal Willis said, raising his brow suspiciously.

That cut Ashlyn a little. She should have, but Tripp hadn't said a word to her since he told her to leave. Though that had only been a little over a day, that said a lot when it came to Tripp.

Principal Willis continued. "Tripp Scott is not expelled or suspended. He's probably not here today because he might have just needed a day away from here. More so, as long as he is present at school tomorrow, know that he will be playing in the game tomorrow," Principal Willis concluded with a smirk.

When Ashlyn closed the door to the main office and made her way down the hallway, she couldn't help but laugh at how ridiculous she must have seemed to Principal Willis. There was no doubt in her mind that her friends would explode in laughter when she told them that one.

She took a deep breath filled with relief. Everything with Tripp was fine, not necessarily between the two of them, but at least he hadn't gotten in any trouble.

She flipped her phone in her hands over and over as she went in the direction of her next period class, the one she shared with Tripp. She wanted so badly to message him, but what she had no idea.

After everything, she had to be the one to pursue him. That she knew.

Ashlyn nearly jumped out of her seat, the biggest grin in the world spreading across her face as Mrs. Cohen announced the next upcoming project. A few nearby students took notice and gave her menacing looks.

Was she excited about a project, definitely not; however, this gave her the perfect opportunity to talk to Tripp rather than having to wait another day, and as soon as the bell rang, that's exactly what she did.

Ashlyn: Mrs. Cohen just assigned another project.

Tripp debated how to respond. When he saw Ashlyn's name come across his screen, his gut churned. A part of him was still hurt. Another part was now embarrassed, both by not giving her the chance to explain and also by vomiting out that he loved her.

He waited at least ten minutes before replying, knowing she'd be in her next class by then, and hopefully unable to continue this meaningless conversation.

Tripp: Individual or partners?

Apparently Ashlyn had ample opportunity to text in her next class, as a text came back within minutes.

Ashlyn: Partners.

Ashlyn's heart sank when she read Tripp's next message. All it said was one word. *Great.*

She could sense his sarcasm through text. If he were excited about working with her, there would have been more, at least an exclamation mark. She could picture him rolling his eyes and tossing the phone as she read that.

* * *

Tripp groaned and tossed his phone to the side as he fell on the bed. Normally he'd be ecstatic for any moment he got with Ashlyn, but not how things now stood.

CHAPTER 37

"I still can't believe your mom is pregnant," Kayla gasped.

Ashlyn hadn't gotten the opportunity to share the wonderful news with her friends, especially given recent events. Also, she wanted to make sure it was alright with her mother before she blabbed.

"No offense," June hesitated. "But isn't she a little old?"

Ashlyn shrugged and spoke through a mouthful of pizza. "I mean, she's about to be forty-one, so..."

"Your mom is good," Emory began. "I mean, Janet Jackson was like fifty when she had a kid."

June gasped. "At that rate, your mom could have like four or–"

Ashlyn began choking on her pizza. "Let's just stick with the one for now."

Her friends continued to talk about their excitement for her. Apparently it was much more fun getting a sibling at their age as opposed to if they were toddlers.

Ashlyn looked up and watched as Tripp sat quietly at one of the jock tables eating his lunch. She would have given anything for him to look up, but that didn't seem to be in the cards. As giggles and happiness continued on around her, she wanted nothing more than to share the news with Tripp; however, that wasn't going to be done by text.

She had resigned herself to the fact that he was mad, or hurt, or a combination of emotions when it came to her, and though he was curt in his texts the day prior, she knew that she couldn't give up.

Tripp wasn't like Eric. She hated how long it took her to figure out that he was different, different in the best ways.

* * *

"I can't believe you followed me," Ashlyn shrieked from the bathroom stall.

"And I can't believe you're skipping class," Emory huffed back.

"I just can't do it. I can't sit next to him and–"

"Then maybe you should have, oh, I don't know...Talked to him sooner!"

"I tried!"

Emory scoffed. "Both of you are being ridiculous, all over stupid misunderstandings."

"Well, those misunderstandings were enough to put us where we are now," Ashlyn pointed out.

"Which is completely and totally in love with each other," Emory cooed.

Ashlyn looked up to her stall's door and shrieked when she saw a bright blue eye peeking through the crack. "I could be peeing, you know!"

"Look, I'm already late to class. Are you seriously going to sit in here for the next forty minutes," Emory asked, growing mildly annoyed at what she thought to be childish behavior.

"Please. Just today. Just let me do this today," Ashlyn sighed.

"You'll be at the game tonight, yeah?"

Ashlyn's face clenched up. The thought of watching Tripp in his element both made her heart race as well as her stomach sick to the core.

"Yeah. I'll be there."

* * *

Tripp: I hope you're enjoying ditching class.

Ashlyn's heart pounded when halfway through a sketch, while trying to make herself comfortable on a toilet, she saw the name flash across the screen. She couldn't believe Tripp was reaching out. Regardless what he had to say, at least he was saying something.

Ashlyn: I wasn't feeling well.

Tripp: You seemed fine at lunch.

Tripp should have been paying attention to Mrs. Cohen, especially after resting at home the day before, and now with a new project just beginning; however, Ashlyn's next text triggered something in him.

He didn't know how to perceive it, whether it was hurt or anger, or something else entirely.

Ashlyn: I'm surprised you noticed.

He could have screamed. He always noticed. Just because he needed space and time to think didn't mean he didn't notice everything about her.

He wasn't about to take the bait, so instead, he veered away from how he wanted to answer.

Tripp: Guess you won't be at the game if you're sick. Wonder who they'll get to cover it for the paper.

Ashlyn's thoughts immediately went to Grace. She knew that Tripp wasn't interested in Grace, or at least he wasn't that day on his lawn. After the cold-ness between the two of them in the last two days, she couldn't be sure if Tripp had given up on her and decided to cut his losses and move on. She hated the jealousy that ran through her at those thoughts.

She hit at her screen harder than necessary.

Ashlyn: I'll be there. Can we meet up after?

Tripp: I don't know if that's a good idea.

Ashlyn dropped her phone inside her bag and quickly tore at the toilet paper on the side of the stall, managing to get enough to cover her face before the tears fell.

Of all the times she cried over the stupid fights with Eric, none of those felt like how she felt now. Though a tiny part of her wanted to give up, a bigger part, a much bigger part, knew that what Tripp said to her that day about his feelings, it wasn't one-sided.

* * *

"Hey, you ready," Deacon asked, as Tripp fiddled with his laces.

Tripp sighed. "I don't know. I'm just not feeling it tonight."

Deacon sat on the locker room bench near Tripp. Most of the players had started to dwindle out of the locker room to the dugout. He rubbed the back of his neck. Though he wasn't big on talking, he'd make a bit of an exception.

"Ellis told me that Ash is here to–"

"Stop," Tripp interrupted him. "That's not helping any."

"Ugh. I can't believe I'm talking about this crap," Deacon groaned.

Tripp turned to Deacon with narrowed eyes. Suddenly Deacon looked uncomfortable and sick.

"Look," Deacon began with a heavy sigh. "I don't know what's going to happen between you two, and now that I see how the both of you are, I get why she never told you this."

"Told me what," Tripp quickly asked. His eyes were now wide with anticipation.

"Eric was a manipulative jerk to her. He even tried to get her to stop being friends with Emory, because of a few stupid comments she made. I guess Ash really liked you and she didn't want you to have to deal with him."

Tripp shook his head, not fully understanding, knowing that Deacon was leaving out a chunk of the story. "I don't get what any of that–"

"Eric thought that Ash broke up with him to be with somebody else. He threatened her, well, not so much her, but he told her that if he ever saw her with another guy…" Deacon's words drifted off, hoping that Tripp understood.

"That this would happen," Tripp finished as he motioned over his face.

Deacon nodded.

"So that's why she pushed me away for so long."

Deacon snapped his fingers remembering something. "Oh, and the thing with Eric Saturday? She found out that he stole some baseball from her father, and she wanted to confront him about that. I mean, I know that doesn't make up for not being there for–"

"It's forgotten," Tripp interrupted, still trying to process everything.

More than anything, he was hurt. He didn't understand why Ashlyn couldn't have told him all of that herself. It seemed so small now.

"Anyway, I don't do this," Deacon grumbled, motioning from himself to Tripp. "That's all I got."

After putting all that information in a file to go over after the game, "Curious, where did you get all that?"

Deacon rolled his eyes and his cheeks turned a little red. "Ash told Emory. Emory told Ellis. Ellis told me."

"I'm surprised Emory didn't just tell you," Tripp scoffed.

"We're not talking lately. Ever since she started dating some dude from Halshire, she's been a pain." Deacon stood and cracked his neck. His annoyed face softened. "Ready?"

Tripp was just about to ask another question but decided against it. That was hands down the most Deacon had ever spoken to him. It was probably his quota for the month, so Tripp decided not to push it.

CHAPTER 38

"I can't even watch this anymore," Ellis groaned as the bottom of the third inning started and Tripp took his first strike.

"Then don't," Emory spat. "Go see Abby and stop your complaining."

"He's just so bad today."

Ashlyn's eyebrows were clenched together, and she bit at her bottom lip. Tripp had never played like this before. Even in the distance, the little she could see of his face, she knew something was off. That playful look in his eyes and that cocky grin was replaced with a mix of confusion and seriousness that she couldn't recall ever seeing on Tripp's face.

Ashlyn's eyes fell to the rows of stands in front of her as a gruff voice called a second strike. She recognized so many people at the game. The one person she was thankful hadn't noticed her was Tripp's dad. He was buried away on his phone, completely ignoring the game.

A couple rows away, she caught several girls, Grace amongst them, glaring at her. She wanted to jump up and scream. She wasn't the one out on the field. She wasn't the one at bat.

She wasn't sure what surged through her when she heard a third strike called, but she immediately rose from her place between Emory and Kayla and rushed down the stands toward the sidewalk that ran along the fence to the field.

Ashlyn didn't know what she was going to say to Tripp at that moment. She hadn't even planned on what she would say if or when they met after the game. All she did know was that she had a sick feeling that if she didn't see him and say something now, he was going to blow a rather important game.

Once Tripp made his way near her, heading back toward the entry to the dugout, Ashlyn began hollering his name, pressing herself as close to the fence as possible.

Tripp glanced in the distance toward the stands, but before his eyes got there, they landed on Ashlyn standing at the fence surrounding the field, her hands clasped in the large wires. He quickly brought his attention toward his coach, who gave him a very displeased look, but nodded for him to take care of whatever it was.

Hesitantly, with nerves finding their way into his throat, Tripp jogged off the field.

"What are you doing," he growled once he was a couple feet away from Ashlyn. He now slowed his steps, unsure how close he wanted to get. It was the first time he had really gotten to see her and talk to her in days.

"More importantly, what are you doing out there?"

Tripp took off his helmet and ran a hand through his blonde hair, which now appeared much darker with sweat. Trying not to come across as too hostile, Tripp simply shrugged. With an expressionless face, "Don't worry about me."

"But I do," Ashlyn stressed.

Tripp met her eyes and he could see the sincerity in those gorgeous blue eyes he had fallen so hard for. He had wanted space, some more time, to just be annoyed with her for a little longer. Then Deacon had to unload all of that on him right before the game, and now here she was, as close to him as she could get at the moment.

A playful glimmer came to Ashlyn's eyes when Tripp didn't tell her to get lost or walk away himself. "Remember in the hall when you wanted to make a bet?"

Tripp narrowed his eyes and softly bit at his bottom lip.

When he didn't answer her, "Do you remember that conversation?"

"I remember every conversation with you," he answered a little too quickly.

In the pit of her stomach, Ashlyn felt something which might be dangerously close to hope, the hope that things could be repaired.

"I accept. Only, with the way you're playing, it doesn't even have to be a home run, just get a hit! For every hit–"

Attempting to make her sweat a little, Tripp interrupted her. "Now who's the overconfident one. What makes you think I still want that?" He took a few steps closer to the fence separating them. "I don't know what you're trying to do, but–"

"I'm trying to make you happy!"

Narrowing his eyes at her once again, "Why do you care if I'm happy, Ash?"

She wasn't prepared for what she was about to say, but it slipped out so easily, to the point that she surprised even herself. "Because I love you." When Tripp's eyes widened and his mouth went slightly agape, Ashlyn knew that she couldn't let those words linger for long. "And...And I care about this game for you...I know...It's important. With the scouts and all...And–"

"Stop." Tripp took a step or two more toward her and he covered one of her hands that was linked in the fence with his. He leaned in so that the only thing more than a breath separating them was the wires of the fence. "You can *bet* that we're definitely going to talk after the game."

Tripp squeezed at her hand for just a split second before pushing off and turning from her, heading back to the dugout.

Ashlyn stood there for a moment, mesmerized by the intensity that was written across Tripp's face when he said that. Her stomach flipped and she thought she might pass out from his touch that still lingered across her fingers.

Then a realization hit her. She had just told a boy that she loved him.

Somewhere between then and the end of the fifth inning, Tripp must have found himself, and was back with a vengeance. At the end of the second, they were losing four to one. Now both teams were tied at five to five; however, Tripp couldn't take all of that credit. He had only gotten one tremendously good hit, enough to bring two players in, but it was Byron who got a home run shortly after.

"What happened to you," Deacon scoffed as they began to take the field for the beginning of the sixth.

"What do you mean," Tripp asked, with a slight smile that seemed to never leave him now.

"You look like you've just chugged a barrel of coffee."

Tripp laughed and headed in the direction of first base as Deacon made his way into the outfield. "I'm just...happy," he replied with a shrug.

He couldn't believe how pathetic he was, but seeing Ashlyn, hearing those words, it did something to him. All his frustrations, with her, his father, worrying about the scouts, none of it seemed to matter. Knowing that Ashlyn had never told her boyfriend of two years that, but could tell him after only knowing him for two months, that made him believe that anything was possible, and any of his worries faded at that point.

At the bottom of the sixth, Tripp took his place on the field. Louis, a senior, had just gotten an out, after failing to make it to first; however, Deacon on third had made it in.

After messing up badly at the beginning, Tripp had watched the opponent's pitching techniques intently. While it was absolutely impossible for anyone to get a home run every time they went up to bat, he was more certain than ever that he could get a good hit, especially if he decided to be the one throwing a curveball.

* * *

"What is he doing," Ellis gasped, rubbing at the back of his neck.

Ashlyn was equally confused as Tripp took his place at bat, on the other side of home plate. Was he confused? He always batted right.

Emory choked on her soda. "Are you kidding me right now? How long was he waiting to show this off?"

Ashlyn and Tripp rarely talked about baseball. She knew what was in his repertoire based on what she had seen at games. While it wasn't completely uncommon, she was pretty sure that no one on their team was a switch hitter. Looking farther onto the field, she could tell that the pitcher was equally confused.

Despite how he played at first, the opposing team now knew he could not only hit a ball, he could bat either way.

Ashlyn couldn't imagine what would make Tripp suddenly switch now. It had to have been something he saw in the pitching, something telling him that he'd have a better shot this way.

When the ball and bat collided in a familiar clank, she held her breath. Waiting. She shook her head and cursed under her breath as the biggest smile came to her face.

Emory jumped and screamed and sloshed soda all over Ellis, despite knowing that there was still more than an inning left.

"What is wrong with you? You're such a Neanderthal," Ellis scoffed, wiping shards of ice off his wet and sticky jeans.

"Oh, shut up, Ellis!"

Screaming ensued around them as the announcer on the speaker yelled out that it was another home run for Raymere Grove.

They would end up winning nine to six by the end of the seventh inning.

CHAPTER 39

As everyone in the stands began rushing out, Ashlyn held back, allowing the crowd to pass, knowing that she needed to see Tripp anyway. Immediately after their win, most of the guys, knowing they'd be going to celebratory dinners, scurried away to the locker room to quickly clean up and change. Tripp was one of them.

"I wonder if that's one of the scouts," Kayla nodded, as she grabbed her purse and stood, finally getting the chance to stretch.

Ashlyn looked in the direction Kayla had motioned toward, only to see Tripp's father shaking hands with a man in dress pants and a polo shirt with an emblem Ashlyn recognized well. Cartwright University.

It was the best university in the state, and not too far away. Most of the students who were lucky enough to get in, or lucky enough to afford it, were able to visit home on the weekends. When Ashlyn interviewed Kyler West, that's what he said one of his biggest reasons for accepting was, despite having full rides to several universities across the country.

"You good," Emory asked before leaving.

Ashlyn nodded. There were still several people lingering about the stands. She knew that if Mr. Scott was present, chances were that Tripp would be around soon.

Another ten minutes passed, and when Ashlyn's phone dinged, she nearly dropped the thing with how quickly she reached for it.

Tripp: Where are you?

Ashlyn: The bleachers.

Tripp couldn't get out of the field house fast enough, so much so, that he wasn't even sure if he had gotten all of the bodywash off his skin.

There were several groups of adults lingering around the stands and field, probably parents waiting to take their sons to a late dinner. Once Tripp saw Ashlyn, halfway up the stands, all those other bodies faded. His heart raced more than ever before as he neared her.

"Son," a voice called from nearby, startling Tripp.

He looked over to see his father talking with some older man he didn't know.

"Hey, dad."

"There's someone I'd like for you to meet," Ronan began, motioning toward the man with him.

Tripp wasn't sure how long that would take. Seeing the look on his father's face, he could easily assume that he'd have to stand there and say more than a couple pleasantries.

"Yeah, sure." Tripp glanced up to where Ashlyn was now standing, grabbing her bag and camera. "Just give me a second."

Ronan's eyes went to where his son's had, and his pleased face went dark. "Tripp," was all he said, but it was the way he said it that put the slightest bit of fear in Tripp.

Normally Tripp would have done whatever his father wanted at the snap of his fingers. "Dad," he began, trying to remain polite in front of the stranger. "This will only take a few seconds."

"See to it that it does."

Without another glance to his dad, Tripp rushed down the sidewalk and up the closest aisle leading to Ashlyn, who was already coming out of her row to the stairs.

"Hey," he greeted, slowing his steps to a more cautious pace the closer they got to each other.

Ashlyn glanced to Tripp's father. Although he was talking with the man from Cartwright, he appeared to be staring daggers at her.

Without saying the smallest of greetings, "I think your dad is waiting on you."

"So," Tripp said, taking one more step so that only a single stair separated them. He then leaned into the railing running down the aisle.

"We can talk another time," Ashlyn stressed.

Tripp chuckled. Ashlyn knew that one well; it was laced with something that didn't resemble humor. "Oh, Ash," he sighed, shaking his head. He then met her gaze, forcing their eyes to lock together. "If you think you're getting off that easily, you're mistaken." Before she could protest, "I only came here to ask you to wait a little longer. Then maybe we could go out to eat?"

"But what about–"

"Great," Tripp exclaimed, turning from her and rushing back down the stairs. "Be right back."

There was no way that he was going to give her the chance to leave without talking to him, not after what she said.

Tripp's elation took a nosedive the closer he got to his father. The man wasn't pleased. Tripp let out a breath of frustration. It was every bit of two minutes.

Without so much as another word with his son, Ronan rushed into introductions. "Tripp, this is Mr. Granger from Cartwright University. Mr. Granger, this is my son, Tripp Scott."

The man held out his hand and Tripp took it firmly, noting how the corners of the man's mouth tipped up as he did so.

"Nice to meet you," Tripp said, wanting to beat Mr. Granger to the inevitable response.

"It's a pleasure. You boys played quite well."

Trying his best not to mumble with the uncomfortable feeling in the air, "Thank you."

"I must say, at first, when I saw you, I was sure I was watching a different Scott than the one I've heard so much praise about."

Tripp could feel his face heating at the remark. "I guess nerves got the best of me." He laughed and gave a playful shrug.

A quick glance to his father and he knew that he didn't share the same thoughts. It was short, but he could see his father's eyes dart behind him to where Ashlyn was sitting up in the bleachers.

They continued to talk for what seemed like an eternity, but it wasn't until Tripp saw Ashlyn walking down a nearby sidewalk out of the main gates, that a feeling of dread and anxiety hit Tripp.

"Anyway," Ronan began. Tripp couldn't help but notice that his father's face held a much happier expression since when he first walked up. "Mr. Granger has agreed to go out to a late dinner with us. Isn't that nice?"

Tripp's eyes widened as he looked from his dad to Mr. Granger. He wasn't sure what the look on his face was projecting, but suddenly his father didn't appear too pleased.

"Oh, it's no big deal," Mr. Granger said, and Tripp tried his best not to let the relief show too much. "I'm sure the boy has plans of his own after a win like that."

Tripp's eyes met Mr. Granger's and he saw the twinkle in them.

"Nonsense. He has time so that we can talk more," Ronan insisted.

Mr. Granger glanced from father to son, picking up on something. He waved Ronan off. "It is late, and I have quite a bit of a drive." Then, turning to Tripp, "We'll be in touch."

Tripp felt a sinking and ominous feeling as Mr. Granger said goodbye and strode away. It wasn't until he was well out of earshot that Tripp knew why that feeling was there.

"What the hell do you think you're doing," Ronan spat.

Tripp had no intention of fighting with his dad. He was having the best ending to a day that hadn't started out as such. So he did what he always did, and played it off, trying to deescalate with joking or playing dumb. It was a mechanism he had begun using early on when he disappointed his dad.

"He said he'd be in touch," Tripp shrugged, pretending not to follow.

The red in Ronan's eyes told Tripp that he wasn't going to get off easy tonight.

"That man holds your future. You should have taken the opportunity to–"

What his father said hit him hard and he was quick to interrupt. "I thought I held my future."

Ronan scoffed and ignored the statement. "Is this because of that girl?"

Tripp really hated that his father kept referring to Ashlyn like that. Knowing that he was about to hit a nerve, "Yeah, I have dinner plans with her."

Ronan's jaw ticked. "No, you don't."

Tripp honestly didn't know at the moment, seeing as how Ashlyn had left. "Dad," he began, rubbing a hand over his face. "She's my girlfriend, and I really like her."

"She's a distraction! You played horrible, no doubt because–"

Raising his voice slightly, "You mean when I got a home run batting left-handed?"

Ronan scoffed. "You should have had five home runs blindfolded."

Tripp shook his head. There was no point in arguing with his dad when he was like this. "I'm not a superhero. I wish you'd stop acting like I can be."

"You can do so much better. Both on the field and in your personal life," Ronan stressed.

At least his anger was calming down to extreme disappointment.

Tripp knew why his father didn't necessarily approve of Ashlyn. It was simple and ridiculous. Aside from her being what he considered a distraction, he thought her choice of hobbies was ridiculous. While Tripp's mother told him that his father had been impressed with Ashlyn's work, overall art was a waste of time, and her pursuing it said a lot about her character. Whatever that meant.

"I like her, dad. She takes me down a notch," Tripp said, a small smile forming on his lips. "She doesn't make me feel like I'm something special just because I can play a sport."

"Tripp..."

"Please, dad. Don't give me an ultimatum."

Ronan grit his teeth and began storming out, headed toward a closer exit than the one Ashlyn had taken.

"Curfew is eleven tonight," he yelled. His voice was probably loud enough that anyone still in the field house heard him.

CHAPTER 40

Tripp was shocked when he rushed out of the exit Ashlyn had used and found her sitting quietly on a bench underneath one of the streetlights.

"I thought you left," he said. He immediately cringed with how panicked his voice sounded.

Ashlyn stood and walked toward Tripp, only for him to nod to his right, for them to continue walking in that direction.

"I thought about it. I'm kidding," she immediately corrected when she heard Tripp take a deep breath. "Honestly, every time I looked up, it seemed like your dad wanted to rip off my head. I just thought it would be best to be out of sight."

Tripp raked his hand through his hair. He had no intention of telling her anything about the conversation he just had with his dad. His dad was being an idiot when it came to Ashlyn; however, Tripp knew it wouldn't just be Ashlyn. If anyone took even the slightest bit of time away from his studies or baseball, they were seen as a problem in his father's eyes.

Ashlyn knew Tripp was struggling to say something when it came to his father, so she quickly changed the subject. "So, a scout from Cartwright. That's pretty impressive."

"I guess so."

Tripp had grown increasingly quiet compared to the confident boy that told her to wait for him. They were just about at his vehicle and they hadn't really spoken about anything of any real substance.

"Look, Ash," Tripp sighed.

Ashlyn swallowed heavily, wondering if this was going to be the ultimate break between them, wondering if his father really had gotten into his head enough.

"I don't want to talk about any of that right now."

When Ashlyn looked up in surprise and met his eyes, even in the darkness with just the parking lot lights shining above them, she could she the glittery playfulness that was Tripp Scott. Then he hit her with a ton of bricks.

"I can't say that I'm not disappointed." When Ashlyn's jaw dropped and she said nothing, Tripp continued. "Deacon told me everything. I mean, it's not so unbelievable. I just wish you would have told me the reason you didn't want to get involved with me. It would have saved us from a lot of back and forth and misconceptions."

"If I would have told you that there was a chance that my crazy ex-boyfriend might beat you up, would you have still pursued me?"

"Yes," Tripp quickly answered.

"Then, we're back to the same place had I not said anything," Ashlyn pointed out.

"But I wouldn't have thought that you were still into him, possibly going back and forth with your emotions. It would have made a difference."

They both leaned against the Mercedes-Benz, their shoulders almost touching.

"We could have just dated in secret." Then, after thinking about if for a second, "I guess that's what we kind of did anyway."

Though Ashlyn could hear the humor in his voice, she didn't see it that way. "You deserve so much better."

Tripp tilted his head so that his eyes were on her. "So do you."

Ashlyn shook her head. "You know what I mean. I've been unfair to you. I'm so sorry for all this," she motioned her hands around, her words not coming to her. "Mess," she concluded.

"It was worth it."

"How so?"

Before Ashlyn could think another thought, Tripp pushed off and turned toward her. He placed both his hands on the side of the roof of the vehicle and pressed himself into her. Ashlyn's sense of smell was taken over by Tripp's cologne, and she thought she might fall into a drunken stupor by how intoxicating it was.

"Hearing you say what you did."

Ashlyn's eyes fell, and she could feel her cheeks burning. She had wondered how long it would be before he jumped to that little confession.

"Did you mean it," he asked. His voice was more strained and gravely than she had ever heard.

Ashlyn brought her eyes up to his and the intensity behind them was overwhelming. "Yes," she managed.

Before another word came from either of them, Tripp's lips crashed onto Ashlyn's and he pushed her farther into the vehicle, the cool exterior doing little to extinguish the fires building between them.

Tripp let out the slightest moan but pulled back before things escalated too far. He still fully intended to take Ashlyn to dinner, and if he didn't show some restraint, that wasn't going to happen.

Once their lips parted, Tripp pressed his forehead to Ashlyn's, their noses almost touching. "After all, I did get a home run," he pointed out, attempting to justify the kiss, yet knowing it needed no justification.

Ashlyn playfully swatted at him. "It would kill you to be serious."

Tripp's smile quickly faded, and with one hand still pressed behind Ashlyn, he took the other and intertwined their fingers together, knowing that the sharp breath of air Ashlyn sucked in meant that she felt it too.

"Can I take you out to dinner?"

Ashlyn wasn't sure why it seemed like a big deal to him. He had said as much when he met her on the bleachers. "Yeah, sure."

Tripp shook his head. "I mean really. Not eating inside a car, not a town over, not some secluded lake, not–"

Ashlyn felt the need to interrupt. "The lake was really nice." It was probably the nicest date she had ever been on.

Tripp's boyish grin graced his face immediately. "What I'm saying is, right now, out in public, where a hundred different people might see us, even if I end up with a black eye."

Ashlyn groaned. He almost had it until that last bit.

"Sorry, I had to."

Not wanting to change the subject, especially with Tripp being so intense and romantic, Ashlyn felt like she had no choice but to say something. She had intended to talk to him about it on his lawn that day, but he kind of told her to leave. "My dad will help, I talked to–"

With a smile still on his face, "I know. We've been in contact."

Ashlyn's eyes widened in shock, surprised that her dad hadn't told her that in the last couple days.

"I am pressing charges," he pointed out.

Ashlyn's next words caught him off guard. "Thank goodness."

They both laughed. Though the tingling pain above Tripp's eye made him realize how fresh the situation was, it was still something he could laugh about now.

"Now, can I take my girlfriend out? For real."

Ashlyn nodded with enthusiasm.

With a playful look on his face and his fingers dancing in hers, "Just one more thing. I think I missed what you said back there." He nodded toward the baseball field.

Ashlyn wrapped her free arm around his neck. She could have toyed with him, teased him, pretended she didn't know what he was talking about, but it had felt so good saying it the first time that she couldn't wait to say it again. "I love you, Tripp."

He wrapped his arm around her waist and picked her up so that she fell into him. "I will never get tired of hearing that." After giving her the softest and sweetest of pecks, "And I love you, too."

Something felt different between them in the best of ways. From the moment of their first meeting, neither could have ever pictured that their relationship would take the course that it had, but it did, and it changed both of their lives for the better.

THE END

EPILOGUE

"You'd never leave me for another girl, would you?"

Deacon closed his eyes and took in a sharp breath. Melody asked him the same question nearly every other day. Her insecurities or jealousy, whatever it was, was starting to irritate him. This was why he never did relationships.

"Why do you keep asking that?"

Melody twirled her dark hair and sipped on her soda. "Well," she began, and paused.

Deacon couldn't imagine how many thoughts were running through her head, and she was going to let him know every single one. He wasn't a big talker; however, Melody was. He didn't know that when he started dating her. She was probably the only girl he could think of that preferred to talk incessantly on the phone as opposed to text. He only knew this now because she called him every single night, and the calls weren't the five-minute ones he was used to with his grandmother. That said a lot.

"My friends and I were talking."

Deacon rolled his eyes and tried not to groan. That was a dumb statement.

"I know you've been out with girls here and there, but I'm like your first real girlfriend."

Deacon felt sick to his stomach. This isn't how it was supposed to be.

"And you're a great catch, not to mention baseball star. Then in the fall, once football starts, I know you'll be one of the best wide receivers our school has ever had. People cannot wait until our senior year."

He let her ramble on about baseball and football, deep down wondering if she really liked him or liked his status around the school.

"Seriously, you could have any girl at this school, and every girl at this school would love a chance with you."

Deacon stopped breathing when she said that and looked up, out into the distance across the cafeteria.

Those words killed him, mostly because they were so far from true. It's not like he wanted them to be true. He wasn't some egotistical player; he didn't want any and every girl. Just one.

"I know it hasn't been but a few weeks, but I feel like you're distant, and I'm worried that it's a me problem."

Deacon hadn't realized how insecure Melody was. He also hadn't realized that he wasn't helping it. He hated that his friends ever convinced him to go to that party, to be open to dating, to actually getting in a relationship.

Most of all, he hated what a coward he was, because he really didn't want to be in a relationship anymore, but he didn't know how to get out without hurting her. Melody was nice, he guessed. To be honest, he wasn't sure. They had gone to a couple dinners, to the movies, they sat together at lunch, but he didn't really know much about her. He felt like such a jerk.

He also knew what she meant with the distant comment. They had kissed approximately twice, and both times he felt nothing. Their kisses weren't even the kinds of kisses that new couples have. They lacked passion and emotion. Melody wanted something more physical, but the thought of making out with her made his chest tighten and his stomach flip, because he knew his heart would never be in it.

That was why he had started dating her to begin with, to move on, to escape inevitable heartbreak. That didn't happen. A part of him couldn't move on.

"You've got nothing to worry about," Deacon finally said.

It seemed to please Melody as she grabbed his shoulder and leaned into him.

It might have felt like a little lie, maybe because it was. There was only one girl Deacon wanted, ever wanted, but she would always be completely off limits. He couldn't ruin his friendship with her. He especially couldn't ruin his friendship with his best friend, which would inevitably happen if Ellis knew that every night when Deacon closed his eyes, all he could see was her.

* * *

"Stop it," Emory huffed as Ellis grabbed one of her fries.

"I'm bigger than you. Plus, you have to keep your cheerleader physique," he pointed out.

Emory's face fell flat.

"Wow," Ashlyn sighed. "You did not just say that."

"I guess that attitude is why you're not eating lunch with Abby today," Emory spat.

Ellis only shrugged. There was no point in mentioning that he and Abby were having another little spat.

Emory shoveled her food into her mouth before Ellis could go after much more. It wasn't until she glanced up and saw a pair of eyes on her, one eyebrow cocked in confusion, that she felt her face heat in embarrassment. It wasn't her most ladylike moment.

She swallowed and nodded toward Ellis then shook her head. In doing so, a small smile spread across Deacon's face, a rarity. Then his girlfriend must have said something, because it faded and he turned his attention back to her.

Tripp took notice. "It's weird not having Deacon here anymore."

Byron shrugged. "Dude never says much anyway."

"I don't get how he can tolerate Melody. She talks way too much," Kayla chimed in.

"Opposites attract," June laughed. "Take Ash and Tripp."

Everyone at the table chuckled, even the two lovebirds.

Emory couldn't help it. "He just doesn't seem happy with her."

"Unlike you and Cole," June teased, only for Kayla to finish with kissy noises.

Emory could feel her face warming. As if on cue, Ellis scoffed, interrupting any pleasant thoughts.

"I still can't believe you're dating Halshire's quarterback," Ellis groaned.

"Well, thanks to your reputation here, and the fact that Uncle Jim is the head football coach," she began, referring to Coach Turner. "I'm practically undateable."

"Whatever," Ellis mumbled. "Just know, we're destroying him this coming fall," he concluded, hoping that the topic of relationships, his sister's in particular, was over.

Once Ellis saw his sister in her cheer outfit freshman year, he had made sure that not a single guy on that team would look at her. He may have even gotten their uncle involved, but what was he supposed to do? She was his little sister, by twelve minutes, and while he knew she could hold her own, he also knew how a lot of the guys on the team were. He heard how they talked in the locker room. If any of them had intentions of dating Emory, they weren't getting within ten feet of her.

Thankfully Emory was a bit of a tomboy, a beautiful tomboy that still wore makeup and had long blonde hair down to her waist, but enough that most guys were already a little intimidated by her. Then, there was her hotheaded attitude. What guy would want to date a girl that would threaten to gut a guy twice her size?

Ellis couldn't help but chuckle at his last comment. "Totally destroying them," he repeated.

Emory glared at him. "You know what? Shut up, Ellis!"